MOONSHINE COUNTY
Keys To Rocky Mount

A Novel

Contents

Dedication

I dedicate this whimsical historical novel to my son, historian, lawyer, and author Andrew Taylor Call, who grew up where this novel takes place and who has written his own stories, three tall tales, and a memoir about this life in his *"Trail of the Appalachian Sunset."*

And I offer it in memory of my late husband, lawyer and historian Thomas Keister Greer (1921-2008) without whom I never would have known of Rocky Mount and The Grove.

Disclaimer

This is a piece of fiction. The history of real places and historical families is accurate to the best of my knowledge. Artistic license was taken with several members of actual families (Hale, Saunders, Hill, Jackson) so they could be characters in the novel. Any resemblance to actual places and people is quite possible, and the author was granted permission by each living person who appears in the novel as a character with another name or, in the case of Virginia painters and writers, with his or her own real name.

"The last enemy that shall be destroyed is death."

I Corinthians 15:26

Chapter One

"For now we see through a glass, darkly;
but then face to face: now I know in part
but then shall I know even as also I am
known."

I Corinthians 13:12
The Holy Bible

     Young Lacey Brew was on her way to south-central Virginia on an overcast day in late spring. She was excited about her future. Her head was packed to the brim, like her luggage, with what she had learned of her soon-to-be new home in Rocky Mount, Virginia. The Old South!

     After living in the suburbs of Denver for years, she thought life in a small town would be a snap. Little did she know. She had not yet learned that if one were a newcomer in a sleepy Virginia town, hoping to know its past as well as its present, one might be a little frustrated. Many adventures and secrets of earlier times were securely hidden...in a Code of Silence. Families often did not know the facts about the doings of their ancestors before and during the Revolutionary War, the Civil War, Restoration, WWI, Prohibition, the Great

Depression, WWII, and beyond.

All lives, like fruits on a tree, are products of their past. Every breeze, every rain, frost, each burst of fickle weather, visiting birds, playful children climbing into the branches, attentive arborists pruning and watching over time, shaped the trees. So it was with a life of a person and even of a town. Time and circumstance. And God, if one let him be counted in the process.

At thirty, Lacey Brew may have thought she had already experienced a lot. An art history teacher changing careers and locations, she was as innocent and naïve in many ways as the young people she had been teaching how to appreciate a Van Gogh painting of an apple orchard. Learning the history of where she was going was not the same as knowing its roots and its secrets.

Ministers new to town, and hired to give sermons and pastoral counseling to the local folks, rarely had an inkling of the dark secrets tucked behind poker faces in a pew on a Sunday. And Professionals, new to the town and eager to run a business, doctor patients in a clinic, draw up a Will, or sell real estate…well, they may have been the most in the dark because no one was going to tell them…the truth.

Secrets were hidden. Like treasures. Like skeletons in a closet. Like dreams hidden behind smiles. Like promises not kept and runaways who never came home. So, do not bank all your hopes on a newcomer if truth is what you seek. But follow her closely. She might lead you right to the truth you didn't expect.

Moonshine Corner, with its heavy trees and tumbled sidewalks, frame houses leaning slightly off-center on tired foundations, and front porches looking into the past, was just a quaint part of Rocky Mount, Virginia, a small 18th century town at the far western edge of Southside, where the Blue Ridge Mountains sloped and slipped down to the farm and cattle lands that rolled east through history and mystery to the Atlantic many hours away.

Early towns, back in the days of carriage travel, were built about ten miles apart, for the convenience of the horses. Rest stops. Later, roads and passenger train tracks linked these small communities together. Ferrum was ten miles from Rocky Mount, which was ten miles from Boones Mill, which was ten miles from Roanoke, which was ten miles to Daleville, and so on.

Towns had also been situated near a reliable source of water. There were many creeks and rivers in that part of Virginia: Beard, Beaverdam, Blackwater, Chestnut, Cooper's, Daniel's Run, Doe Run, Falling,

Foul Ground, Fuckin (later renamed), Furnace, Gills, Indian, Linville, Little, Luck, Maggotty (later Magodee), Mill, Nicholas, Otter, Pigg, Roanoke, Runnet Bag, Shooting, Simmon's, Snow, Soakarse (later renamed), Staunton, Stony, Story, Turkey Cock, and more.

And in between these small towns lay forests, caves, pastureland, and farms. There were also old copper moonshine stills forgotten in woodlands near creeks and old cemeteries whose stones had almost sunk and faded into the red soil, families forgotten. Clearings in the forest in the middle of nowhere might once have been a cluster of chestnut trees, killed off by the blight in the early 20th century. Chestnuts had brought in money. So had "white lightning," another name for corn whiskey, made since the first European settlers arrived from the Old Countries.

The Blue Ridge Mountains were part of the eastern range of the ancient Appalachian chain that ran diagonally from NE to SW across the western third of the state. They wore many shades of blue, lavender, or grey at different times of day. Ancient, like the Alleghenies to the west of the great valleys, these proud mountains had been worn down to rounded shapes, countless hollows, caves, and gentle ridges, very unlike the younger Rockies far to the west.

In the forests of the Blue Ridge, many trees were now grotesquely veiled and braided together by the invasive Kudzu vines into towering, unearthly, menacing green shapes. These hidden trees stood silent under their green capes, like the listening Indians who once walked the same forests. The vines that cloaked the forests, the haze that charmed the traveler, the mist that delighted the painter, the storm clouds that thrilled the dreamer all covered terrain that held secrets from long ago.

There was a kind of randomness to a region that had no zoning and where most people pretty much stayed put and carried on exactly as their forebears had. There was no zoning in Franklin County, Virginia, Lacey Brew's destination. They could put an ice cream and hamburger shop next to a funeral home. A dairy farm could have a beauty salon next to it, with a used car dump of rusting vehicles on its other side. Random. People thereabouts did not like to be told how to live.

Ah. That was a key to everything. Independence. Could be called stubbornness or hostility to change. Might be tradition or resistance. Could also be called courage and confidence. Kind of depended on who said what. What was said, repeated, twisted, gossiped about, and reported...was *news*. And news had always traveled faster than any carriage or train, faster than a Red-Tailed Hawk, a forest fire, or a mountain rain. Faster than a Carrier Pigeon. Faster than a runaway boy looking over his shoulder.

News, secrets, and knowledge could also be hidden in those mountain mists that shrouded the Blue Ridge peaks of Cahas, Grassy Hill, Bald Knob, Scuffling Hill, Tough Ridge, Cook's Knob, Ferrum Mountain and the other innocent-looking foothills that stood sentinel around Rocky Mount.

Long, long ago these forested mountains had been inhabited by Native Americans. These spaces had been farms, hunting grounds, sacred places, towns, and gathering places for tribes that were part of a vast Algonquian-speaking Powhatan Paramount Chiefdom and then Eastern-Siouian speakers of the Catawba, Saponi, Tutelo, Monacan, and Chickahominy tribes, which were all part of the same group. After most of the Native Americans were pushed on, only the Monacans were permitted to remain, and settled mostly near what became Amherst, northeast of Rocky Mount. Small groups or individual Shawnee and Cherokee hunters or warriors occasionally passed through to hunt or to raid. And later, when the United States Government forced Indians to march west and vacate their eastern lands, pockets of Cherokee hid in the forests. They are there today, scattered across the lands. Their traditions, place names, and lore are deep in the soils, plants, trees, winds, and birds of the area. Their totems may be invisible. Wisdom lives on. Wisdom and Time, like wind and sun, sustain life. And God, if you let him.

In the 18th century, the region filled up with frontier forts, English-speaking pioneer farmer settlers, mountain folk, and miners. Land once worked by Indians became tobacco country, including plantations worked by slaves and white farmers. Even later, these small tobacco or dairy farms and former plantations were owned and worked by freed black slaves, mulattos, Scottish-American, English-American, and German Baptist and Moravian farmers. Each group contributed its traditions, music, religion, and skills to the growing region. Farming, timbering, market days, Court Days, laws, and making corn whiskey flourished.

The last of the tobacco barns still stood in fields stretching across Southside.

But tobacco as a money-making crop was over. The old plantation houses had mostly fallen down, leaving only burnt chimneys, piles of hand-made bricks, hewn beams, and toppled tombstones amidst copses of ancient trees. Lots of things were over, yet that was the beauty of a place rich in history, that new life came from the old, when least expected.

Trails and wagon roads ran from northeast to southwest. They followed what had once been the Great Warrior Path of the Iroquois. The Cherokee Trail and the Great Wagon Road, known here as the Wilderness or Old Carolina Road, paralleled the mountains and valleys and led travelers and settlers from Philadelphia to Georgia. Railroads started to criss-cross Virginia before the War Between the States. After the 1860's there were railroads for passengers as well as goods, dirt roads, and finally paved roads for cars.

In recent decades only coal had been carried on the freight trains that rumbled without stopping through the quiet towns. Where eighty years ago small children used to scurry to grab fallen coal to take home for their families' stoves and fireplaces, now only feral cats and tourists wandered along the tracks, enjoying the sun. It was here, in the shaded patch of history beneath Tough

Ridge and Grassy Hill that the story unfolds.

Sometimes change happened slowly, sometimes quickly, in a small town with a neighborhood named Moonshine Corner. Nothing went unobserved. On Cottage Hill Drive, the drooping limbs of the old Willow Oaks blocked the view from passersby of a row of frame houses. Whether those folks were on foot, in a cart, a carriage, on a bicycle, or in a car, all they could easily see were narrow houses behind street-side trees. The frame houses lined the street like serious, somewhat tired, dignified and wise grandmothers in rocking chairs.

The houses were full of secrets, the kitchens rich with pies, canned fruits, and canned meats, the attics full of the Past. It was not a fancy neighborhood. It was worn and full of stories. Under the right kind of moonlight, Moonshine Corner was translucent in its history. It was practical, ornate, and delicate like the once popular linen antimacassars draped over the high backs of wing chairs to protect the fabric from the Macassar Oil used by dapper men to slick back their hair. Moonshine Corner was both delicate and sturdy. Every window, every sidewalk, every tree, and every old brick could tell a tale. Moonshine Corner was much more than it appeared to be.

Time hung still, like an organdy

curtain on an open dusty window, wavering back and forth, back and forth, fooling the senses in its ghostly way, on Moonshine Corner.

Though often poor in paper money or fancy clothes, people here were rich in stories and heritage. Shallow closets and hot attics held letters and medals and swords from the terrible losses of the 1860's. Cool basements held shelves of mason jars and jugs from the era of Prohibition and illegal moonshine of the 1920's and 30's.

Front porches sloped gently towards the street. Nothing was quite level or perfect on Moonshine Corner. Chimneys leaned. Doors stuck. Clotheslines sagged with the weight of wet garments and with memories and tales. If you dropped a marble at midnight and saw where it rolled, it might roll way back....

At 5:22 p.m. on a Monday in May, Lacey Brew pulled her white Kia up to a frame house beside an empty lot near a corner at the east end of the street known as Cottage Hill Drive. This was her first visit to the Virginia town of Rocky Mount. Scudding clouds were turning the evening sky dark grey and a stiff west wind blew through the branches of two trees, maybe 50 feet tall, with willowy limbs, that stood like old sentries at the beginning of her sidewalk.

She shivered from nervousness and excitement. Then she laughed. What an adventure. She had sold her house, quit her job, answered an ad, and driven across country in less than two months. *Wow. Just wow.* She sat back against her seat and yawned. She had driven over 250 miles today, coming in from I-64 in Kentucky. A few days ago, leaving Denver on I-70 on a chilly morning and heading for Salina, Kansas, she had begun her journey east. High plains and yellow grasses. Eventually, in her rear-view mirror, the last evidence of the high and majestic Rocky Mountains had disappeared from view, a mere squiggle of a line on the horizon and then, gone.

The second day had been across the cattle country and wheat fields of Kansas and Missouri to the Mississippi! Her night on the western outskirts of St. Louis had been educational, with her reviewing the history of pioneers who had been going the other way from that old "Gateway" to the West. Yesterday she had seen the Arch from her car, and had watched as it disappeared from her view. She had not known how very, very wide and muddy Old Man River was until crossing into East St. Louis and heading east on I-64 to Kentucky.

Crossing the top of Kentucky on I-64, watching the wide Ohio River at Louisville and the stately thoroughbred horse farms near Lexington, Lacey had visited the Kentucky Horse Park and had done a quick tour before it closed, and then stopped in Winchester. Today she had been eager to enter the Old South when she arrived in Virginia at the other Lexington, home of the Virginia Military Institute and Washington & Lee University, where she would pick up I-81. She had stopped for coffee and to stretch her legs on the brick sidewalks in the old part of town. Set into the brick walk was an historic plaque noting that in 1777 the Virginia Militia had killed Shawnee warrior "Cornhusker" nearby. She also saw signs for "Stonewall" Jackson's House and other landmarks. Little could she know how important the markers and Civil War homes and statues would soon be to her!

I-81, a hilly interstate that angled southwest from upper New York State to Tennessee, had been full of speeding trucks and traffic. She drove beside tall rock walls part of the time, where the interstate had been cut out of the mountainsides. Most of the drive took her down the middle of the Shenandoah Valley, with the Blue Ridge Mountains to the east and the Alleghenies to her west, as she made her way towards Roanoke, the "Star City" of the South. To get a break from heavy truck traffic, Lacey got off to take parallel Route 11 for awhile, and followed the old wagon road. She stopped to stretch her legs at Natural Bridge. Caves and a Monacan Village, as well as the huge stone arch, intrigued her. When she crossed the James River at Buchanan, she thought of the same river at Jamestown and Richmond and felt she was entering old Virginia, of flat boats and pioneers.

At Roanoke she had had to take a spur, 581, above the city. The skyline was dominated by four very distinct eye-catching things: a Neo-Gothic Cathedral; a pointed, copper-topped skyscraper; a super-modern metal and glass building pointed at the road; and a huge star on a mountain ahead of her. Old and new! There were two neon-signs which entranced her as she went by. One was a Dr. Pepper sign, a big bottle cap. The other was a coffee pot and cup. She loved that they welcomed her to the city. She sipped her coffee, still warm from when she had bought it in Lexington, just forty-five miles north.

The skies were turning dark from rain clouds as she found that 581 became 220 South, and that she had only 25 more miles, crossing east through the mountains, into what Mr. Ruter of Glass & Howe Realty, her new employers, had called "deepest Franklin County." Her route was lined with mountains, trees wrapped in some kind of weird vine, old signs about an Apple Festival, small farms, a scattering of small businesses, and billboards.

Finding her way off 220 into Rocky Mount and allowing her GPS to take her to her new address, she realized that a storm was about to pour down on Rocky Mount. Her new Rand-McNally spiral-bound map of the USA sat beside her and her navigational system, plugged into her electric outlet on the dashboard, was repeating in its mechanical tones, "You are at your destination." She had arrived!

As she looked for a driveway the rain started. She pulled up in front of the house. The rain blew in sideways, silken sheets, obscuring the street, the cottage, and the road. She could sit it out in the warm car or make a dash for the front door and get soaked. The car radio crackled something about a severe storm-watch with dime-sized hail and, sure enough, right on cue, the beautiful little ice balls filled the air and clattered off her car. She took a sip of her cold coffee and waited. Turning the engine off, she was alone in her world, alone in a new town, alone in life. She tried to smile, but could not. The smile just would not stay in place. *Buck up, she told herself. You can do this.*

Beside her a limb fell noisily onto the lawn. It had missed her car by only a few feet. The street was pretty dim now, too early for lights in the houses, no other cars parked along it. Some storm. Some welcome. Well, she might be safer inside, she reasoned, gathering a box from the front seat to take with her on her dash to the door.

As she hurried up the walk, a gust of wind seemed to hold her in place, and then, just as suddenly, pushed her forward, through a mass of cobwebs strung between the big trees. Oddly, it felt almost as if she had broken through some invisible barrier. The last few steps took her onto the porch. She paused to catch her breath and wipe the rain out of her eyes and the cobwebs off her body. Looking back over her yard she saw hundreds of tulips bending in the rain.

Her new job at Glass & Howe Realty would begin the following morning. Shifting from life as a high school art history teacher to a realtor had not exactly been in her plans. But when she had been in a bad car accident two years ago her world had crumbled apart. Then, during her hospitalization and long recovery, her boyfriend had dropped her. After a half-hearted attempt to resume her job, she decided that a fresh start somewhere across the country would be the best thing for her. Okay, so the decision had been made after crying through a melodramatic movie on Lifetime TV, but if those people could start fresh, so could she!

Standing under the roof safe from the storm and curtain of dripping leaves between her and the street, she could have been anywhere on earth. The peeling paint on the gingerbread trim of the porch, the warped boards of the porch itself, and the sound of heavy rain pounding the tin roof made her wonder if she had been too hasty in choosing this cottage sight-unseen. A "virtual tour" online, posted by Glass & Howe Realty, with quite a large discount on the purchase price of this property, had shown her every room and vista from the many windows, but had not shown peeling paint and uneven floors. Oh, well. A brand-new adventure!

A clop-clopping sound drew her attention. Could that be a cart pulled by a horse going by outside? Sure sounded like one. Maybe they used carts and wagons here to bring garden produce in to the Farmers Market, she mused. She had read about the Market and the German Baptists from the outlying farms who sold produce and baked goods there on Saturdays. She was confused about the difference between German Baptists, Dunkards, and Mennonites. Were they like Amish but with cars? She had no idea.

Up the street a dog barked. Another tree limb fell to the ground somewhere in a rustle and swoosh of noise muted by the rain. The wind was strong. People probably were already home from work. The storm would be keeping children inside. It was hard to tell what kind of neighborhood it was. Would she be the only single woman?

The keys. Did she have the keys? Where had Mr. Glass written her that they would...be... Aha. Under the vinyl cushion of the swing where the porch bent around the house to the west. She found one. It was a large key with a hole for a silk tassel. Very old, like a key from a fancy hotel 100 years ago. The tassel was a ruby color, and damp, slimy. Ick. Lacey went back to the front door and tried the key. It took almost a full minute for her to get it positioned properly in the old lock. It did not quite fit. When she pushed on the door it did not budge.

In frustration she went back to the sofa cushion and felt around beneath it. Her hand touched metal and she pulled out a key ring. It had two more keys on it. One was scuffed and dull and the other quite shiny. Chilled by the late spring rain she tried the larger of the two newer keys, the scuffed one, and the door finally opened. It acted warped, as if it had not been opened in a long time. She tucked all three keys into her pocket, wincing as she touched the slimy one.

Inside the room it was as dark as dusk. The air was musty but not unpleasantly so. There was an ironed linen, fried chicken, old fireplace, cornbread kind of blend of homey scents. Like a Cracker Barrel Restaurant when the fire was lit, she laughed. Sort of as if candles had been snuffed out or a fire let to burn out not long ago. Maybe someone had burned a candle called "Cozy Home" or "Cornbread" in here. Lacey loved candles.

She felt for a light switch and found a round porcelain knob on the wall, unlike any switch she had ever handled. When she turned it, the room glowed from several ceiling lights under etched glass domes. She smiled and looked around. "Vintage," as in mid-20th century or earlier. This was clearly the main room, large enough for her living room furniture and with a wall of front windows and one on the left...hmmm, the east. Smooth, worn hardwood floors, lots of busy faded floral wallpaper, some built-in bookcases, a tiled-up fireplace. Two rooms opened off to the right, both the size of smallish bedrooms. An old-fashioned tiled bathroom with a porcelain tub with claw feet was straight ahead, and through a door to the left, beyond the living room was a large room, a dining room with built-in shelves and cabinets with glass doors. From that room a door opened into…the kitchen.

Ah, the kitchen was large. Wooden counters, warped and cracked with age. Linoleum floor. Where was the refrigerator? A porcelain sink with those old-fashioned ridges on the side for drying plates, a double faucet, one hot and one cold. The walls had windows on the east above the sink and on the south, and a door on the west that opened into a kind of mud room. The laundry room, she deduced. There was a big metal tub tipped against the wall and a canvas sling bag of clothesline and clothespins attached to the wooden wall. Old, but very handy. Hmmm…no visible washer or dryer. Had there been a dish-washer?

The rain let up enough for her to run back up the wet walk through rain puddles to her car. She made several quick trips for bags and two small boxes of essentials in case the movers did not bring her things this evening. She had packed her coffee maker, coffee, tea kettle, paper products, radio, a sleeping bag and pillow, thick bathroom towel, shampoo, soap, and her favorite mug in the car. Her furniture was due to arrive this evening before 7:00. Comfort was made up of many little things, she had learned. Ambiance, books, music, coffee, good light, healthful foods, rest, and memories were all part of her survival and need to move forward.

Glass & Howe Realty had arranged for a local moving company to bring her things over from Roanoke. It was already 6:00, so Lacey shoved her bags and boxes into a corner and put all the lights on, one round switch at a time until the interior was as mellow as a stage set waiting for the actors to walk on. The virtual tour had not shown the neighborhood, or many details of the interior rooms. Her realtor had assured her it was "very nice" and to go ahead and buy it!

Her coffee brewer would not plug into any of the kitchen outlets, all missing the third hole. These outlets were old. She would have to get them up to code! So she heated water on the gas burner of her scuffed white stove and poured it through the carafe filter into a mug. The cottage took on a fresh aroma as her organic, Fair Trade Sumatra's bouquet wafted through the small house. She stepped out onto the porch and, by the light of the streetlights, she could see that there were empty lots on either side of her. And the narrow driveway! Good! No noise from immediate neighbors! That was such a blessing, she thought, almost giddy with the revelation. And even though this was the South, and not the hill country of Colorado, from where she had moved, she kind of hoped the neighbors would not be too "friendly."

As soon as she thought that, she felt guilty. Yet she had never been the kind of neighbor to show up with a plate of cookies when someone moved into a neighborhood in which she had lived. Of course, at 30, she had not lived in that many places, but still...
It was not long before she saw a van drive up and park and heard doors slam. Three youngish men started to carry boxes to her front door, as if they were completely certain that this was, indeed, 33 Cottage Hill Drive, Rocky Mount, Virginia. She propped open the storm door (which she would replace with a pretty door as soon as she could) and welcomed them in.

"Hidden Attics Movin' and Shippin', ma'am," announced the first man, nodding his head in greeting as he set a large box on the floor out of the way of his associates. "Pleased to meet you, ma'am," he added with a shy smile. "You will like livin' at Moonshine Corner," he said, not waiting for a reply.

"Uh, yes, um, hello," Lacey replied

awkwardly, never having been called "ma'am" in her life. *Moonshine Corner*. A few seconds later the other two men arrived with her couch, carefully shrouded in heavy plastic. They tipped their heads and greeted her in the same quiet, polite way. They placed the chenille-covered couch in front of the main windows at the front of the house and retreated for more furniture. They set her bed up in a back bedroom. A few arm chairs, a dining room table and chairs, a dresser, eight bookcases, and one hundred and forty boxes later, they held out some papers for her to sign, and were off. It had all happened so fast that she blinked, amused that within two hours of her arrival her new house was almost ready to live in. How on earth had they moved her into this house so quickly?

Lacey tore the plastic off her couch. She poured herself another cup of her coffee and sat down. It would take her awhile to figure out where to put everything. She thought that she was too tired this evening to unpack more than a few boxes of clothes and kitchen things. One of the side rooms would become a television room/den, if she could locate a cable or connection in a wall. The movers had placed several bookcases in there already and the rest in the living room. Many of the boxes were full of her books.

Art books were heavy. A few wardrobe boxes had been placed in the second bedroom, the one towards the back of the house. Her double bed had been set up in there already. All she had to do was find the bedding and have a good night's sleep later. She smiled. What would her old beau, James, have thought of her moving across the country to this small town in the foothills of the Blue Ridge, changing careers, and starting over?

She did not let herself dwell on the accident and its aftermath, knowing that they dragged her down into the black, inky depths of depression. No, this was her new beginning, a way to move forward after losing her job and him and all that she most loved. He would never have believed she could leave Colorado and their friends to move somewhere brand new. She had to let go of the past if she were to have a future. This new job and little cottage in Rocky Mount represented courage and daring. It truly was a second chance for her.

A creaking noise brought her back from her reverie. Had the noise been the back door? Lacey quietly hurried into the kitchen. No one there. But she did see a small flap on the door to the back porch moving...a doggie door? She opened the door all the way and saw a calico cat staring at her from the covered part of the wet porch. It came toward her and she stooped to pet it. "Aw. You are so pretty," Lacey crooned to the beautiful cat. "Did you used to live here?" The cat had no collar. It looked thin. Glancing at the "cat door" she decided to get some cat food tomorrow and see what happened. It might be good for her to have a cat. She had not had one since before her relationship with James. He had been allergic to them.

Back inside, looking through each room, she saw that there were no visible phone outlets. But there was an old black rotary dial wall phone mounted in the kitchen, the kind of phone one could buy from a catalog of antique reproductions. Well, it fit this kitchen, she admitted, smiling. Maybe she would make do with this one phone and her mobile phone and save some money. And she would ask about an electrician.

With a sudden burst of energy, after the remains of a lunch salad, an apple, and her coffee, Lacey spent the rest of the evening listening to the local classical station ("Piano Jazz") on her portable radio and sorting her books. Her collection of landscape paintings got propped along some of the walls where she planned to hang them after she knew where her furniture would be.

Her newest purchase, called "Chestnut Mountain Homeplace," would hang in the living room. She had found it online through an art gallery of artists from this county. It was by Jane Stogner. It was a pastoral landscape with fog-shrouded Chestnut Mountain in the distance and an old homestead surrounded by trees, fields, and a small family cemetery. The foreground was a dirt road and the dirt was native red clay. The scene was timeless.

In searching for artists in this part of south-central Virginia, she had been surprised to learn that Rocky Mount and its neighboring towns, Boones Mill, Ferrum, Callaway, Roanoke, Bedford, Floyd, and Lynchburg, were considered art colonies! She was eager to visit all the galleries and festivals! And she was looking forward to buying more local art. Landscapes were her favorites.

Her cookbook collection went into the roomy kitchen, where she would get a bookcase for the wall near the porch. For now, the three piles of cookbooks could sit on the counter. It was an eclectic collection of Italian, American, Hungarian, low-fat, Junior League, and dessert cookbooks, some inherited from her parents. Missing were Southern cookbooks! She had only one, *"Southern Sideboards,"* an older Junior

League cookbook from Jackson, Mississippi. Its delicious "Country Captain" curried chicken recipe was her favorite, and had been made for President Franklin D. Roosevelt! His favorite, too. It would be fun, she thought, to hunt for more Southern cookbooks.

Cornbread, spoon bread, Sally Lunn Bread, hoe cakes, Smithfield Ham, fried chicken, peanut soup, and grits were about all the Southern foods she had heard of. Lacey loved to entertain, but it had been years since she had been able to. James had not liked having people over.

The cat was curled up by a radiator which, when she touched it, was barely warm, but was taking the chill off the cool spring night. Her cell phone rang and she answered it with a simple, "Hello."

"Ms. Brew? Lacey Brew?"

"Yes, this is she."

"Well. Welcome to wonderful old Rocky Mount!" exclaimed an older man, chuckling. "Mr. Glass here. Jim Glass. We wanted to make sure you were here and that you would be able to start work tomorrow in the morning. There are some clients looking for a small frame Victorian. If you come in by 8:30 we will get you settled and show you the ropes. Your first week will not be terribly busy, dear. We want you to take it at the pace you want."

"Thank you!" answered Lacey, hoping she would be able to wake up early enough for the new job. Her body was still adjusting from Mountain Time. "I will be there at 8:30 and am eager to begin."

"We are a very small staff over here," he added, "and the town is small enough for you to become familiar with the listed properties right away. See you tomorrow, then. Oh, by the way, there is really just one other realty company in town, and it is pretty competitive. It is called Beach & Bowers. Its large staff is competent and very professional and their office is larger than ours. Just thought I would warn you. Ha ha ha," he chuckled as he signed off.

Lacey curled up on her sofa by the window in the mellow room with a legal pad and pen and jotted down notes on what she already knew, from reading up on the Internet about her new home.

Rocky Mount had about 8000 people and had been a busy timber and furniture town until recently. It had been very famous, or infamous, for years for the making and transporting of "moonshine," corn whiskey, in the early 20th century. The Scottish settlers had brought their whiskey-making skills with them and made whiskey all along, whether the state or country approved, or not. When making and selling moonshine had been illegal all over the country during Prohibition after the Volstead Act of 1920, many families in Franklin County and elsewhere had gone underground to make and transport it for sale, sending much of it to Canada, to make a living. Before and after Prohibition, which ended in 1933, they refused to pay federal taxes on the sales. Such blatant illegal behavior had brought the county to the attention of the Federal Government's Regulators. She had read up about it after learning that moonshining had pretty much put Rocky Mount on the map long ago and was still a popular tourist attraction, when people wanted to see where it had all taken place. She had read that some folks around here still made illegal liquor, ran drugs, or worked meth labs. Hard drugs, abused prescription drugs, and addictions. Sad.

Well before the notoriety of making so much moonshine, though, the county was known for having produced two very famous and very different kinds of 19th century leaders: Jubal Anderson Early, a lawyer with his pre-Civil War law office on the grounds of The Grove, and later a General, and the only Confederate General not to surrender, and a much younger man, of the same era, Booker T. (Taliaferro)

Washington, who walked out of the county as a freed slave in 1865 when very young, became educated, and went on to do great things, including founding the Tuskeegee Institute.

She loved details. That love had helped her as an art history teacher and it would help her now as she absorbed all she needed to know to be a successful citizen and realtor here. Lacey still wondered at her good fortune at getting her new realty job as an out-of-towner. She had been phoned in Colorado by the real estate company. Luck, sheer luck. The wonders of online life. Click and find. She might ask why she had been recruited for this position.

According to what she had read, there were lots of people out of work, especially in Henry County just south of this one, where the furniture and textile mills had closed. Many others worked in construction, at Ferrum College, in health care, at the local hospital, and in tourism and the growing arts community. Music was another big draw hereabouts, it seemed, and the town was the beginning of the famous "Crooked Road Music Trail," celebrating and preserving the state's long tradition of country and bluegrass music and festivals. A brand-new music hall, The Harvester Performance Center, had just been established a few blocks from her neighborhood, and was already bringing hundreds of people in for each musical act.

She wandered out onto the front porch and could hear the water still dripping from the leaves of the trees beyond. Overall, the neighborhood seemed very quiet. Almost as if no one lived here. Through the mists or fog rising from the recent rains, lights on houses up the street twinkled like small Christmas bulbs, white and beautiful. In the golden glow of streetlights, the view, from her porch, of roofs and trees with a distant church steeple pointing up above the treetops, reminded her of a favorite Utrillo print she would hang. It was of a rainy view of a quiet street and park in Montmartre in Paris with *Sacre Coeur* Cathedral in the distance. She sighed. This was hardly Paris, she told herself. But it is peaceful. And it is my new home.

Before bed, she blocked the doggie door so the cat could not come and go until she had picked up a litter box and water dish, and had taken Callie, her name for the pretty cat, to a vet's to be checked over.

Sleep came quickly. But just before she slept, she had the scary sensation of falling into a black hole. The doctors had warned her that she might feel that way for years, after her near-death experience, the coma, and her recovery from the crash that had changed her life. She clenched her fists onto the sheet and willed herself back awake and then let herself fall asleep gently.

She soon fell into a deep sleep with vivid dreams. She was in what looked like her own new kitchen, drying a dish by the porcelain sink. Beyond her, people were talking loudly.

"You talk, you die," the old man said, *leaning into his future son-in-law's face. "I am Clive McCain. I make the decisions." He took a deep swig of whiskey and plunked his bottle down on the kitchen table next to a glass jar of tulips, shaking the plates that had held fried chicken and cornbread and bowls of beans.*

"If you want to be part of this family, you need to know a few things." He stared hard at the young man's face. "If you won't stay silent, then get out. There's the door," he pointed, not turning to look. "This is 1933 and no one, 'specially the Feds, will ever tell a McCain what to do. Prohibition is coming to an end. You tell your Pa that."

"Papa," cried a pretty young woman, "Bobby understands. Don't scare him off. He won't never double-cross you. Will you, Bobby?" she whispered. "We know that Bobby has come too far now, courtin' me, to

be left alone by you and your men. His life would be in danger if he backed out now. And it would not be in danger from you, but from the hidden men who control all the moonshinin' families hereabouts. The men who collect the 'granny fees.'"

"What d'you know, Ann, about any 'granny fees'?" her father cried, coming towards her.

"I know they are the payments y'all have to give to the deputies and sheriffs and their boss or bosses to keep them from reporting the illegal activities." She paused, her face flushed. "I seen you payin'."

"I know all about it," quipped Jack, a young boy, of no more than 13, from the doorway. He would regret that bragging in another minute as his Pa stepped backwards, quick as a hornet flying in an open door, and slapped the boy across the face with an open hand. The child cowered and ran outside, paying no mind to the sheets of rain blowing in from the north across Cottage Hill. Their calico cat ran after him.

"I will stay quiet," Bobby Grierson replied, startled by the sudden violence that had driven young Jack out in the storm. "I did not know until recently, sir," he added, "that you all made 'shine. My family transports it, over near Maggotty and

Soakarse Creeks and into the next counties to the east. We all are protected by the law to the county line. After that, each man is on his own. But I expect you know all about that."

Clive McCain spoke again, more softly, fists clenched. "Hereabouts, if'n a woman marries into a family that makes 'shine, she has to go along. No talking. Ever. Same with a man. If you marry in, you keep silent." He paused, looking into the strong face of the younger man.

"We make it. We drop it on Callaway Road, on this side of the valley, and then we do not see it again. Sometimes we drop it here in town, on Coal Street. Whole street is all 'transportin' families, maybe like yours. They carry it up Shootin' Creek Road into Floyd. We do not work past the Old Wilderness Road at all. That's someone else's territory.

"You tell your Pa and your Pa, alone, you hear me? Have him meet me on the Callaway Road at the store by the school. Have him come over here alone within a week. How about noon next Saturday? We need to talk. I hear that the Feds are being called in and we need to be together on what to do or say from now on. No loose tongues. Hear me? Our boy, Jack, hears too much," he added angrily. *"Going to get him, or all*

of us, in trouble with the law, the few that ain't paid off by Mr Big," he muttered. "Or maybe killed to shut us up if anyone wanted to talk."

McCain strolled over to the fireplace and sat down. The conversation was over. Behind him his wife cleared the table, darted her eyes to her husband's bulk in the old chair, and threw a cautious look at Ann and her Bobby, who were standing still as statues, scared stiff. Ann went out to look for the cat, calling, "Cleo?"

The noise of a car back-firing somewhere along the street broke the quiet and the dream receded into a fog as Lacey awoke before 7:00. As she came awake, she felt drugged, as if she had had too much cough syrup or wine. The dream had been so vivid. *Wow.* She must have been really, really tired. Bathing in the shiny tub (there was no shower) and dressing in a pretty linen-silk sleeveless blouse and black pants and jacket, with red shoes, she studied herself in the little mirror and decided she looked fine for her first day on a new job. Slim, pale from a Colorado winter, a little tired, she seemed all of her 30 years. Her hair, worn loose, softened the angles of her face. How much weight had she lost since the accident? She felt light on her feet as she peeked around her new home in the morning light.

The kitchen was a pale yellow. The walls in the other rooms were either painted white or had faded wallpaper. She could change that. This would be a good house to decorate. It had good bones. She smiled. Knowing that the bigger grocery stores were clear across town, she left early to explore and found a fast food restaurant for breakfast. Sitting inside on a red vinyl seat, she saw that the place was full of older men, "country" men, some in overalls, talking loudly over coffee and biscuits. They all glanced her way and then away. Not unfriendly. Just curious, maybe. *Overalls.* That was new for her. They seemed to be talking about how little money they had and how bad it was that the Government was so involved with their lives.

Her breakfast was a cup of coffee and a fruit and granola parfait. And it was only a quarter to eight. She was due at work soon, but it was very close to this place. She knew that from memorizing the town map. Lacey pulled up into the little parking lot behind the businesses on Main Street, the main thoroughfare, known also as 220 Business, of Uptown Rocky Mount. Main Street crested right at the Courthouse across from Glass & Howe Realty.

The parking lot behind the row of small businesses was level, but the sidewalks out in front sloped. All along Main Street flower baskets full of spring flowers hung from lampposts. Vertical banners proclaiming "Spring" were attached to the posts. A few people were walking towards law offices and the Courthouse. There were two banks and a small coffee shop, The Daily Grind, within sight of the real estate office doorway.

She entered through the front door and was pleased to find an attractive room of leather chairs, antique tables, a huge gilt-edged mirror, an Oriental carpet, and two walls of nicely-framed landscapes and folk art portraits. To her trained eye the landscapes resembled the best of some of the English and Dutch landscape painters, Constable and others, with villages and church spires peeking out from behind lovely copses of tall trees. Bucolic. The artists' names, Penny Simmons and Anne Way Bernard, were familiar to her from her online search. They were local painters. A clever modern "folk art" portrait with a repetitive and colorful border of tobacco leaves and books, was of Booker T. Washington. It was by Kanta Bosniak.

"Ms. Brew. Welcome, my dear," said a tall man with white hair and glasses, wearing a dark suit. "Welcome to Glass & Howe, 'where *everyone* can find a perfect new home.' I am Jim Glass, co-owner with Coy Howe."

"Hello," she answered. "And you all may call me Lacey, if that is okay," she added. "And Mr. Ruter ?"

He tossed back his head and laughed heartily, pointing to a framed photo of a man on the wall, but did not respond to her comment. "Ah, yes, quite...," he said, not answering her question. "Lacey. Your new start here will be a refreshing new beginning. And you have much to offer us, too," he said kindly.

"But I am so new at being a realtor..."

"Not at all. You will be perfect for our needs. Let me show you your office. You will have a desk right here in the back of the front room, here by this sitting area, and your own small office at the back of the building. It used to be a large storage room and I have asked the others not to bother you in there," he added with a wink. "I suggest you keep your working papers in your own room and keep a nameplate, which we are providing, and business cards, and brochures for available properties, on the front desk. You will be paged or phoned by any one of us if you happen to be in the back or out."

Down the hall and through a new door, from the looks of it, he led her into a newly renovated room, at the very back of the original brick office. In fact, she did not even recall seeing this addition from where she had parked. Her office was spacious. There were a laptop on an antique desk, a floor lamp, two small brown leather chairs, and an antique table. In the hall beside her door there were a tiny galley kitchenette and a room like a deep closet with another door in its far wall.

"I am back here by myself?"

"Yes. This is a new addition for our newest clients, who can come and go through the back entry." He gestured to an almost hidden door beyond the closet. "It opens right into a tiny patio and then the parking lot. Very handy for people who park in the back. And it lets more clients come in unseen," he added mysteriously.

"This is wonderful," Lacey said, meaning it. The room was serene with ivory-silk curtains and pale grey walls; there were three more lovely landscapes. She checked the artists' names: Jane Stogner, Karen Sewell, and Anne Way Bernard. Their styles and palettes were completely different from each other. But each painting contained trees and a house. On the powder room wall was a pastel of a calico cat by Gretchen Gilbert St.

Lawrence. The cat could have been Callie.

"Here," Jim Glass said, pointing to a booklet on a table, "is what we put together with the Historical Society, from notes we all have gathered over the years and from various studies about the history of the area. I suggest you work your way through it when you have a chance, so you will be able to answer questions when you show houses in town or the county." He smiled. "It is a treasure trove of facts."

"I will," Lacey replied excitedly. "I know so little."

"I am glad you like your office. The rest of the staff will be here at 9:00. Every Monday we have a morning meeting in the conference room, down the hall and up the stairs, at 9:15. If we need to meet during the week, someone will let you know. We take turns making coffee and bringing snacks. There is a refrigerator up there and a microwave. Today is my turn and my wife, Hattie, sent cupcakes and muffins from the new bakery, Blue Ridge Cupcakes. Your turn will be one of the Mondays coming up. Kim will probably schedule you soon. There are five people," he finished, smiling. "Kim Bellows, Mary See, Coy Howe, you, and me. The family running Blue Ridge Cupcakes just bought a house through us, by the way, over on Windy Hill, off 220, the road to the city."

Lacey wondered how Ned Ruter, who had also phoned her in Colorado, fit in. "I am eager for it all," Lacey replied. "What do I need to do first?" She did not have a chance to ask about Mr. Ruter.

"For right now, just skim though the booklet on the town and codes. You will be handling private homes. No apartments or condos. There are 23 homes for sale right now in the town limits. They vary from a seedy frame Victorian with promise, to a Foursquare with structural problems, to a neo-Tudor with cosmetic problems, to a new modular, to a deluxe mansion with history. The mansion, The Grove, is on the market for the first time since 1959. You have your work cut out. And most are Multiple Listings, so Beach & Bower Realty and a few Roanoke companies might also be showing them. And there are lock boxes containing several keys on each property."

Mr. Glass slipped out quietly as she started to read about area real estate and Town zoning, codes, and local laws. The booklet was well-written and easy to read. Maybe, she mused, she would be able to be a realtor after all. She had been so worried about changing careers.

At 9:10, Lacey made her way up to the conference room where the rest of the staff was assembling. She was introduced to everyone and made to feel comfortable.

"Lucky you," exclaimed Mary See, "to have two couples signed up for today for seeing private homes. I handle the rental market as well as the lake. I have not had anyone in a few days except two faculty families looking for two-year rentals not too far from the community college, Westlake C.C. It is between town and our lake. But interest in all the empty or foreclosed condos and mansions at the lake is picking up. And they are all mine," she smiled.

"I did not realize there were two colleges here," Lacey commented, biting into a lemon muffin.

"There are two here now, Ferrum College," Kim said, "a four-year school that is 100 years old, and Westlake Community College, a brand-new campus closer to Smith Mountain Lake east of town. Virginia is really into community colleges. If a student attends for two years, he can then apply to any state university and have a very good chance of transferring. It is a great deal all around. My brother is starting up here at W. C. C. and hoping to transfer into George Mason near D.C. in two years."

"I will be sure to go see both colleges here," Lacey mumbled, over her last bite. The coffee was excellent, too. She smiled.

This seemed like a very pleasant work environment. There were more paintings on the walls in here, including one of Robert E. Lee, done by Kanta Bosniak who had portrayed Booker T. Washington as a folk portrait. Unmistakable style.

"Have you seen today's paper, Kim?" Mary See asked, holding up a slim newspaper. "That story about the missing teenager is in it again."

"Oh. Not more bad news, I hope," cried Kim, reaching for the paper.

"Seems that the family has decided to stop searching for Jack," Kim read aloud. "It has been over three months and they figure he ran off and will just head home when he feels like it."

"That can't be right." said Mary See. "If it were my son I would never give up."

"What happened?" Lacey asked. Jack? Had there been a boy named Jack somewhere she had been...? Why did that sound kind of familiar?

"Well," Jim began, "sometime last winter a man came into the police station claiming someone had stolen a truck out of their yard and that his stepson, Jack, had not come back home after being out over the weekend at a friend's house. He suspected that Jack and the missing truck might be linked. A theft or kidnapping or a runaway.

Jack's mother was home sick at the time and did not say anything to contradict her husband, so his story is all we have. But this article says the truck has been found submerged in the lake south of town. It could have been there for months. It is a lake with a rugged shoreline of cliffs and many coves. Few people live there. But there are some developers trying to make it a fancy place to live. And every house, so far, that has been built, has sold, and at a *big* price."

"Do you think Jack stole the truck and ran away?" Lacey asked the group. She got nods of the head for "yes," and for "no."

"I think there is foul play, myself," said the dignified Coy Howe.

"I suspect a runaway," added Jim Glass.

"I think it was drugs and murder," whispered Kim.

"What?" gasped Mary See. "Why a murder? Why on earth?"

"Well, I heard that Jack's mom and step-dad fought a lot. And the step-dad has been arrested before for Oxycontin abuse."

"Oxy-what?" Lacey asked, puzzled.

"Oxycontin or Oxycodone, addictive opoids. Over-prescribed by doctors and abused by people who get addicted. Sad," replied Kim. "Lots of it around here."

"Problems at home would suggest a

runaway," said Jim Glass decisively. "Well, let's get on with our meeting, folks."

They each sat around the oval table. At each place were a crimson folder and a pen. Kim was using a Tablet. And Lacey pulled out her IPhone.

Inside the folders were all the new listings for the region and a list of the G & H listings in the town and county. They talked for fifteen minutes about possible new clients, returning clients, mortgage news, news about town water being expanded into the county near the big lake, and how an upcoming rain might affect an Open House to be hosted by the staff next Sunday afternoon at a foreclosed modular house in a new subdivision in Callaway very near the wedding and event venue called Mysterious Ridge, owned and run by Alicia Molina and her family.

Lacey listened carefully and made notes on paper and added events to her electronic Notes. She could begin to see that Mary See was a mover and shaker, probably even socially, in town. Her comments sounded like insights about people's prejudices and notions about change and progress. Kim, younger, maybe in her mid-twenties, said little but was clicking away on her Tablet. Jim Glass and Coy Howe, old pros and natives of the town, spoke easily and fluently about trends to notice, what young couples wanted in a new home, estate sales, and so on. No one seemed to harbor any ill will towards her being the new person aboard, Lacey thought. For that, she was grateful.

They all left for their own spaces in the building and Lacey went back to her room. When she crossed from the older part of the building into the new part, she had that same funny sensation of passing through a kind of cobweb…as if an invisible barrier were in place. Odd. There was nothing to be seen at all. Just air. Maybe she was still tired. She checked her mobile phone: 10:00. Just 8:00 in Colorado. Her body might be reminding her to take it easy until she adjusted to a new time zone. She would remember that thought later that day.

Chapter Two

"My times are in thy hand."

Psalm 31:15

As Lacey sat at her desk she sensed a stirring in the air, as if someone had turned a fan on. They had! There was a box fan near the door which was whirring softly, bringing fresh air into the room. She had not noticed it before, nor how it suddenly came on. It felt good, though. She lifted her shoulder-length hair off her neck and fastened it into a pony tail. She smoothed her jacket and skirt and wondered if there were a track or indoor fitness center in town where she might walk and exercise. Back home, she had taken a long walk through her neighborhood almost every morning except in snowy weather. And she had even done a 5K before the accident. Of course, she could continue to walk right in her own neighborhood.

Someone knocked on the door. Standing to cross the room and open it, she caught something out of the corner of her eye. A woman was standing in the other doorway, disoriented.

"May I help you?" Lacey asked as she unlocked the outer door to admit an elderly man and woman, who walked right in without so much as a greeting.

Confused that not one of the three had yet spoken, she glanced around and gestured to the chairs. "Please, have a seat." They did.

"There you are. We have been huntin' all over for you, deuh," the older woman cried out happily, smiling at the younger woman in the far chair, who smiled back.

"Been raht with you the whole time, mama," she said in a local accent.

"Never thought we would be searchin' for new digs," said the man. "Not now. Not evuh."

"Well," Lacey broke in, "I am Lacey Brew, the realtor here to help you, I believe," she said cheerily. They turned to stare at her.

"We nevuh dreamed we would be using a realtor," said the older woman. "Well, I am Maisie Field and this heyuh is my mistuh of 56 years, Sim Field, and our daughtuh, Brenda Field Marks."

"And it seems like we are needin' a house for the three of us, ma'am," said Brenda.

"All together?" asked Lacey, feeling dumb.

"Yes, ma'am. All togethuh. Forevuh," smiled the mother with what almost seemed a smirk.

"Fine. And what kind of place do you hope to see or to buy?" Lacey asked, ruffling though the print-outs of available properties.

They all answered at once: "at least three bedrooms," "a huge country kitchen," and "a media room." This last item was said by the daughter.

"What in the heck is a media room?" asked her father impatiently. "What we need now is lots of space, lots of room. We are goin' to be togethuh now a long time, and we do not need to be on top of each othuh."

Suddenly a young woman appeared in the doorway with a tray of coffee and mugs. Lacey had not seen her before.

"These are for all y'all," she said quietly, setting the tray on the desk and backing out.

Lacey offered coffee to the three visitors and each took a cup, and they each drank it black.

"Kind of odd-tastin' coffee," Mrs. Field chuckled. "Don't taste per-cah-lated." Her husband swallowed his in a few gulps, and Brenda held her mug as if it were made of fragile glass. "Ah," she sighed. "Nahs. Very nahs."

"Would you prefer a house on some land? One or two floors? A garage?" Lacey asked.

"Oh, my. No land this time," retorted Mrs. Field.

"Yes, of course, land," cried her husband.

"Just so it has modern bathrooms and a kitchen with granite counter tops and stainless steel appliances," Brenda said, sounding as if she had watched a lot of television about real estate.

"Well," smiled Lacey, "this will be quite an adventure. Do you have any particular house or property in mind? Perhaps we should start with that."

A clock chimed in the hall and each of the visitors paused and smiled. Lacey checked her watch against the chimes. The clock was off by about five hours. Maybe it was just another antique, not meant to be listened to for real time.

The group exited through the back door and Lacey offered them seats in the G & H van that she thought was hers to use for clients. She typed an address into her portable GPS. The wind was blowing hard enough to launch old leaves from the previous autumn and delicate Dogwood blossoms from the nearby pink trees across the tarmac of the back parking lot; they skittered like dancers. The driver of a newspaper truck almost backed into her, and Lacey braked just in time.

"Sorry." she said to her family of clients. "I do not think he saw us." They drove down the street and turned left at the Farmers Market, drove several blocks and turned right, climbed a hill and stopped. "This house is available," Lacey remarked, glancing at her GPS and papers.

"Oh, my Lawd amighty," crowed the mother, "this is really somethin' special. Moonshine Cornuh."

"It is raht in town," commented her husband grumpily.

"Let's see the inside. I love that full porch," Brenda added.

They all four stepped out of the van and stood staring at the house, a two-story yellow frame Victorian with a nice, tidy flower garden full of tulips along the sidewalk. Lacey approached the house to find the lock box, which was next to the front door. Fumbling with it for a few seconds, she finally was able to reach in and remove two keys. Two? She studied them. One was a large key and the other a small one. She tried the large key first, and momentarily lost her balance, swaying a little, and steadying herself by grabbing the door frame. Maybe her shoes were making her topple, she thought, thinking that she should not have worn new *espradilles* out on her first day.

"How nice," Brenda said, looking at the porch. The four of them all filed into a front hall flanked by doors at the far end on each side. Ahead of them was a staircase. A hall beside the staircase probably led to the kitchen.

"I like this raht fine," the mother said. "I want to see the kitchen." She headed off down the hall. Brenda stayed put, as if rooted to the hardwood floor. She was staring up the staircase. "I think I saw a person," she whispered, turning to Lacey.

"I, um," coughed Lacey. "Hello? Hello," Lacey called into the quiet house. Lacey walked farther into the house and right through what felt like a huge cobweb. "Oooh. I just went through a cobweb," she said to Brenda, who had already headed upstairs. Lacey shrugged and hurried after her. The walls were all white. The floors were wood. There were several fireplaces with andirons in place.

"There does not seem to be anyone up here," Brenda said as Lacey reached the upper landing. They were standing outside a spacious bedroom with large sash windows.

Just then, Lacey's mobile phone rang and she excused herself to take the call.

"Ms. Brew? Ms. Brew? This is Mr. Glass. Where are you?"

"Oh. Hello. I have the Field family with me at 23 Oaklawn."

"Oh, my," he sighed. "I did not get the word in time," he said quietly. "Try to speed them through there by telling them there seems to be a contract on that house, all right?" he asked. "Wrong keys."

"If you say, so, Mr. Glass," Lacey answered, totally confused. Her papers for today had this house clearly listed as available to any client. She found the Fields all upstairs, bickering over rooms.

"I do not want to be in town," said Mr. Field. "And I have a say in this."

"I love this house, though," said his wife. "Oddly, though, there is not a thang in that kitchen. They must have taken everythang with them. We would have to buy all new everythang."

"I think it is kind of creepy, actually," Brenda added. "Let's try another one, Okay?"

They returned downstairs. The rooms were empty. An old glass lamp hung from what must have been the dining room ceiling. Oil burning? There were no bulbs, just a wick. Lacey peeked into the kitchen and saw only an empty room with a wooden floor, a very old stove, a washtub, and a wooden table. There were no cabinets, no appliances, and no evidence of electric sockets for anything. It was all odd, very odd. Suddenly, a woman in a long dress walked up to the cook stove and put a skillet on it. The vision went as fast as it had come, and Lacey was far too startled to say anything to the Field family. Time to get out of here.

Outside, she put the big key back in the lockbox. Then she tucked the smaller key in beside it. The Fields had traipsed back to the van. There were no other cars anywhere to be seen. Lacey saw what seemed to be a horse apple on the pavement. It was still steaming. Had a horse gone by? What on earth? No one had told her that carriage rides were popular in Rocky Mount.

"Mama," cried Brenda, "look at how that woman is dressed. Old-fashioned like. I love her clothes."

"It be bad luck, don't you know, to see a woman walking by herself in the morning," retorted Mrs. Field. "Means there'll be a death!"

"That hardly bothers me," snorted her husband. Brenda laughed loudly.

All of them except Mrs. Field turned to see whom Brenda was watching. Lacey saw a white-haired woman, her hair over her shoulders, with necklaces and bracelets, in a long batik skirt and ruffled blouse, strolling casually along the street and carrying one of the new reusable grocery bags, filled with breads. There was a baguette sticking out. The woman turned and waved with a beautiful smile. Lacey waved back. A Corgi was following her on a leash. Lacey thought it a charming scene.

While they prepared to leave, a group of people on bicycles passed by in the street and waved. The leader of the group called to them, stopping his bicycle at the curb. "Hello? Can you please tell me where the Post Office is from here? I took a wrong turn back there in town!"

Having just come that way, Lacey knew the answer! "It is back two blocks towards that church steeple over there and to your right," Lacey answered, as his fellow riders pulled up behind him and waited. They each wore a shirt that said "Gallant Bike Tours. Bike it and Like it!"

"Thanks a bunch," he said. "I'm doing my first tour of Rocky Mount and missed a turn! Mike Gallant of Blacksburg," he said as he peddled off, his helmet making his head look like an eagle.

She checked her list again and headed off down the street to another house, a one-story arts and craft bungalow, not unlike some on her own street. The Fields got out and walked up a curved sidewalk to the porch. The wind had blown a screen door open. It was flapping against the wooden house. The house appeared neglected to Lacey. Was it even ready to be shown?

"I love this bung-galow," Mrs. Field sighed. "It has a yahd large enough for pawpaw to have a garden. And we could put a porch swing raht over heuh." She wandered around the long porch while her family waited to enter. Lacey wondered at that double "g." Was that a local dialect? Lacey hurried to undo the lock box. This time there was just one key and it opened the front door easily. Her phone rang again.

"Ms. Brew? Lacey? This is Mary See calling. I wondered where you had gone with the van. I needed it for a very important client today. And you did not check it out. I had signed up for it. And Coy, Mr. Howe, said he knew nothing about anything. No one knew you were out with clients. Are you?"

"Oh. I am so sorry, Ms. See. I have the Field family with me, hoping for a three-bedroom. I can have the van back in an hour. Is that too late? I did not know about signing out for the van. Is that soon enough? This family wants to find a house today."

"No. I need it now, dear." Mary See said, making Lacey feel like a child being talked down to.

"I will leave the Fields here, then, and bring the van back, and take my own car back over here," Lacey said, gritting her teeth, trying to sound patient and friendly. It would not do to alienate Mary See on her very first day at G & H.

"Excuse, me," Lacey called into the house, "I will be right back. Will you all be okay in there until I return?" She hurried down the walk, passing through yet another cobweb.

"Certainly, young lady," said Mr. Field, bending around a wall where his wife was examining the plasterwork.

Lacey paused before backing up, to let a slim woman jogging with three large Golden Retrievers pass by. The woman waved. Friendly place, Lacey thought happily, some of the stress melting away. She managed to get the van back to the G & H lot in just under two minutes. One of the big advantages of a small town, she thought to herself with a smile. And when she rushed into the front hall through the back entrance, she caught her breath, as if the air had momentarily been squeezed from her lungs. She needed to slow down. Be calm.

"Here you are, then," exclaimed Coy

Howe, standing next to Mary See by a desk.

"I do apologize," Lacey began, but he waved away her words. "Not a problem. Here is the sign-out sheet for the vans. We have three vans. All are booked right now, so if you can use your car today, until we get you on the list...my error...it would help," explained Coy Howe.

"Mr. Ned Ruter..." Lacey began, but was stopped by a quizzical expression on both of their faces.

"Here he is," gestured Mary See, impatiently, pointing to the wall, where an old photo framed in a gold frame hung next to some other very old photos of what must have been the early days of G & H.

"But, but..." Lacey stammered....

"He founded Ruter & Howe in 1928," Coy Howe explained.

"Excuse me," interrupted Jim Glass, peering into the room and gesturing for Lacey to come closer, "I need to talk to Ms. Brew for a minute." She followed him into his office where he pointed to a chair and then closed the door behind them.

"I need to get back to the Fields..." she began, and he put his finger to his lip and sat down. He sighed.

"Ms. Brew, um, Lacey, I need to fill you in. Coffee?" She nodded that she did not want any.

"Well. First of all, how has today been?" he asked kindly.

"I had a family of three come in, through the back entrance, this morning and they were hoping to find a house today…" she started to reply when he held his hand up to stop her.

"Aha. So that is how it happened. The new back entrance. That explains why no one in the front office knew that they had come in or that you all had left…through the back door, I assume? Yes, yes. It worked." He grinned and tipped back in his swivel chair and laughed aloud. Lacey was so confused. "I was not nearby to point out the, um, the other van for you to use today," he smiled. "My dear, how can I explain all of this," he asked, staring straight at her with a serious expression, all traces of humor or laughter gone. "How about if you start first, with what happened."

"I simply put the Fields in the van out back and punched in the address for the Victorian on Oaklawn. They each had very different ideas about what they wanted in a house."

"Yes, yes," he murmured, "they would. Of course. Go on."

"When you called me, while I was over there showing them the house, I was surprised to learn there apparently already is a contract on that house, so I drove them on to the bungalow, where they probably still are," she said worriedly, glancing at her watch. "I had best hurry back to the Fields," Lacey said, getting up from the chair and heading to the door. "Can we talk later?"

"One question," Jim Glass said, holding out his arms as if to rescue a falling child, "Have you noticed anything odd since you left G & H today?"

"Not really, just cobwebs and lots of keys and I think I must still be tired from my drive," she said with a grin.

"All right. We will talk later on then," he said. "And maybe you can tell me about your interest in Mr. Ruter," he said, pointing to the picture on the wall.

"Oh, it is nothing much," Lacey replied, going out the door. "He first called me in Colorado before I got the job. Then you called me and offered me the job, on the phone and in a follow-up letter." She watched as Jim Glass's face became pale and sweat seemed to appear on his face. "What is wrong?" she asked, starting back in.

"My dear girl," he started, wiping his face with a handkerchief, "Please come over and look at the photos on my office wall, to begin with," he suggested, still pale. "What do you see?"

Lacey hurried back in and stared hard at the photos. "Well, here is a photo of a Mr. Ruter and a Mr. Howe, taken in 1928. Must be Mr. Ruter's father and Mr. Howe's father. And here is one of the original building taken the same year. It has 'R & H' on the front. 'Ruter and Howe,' I guess. Then there is a photo of the building much later…yes, 1959, and it says 'Ruter & Howe' on the sign. And here is one of you, taken a few years ago. Oh, Mr. Glass, Jim, I am so tired from my trip. Maybe we could go over these nice photos later on? I feel I need to get back to the clients."

"You are too tactful," he interrupted, smiling. "That was taken in the 1970's. I had just been hired here, to, um, to replace Ned Ruter. I am standing next to Coy Howe, who did take over from his late father. I think we can cover this right now, dear."

"To replace him?" she asked.

"Yes. Ned Ruter was in a plane crash in 1969, coming back from New Orleans. Plane went down in a bad storm, no survivors. It was deadly Hurricane Camille, actually. Terrible storm! Devastated the Gulf and then stalled over Virginia and killed hundreds up in Nelson County, south of Charlottesville."

"But that is…impossible…."

"He had not finished what he wanted

to do here," Jim Glass continued.

"You mean, he died. He died? And you took his place here. And his son, Ned, works here now, too?"

"There is no son named Ned. He had no children. He was a bachelor, never had married. He was a graduate of Hampden-Sydney College, Class of 1925. His own family had owned a lot of land in the county, and Ned had the brilliant idea of starting a company that would help people find land and houses. It was the very first real estate office here. It was called Ruter and Howe. The name changed to Glass & Howe after Coy and I took over. Afterwards."

"I am so confused," Lacey said, putting her head in her hands. "A Ned Ruter called me, called me twice."

Just then the phone rang and Mr. Glass leaned over to take the call, and gestured kindly that she could leave. "Don't worry about the Fields," he said nicely, "I will go take them around. You can go ahead and meet the Californians coming to see The Grove."

Lacey hurried from the room, out the front door and around the side of the building to the parking lot where her white car sat alone. No vans were to be seen. All the agents must be out showing houses, she thought, heading back out. Her head was swimming. She was totally confused.

Lacey took her car to meet the people coming to see The Grove. She had not had time to read much on the history but knew that the house was one of the oldest plantation houses in town, and had Civil War connections. She was eager to see a Southern plantation house! Before all of this, the Confederacy for her had just been history in a history book.

Sure hope these clients are ordinary people, with money and ideas, because I do not think I can handle much more weirdness, she mumbled to herself as she drove past the Farmers Market and on to the old estate. The streets were dry, the breeze soft, the spring trees beautiful in their blossoms. Blossoms like crosses blew in drifts along the street and through the air. Dogwood blossoms. Nothing like them in Colorado. Lacey was eager to learn the Virginia trees and flowers; she hoped for a small garden in that backyard of hers.

Running along the side of the street with three Golden Retrievers on leashes was the same beautiful, lean woman with short hair. Lacey slowed her car, letting the woman pass. But the woman waved her to a stop right inside the elegant driveway. Lacey leaned out of her window and smiled.

"Hello! I am Lacey Brew, the new

realtor at Glass & Howe," Lacey said with a smile.

"Hi, I am Leila Park and I live right over there around the corner," she replied with a huge grin. "My husband is a Judge. I run the dogs through this property almost daily, but if you all want me to stop, just let me know. Nice to meet you, Lacey." With that she loped off, the big dogs tugging her along towards the corner.

Pulling past two columns made of river stones on either side of a brick driveway edged with English Boxwoods, Lacey made her way down to the large brick house. There was no other car there yet. Which door should she use? The real front door flanked by symmetrical windows with dark shutters was on the façade facing the street but another door on the side of the house was closer to the driveway and...had the lockbox on it.

She jumped out and walked over to the side door with a realtor's lockbox and consulted a paper with the combination. With a little pulling, she was able to unlock the box, get the keys out and open the door.

The heavy black door opened smoothly, opened into a kitchen with a hardwood floor and old cabinets. There was a faint scent of food, very faint. The room was immaculate, the ceilings tall...maybe 12 or more feet. Glass windows, transoms, above the two doors in the room were shut. The doors were massive. She checked her watch. She would just have time to check out the downstairs before the couple from California arrived. On the blue countertop in the kitchen she saw a small pile of booklets. There were several copies of "The Grove: History of a House." She nabbed one to skim before the clients arrived.

She turned right and opened a door into a large dining room, empty, with tall windows and built-in shelves and an enormous gilded mirror above a fireplace. It was chilly in there. She passed out of the room into a front hall, and saw at the end of the foyer/hall what had to be the elaborate front door, flanked by more leaded glass and with another transom above. The front staircase was worn but the railing gleamed. Across from the staircase was the entrance into a fancy square room, a formal parlor with decorative plaster trim and a large plaster medallion from which hung the most beautiful crystal chandelier she had ever seen.

What an amazing room. What stories it could tell, she thought. Beyond the parlor was a narrow hall with parquet flooring, and windows on the front and a granite bar on the back wall. This passage led to a large rectangular room with another fireplace, four huge windows with shutters opened, and a wall of built-in bookshelves built to the ceiling.

A "clank" sound startled her and she brought her hand to her mouth to stifle a small scream. She heard it again. The radiators. Every room had radiators, beneath a wooden seat, beneath most windows. The rooms were cool enough to warrant the heat being on. Lacey wondered why the rooms were cool. Cold, almost.

Lacey hurried back to the kitchen door and waited for her clients. Stepping out onto the landing she watched as wrens, cardinals, chickadees, mourning doves, and squirrels darted in and out of the foliage and vines beneath the poplar trees and pines. It was almost a forest back here.

She skimmed the history of this house. Built in 1854. Greek Revival. John S. Hale, wealthiest planter in the county, widower, late wife had been sister of Jubal Early. There were five original frame or brick 19th century outbuildings, known correctly or historically as "dependencies." They included a law office, a smokehouse, a cook's family's house, and two frame buildings for storage. Had there been slaves here? The thought gave her a chill. Across the lawns she saw a man pushing a wheelbarrow and carrying a shovel. The gardener, she thought, unworried.

Tucking the keys to the house safely into her jacket pocket, she leaned back against the brick wall and closed her eyes. There was so much to know. Her talk today with Jim Glass had bothered her. What was the big mystery about Ned Ruter? He must be on vacation.

Maybe it had been a kind of joke. Maybe Mr. Glass was teasing her. That had to be it. She was still very tired from the drive, from the move, from that weird dream that had been so vivid it had seemed that she were hearing real people nearby. She hoped she could sleep better tonight.

This was just a normal small town, one most people would never hear of, unless they were Civil War buffs or fans of all kinds of music, she told herself. The town was on the map for lots of things. Okay. It was an okay place. She should stop trying to over-explain every little thing, or "thang," as Mrs. Field had pronounced it!

Her thoughts were interrupted when a large SUV pulled up outside in the driveway, scattering birds. A young couple got out and started toward her.

"Hello." Lacey greeted them with handshakes. "Welcome to The Grove. I am Lacey Brew."

"Tiffany and Chip Keller," said the pretty woman, staring past her into the kitchen. "We only have half an hour. I'm sorry. We have to see another house at the lake today," the young woman said somewhat curtly and dismissively. Tiffany stepped into the house and her husband, with a handful of papers and maps, followed.

"Would you like to hear any of the history of the house?" Lacey asked with a smile. "I have a short history here that was left for potential buyers. You may take one."

"Not right now, thanks," Chip replied impatiently. "What we want to do is to zip through and see what is here." With that, they headed off on their own as if Lacey were not even involved.

Her first day as a realtor...she wondered if this were typical. Had she been aggressive enough? Been too personal? Invisible? That thought gave her goose bumps. She had abandoned the Fields. And now the Kellers had abandoned her. Welcome to real estate.

Lacey followed the two Kellers around downstairs as they murmured to each other about antique window panes, the cost of heating with electric hot-water heat, the floor-length boards of the hardwood floors, the parquet, the high ceilings, the bar with the granite countertop.

"This is perfect. I can see us using this bar for all kinds of parties and receptions," exclaimed Tiffany, stroking the countertop with the enraptured stare of a wife on House Hunters who seemed to live for granite and stainless steel.

Lacey consulted her notes. "The bar was redone three years ago, as was the facing on one of the working fireplaces downstairs…all in the same grey and pink granite."

"We have to have granite," Tiffany declared, pushing her windblown hair back as she critically examined the plasterwork of the fancy ceilings. "And, Chip, look," she gestured, "we could replace that chipped plaster with newer molding so it looks perfect. Perfect. It all has to look perfect."

Tiffany glanced over at Lacey and continued. "I am a doctor. Chip is a Developer. We will be running a very upscale retirement home for wealthy California clients who want to move away from the drought and earthquakes and have peace and quiet for their final years. This house *is* handicap accessible, of course?"

"It has an elevator," Lacey replied. "And these wide, old 1850's doorways will accommodate a wheelchair," she continued, reading from the notes.

Tiffany laughed. "Heavens. All of our

clients will be ambulatory. They might use a cane, but only a fancy cane," she laughed. "This will be the first place in the country…um, wherever we end up buying, I mean…for wealthy assisted living in an historic home in the South."

"But I still do not think of Virginia as the South," her husband retorted with a snort. "South is Gulf."

"Well," Lacey interjected, already feeling defensive about The Grove and Virginia, "actually, Virginia is considered by almost all historians as the 'mother ship' of the South. Its history, its many famous presidents…"

"Ha, ha, ha," laughed Tiffany. "You are right, we are sure. But Chip went to LSU and he thinks you have to be on the Gulf to be Southern. I am from Connecticut. I know historical places and I know that Virginia is 'Southern.' But you do not sound like you are from here."

"I am not," Lacey replied, deciding not to divulge anything about her life to these people. They were not going to buy the place. Wait until they saw the kitchen and vintage baths mentioned in the papers.

"Well, we looked it up, and Virginia does not have as many regulations as California, where we moved from…La Jolla…for 'nursing homes,' and we know we can make it work. We already have people signed up to move." Tiffany dismissed Lacey and hurried off to other rooms. Chip remained behind, studying his Iphone messages.

Lacey found Tiffany in the kitchen, with a laser measuring device, apparently getting the dimensions of the room while she talked aloud. "Needs a new floor. New countertops. New stove. New island. New cabinets. New doors. New lights. New refrigerator." Lacey saw that Tiffany was dictating into a hand-held recorder. Pretty neat.

"Hon, let's hurry it up," called Chip as he peeked into the kitchen. The sun was striping the beautiful wooden floor. Branches of a redbud were tapping the huge window. There was a mellow, homey feeling to the room. It did not feel at all as if it had been unused and empty for any time at all.

"We could fix the kitchen, modernize it, sweetie," Tiffany said, hurrying past Lacey and taking the back stairs in leaps. "But we will have to sink a lot of money into renovations."

Chip and Lacey followed her up the stairs. She had studied the house notes long enough by now to know how to answer questions about the back stairs, the walnut railing, the worn treads, that it had been a servants' staircase until well into the 20th century. But they did not ask questions and left her no chance to offer information. They almost ran from bedroom to bedroom, glancing at the huge sash windows, chair rails, crown molding, wainscoting, closets, floors, and electrical outlets.

"I know we have to cut this visit short, but we want to come back tomorrow and look some more. Is that okay?" Chip asked, standing by the fireplace in an upstairs sitting room.

"I am sure that can be arranged," Lacey smiled. "What time would you like to come?"

"How about 9 a.m. tomorrow, rain or shine," Tiffany said smartly, staring at the covered radiators. Outside, the ancient trees swayed in the wind and provided shade for the house. Very peaceful, Lacey thought, as she followed the couple down the front stairs with its cherry railing into the main hall. She let them out the massive front door, locked it from the outside with one of the keys, and said goodbye. She watched as they stood back and stared up at the façade and then made their way over to the paved driveway on the curving brick sidewalk bordered by flowering bushes and a lovely lamppost.

When she was alone again she made a note to check on rules and regulations for assisted care facilities in Virginia and whether or not the State, County, and Town had rules. Surely, they must. She dropped the keys into the lockbox and headed out to her car, and was about to get in when she wondered if they had turned lights on or off upstairs. Darn.

Lacey hurried back over to the lockbox, grabbed the keys to the front door, and ran up the front brick walk, seeing for the first time that white marks on the brick remained where something had been attached…a portico…at one time? It needed a pretty portico or *porte cochère* or awning or something, she thought, to protect people from wind and rain as they came and went through the beautiful door. She fumbled for the keys and found them. Inserting one into the door she stepped in and at once felt a difference.

Where the rooms had been cool and slightly musty from disuse just minutes before, now the hall was warm and had the distinct aroma of…meat? How odd. She inched further into the room and walked slowly towards the smell. Rounding the corner off the front hall into the dining room she almost screamed when she saw a black woman in a long dress setting a platter of pork chops onto a long table covered in a damask cloth. The table was set for four. There were shutters on the inside of the windows. The room was cool but smelled of candle wax. Candles were lit and burning, their flames flickering. A silver baby cup sat at one place. The plates were a blue and white pattern of trees and people, an early Wedgwood. She stepped closer. The woman did not seem to sense her there.

"Gots to be gettin' the plates ready, Tiddy, gots to get them here 'for Mistress Hale comes in with the young'uns. No gennelmen tonight, just the young'uns. But I gots to get the salat on and the cider. Mercy."

With that the woman hurried out of the room, going through the door to the kitchen. Lacey tiptoed after her, startled when she stepped into what she thought would be the kitchen she had recently walked through, only to find she was outside, on hard packed dirt covered with straw and that there was no kitchen there. She hurried along, following the woman who had stepped into…hey, she had stepped into that smaller brick building sitting behind the main house. Lacey followed.

The rooms were small with low

ceilings, plastered brick walls covered with hooks for hanging pans and pots, a large brick hearth with a fire. A young black child was stirring the fire. A large pot hung from a hook and an iron skillet with three legs sat on the coals. It had a lid. The woman lifted the lid and lifted out a big circle of bread. Cornbread. The pork, what remained of it, was still in another iron pan. Something green was simmering in another. The smell was unfamiliar to Lacey. A jug of pale cider sat on a wooden table with pewter mugs. The woman put the cornbread and cider on a tray and hurried back outside and crossed over to the back of The Grove and placed the foods on the table just as a middle aged woman, about 46, and a boy of about 10, a girl of about 8, and a small girl of about 5 seated themselves in the dining room. Following the child was a calico cat. It came over to Lacey and wound itself around her ankles.

"It must see me," she thought silently, fascinated by the scene before her. "My Lord, it can tell that I am in the room."

The woman and children started to eat after a silent grace. She could hear them speak. She moved closer, oblivious to the cat, which screeched when she stepped on its tail accidentally.

The youngest child turned when the

cat screeched. She seemed confused.

"*Let us have our supper now, John, Mary, Jannie,*" *their mother said sweetly.*

"*Mama? Mama.*"

"*Yes, sweet Jannie,*" *her Mama replied, lifting some food onto her pewter fork.*

"*There is something wrong.*"

"*No, no,*" *she laughed indulgently.* "*There can be nothing wrong, Jannie. All of us are here, safe and well. Your Daddy is away for a day or two but he left Big Tim and Nanny Tim and Tiddy in charge of everything so we will be fine.*"

"*But, mama…*"

"*No more,*" *she chided her gently.*

"*Jannie,*" *said the boy,* "*Why do you always think there is something wrong?*"

"*Because Celine screeched, that's why, John, and she had no reason to,*" *his little sister Jannie whined.*

The other daughter, Mary, answered. "*That cat is not right. You know how she acts sometimes at night. Sniffing around and not a mouse to be had…just her checking things, looking, maybe looking for Uncle Jubal. She was his cat,*" *Mary said.*

"*Where is Uncle Jubal, then? Why did he leave us?*" *Jannie asked.*

"*Now, children,*" *their mother said,*

looking at her middle child, "Your Uncle Jube and all the brave men are away in the War. You know that. Your half-brother Sam is riding with your Uncle Jube and General Gordon."

"Daddy is not away in the War," countered Mary, stabbing a piece of pork with her small fork.

"Your Daddy wanted to join the Army but Governor Letcher asked him to stay and make sure our troops got plenty of food and tobacco. That is what your Daddy does. He farms."

"He does not farm, not really," replied John. "He has 250 slaves for that."

"Well, he manages farms. The workers do the work on the farms. And what your Daddy does is very important for Virginia."

"I wish I could be with Uncle Jube," John remarked somewhat angrily. "I could have been a good soldier. I know I..."

"John, you know what Daddy said, and what your Uncle Jube said about that. You are only ten. And your sisters are eight and five, and we need you here. You are needed right here while the men are at War. Someone has to help keep things going."

Margaret Hale lowered her voice to a whisper and continued. "Your uncle and the others think the servants are restless. Some over in Eastern Virginia have been freed. If we win this war maybe things will stay as they are, here. If the South does not win...no one knows what could happen. The servants might stay here and work. But they might not. What would happen to our lands and farms and crops if the workers all just left? Your Uncle Jube wrote us that servants are free in Winchester, up the Shenandoah Valley."

"Is that far away from here, Mama?" Jannie asked. "I'm scared, mama," she whispered," spooning some food into her mouth and glancing over at the cat.

"Is our brother Sam coming home, Mama?" John asked, looking at the cat across the room, who seemed to be playing with her tail.

"It has been just a year since our friend General Thomas Jackson was killed at Chancellorsville. So tragic," Margaret Hale said. "And Anna Jackson wrote to me from her home in Cottage Home, North Carolina, that she probably would not be able to visit us at all, here in Virginia, until the war ends. Your Daddy and I were guests of theirs in Lexington just the one time, when he was teaching at the Institute."

Celine was circling Lacey's left foot, purring. Lacey was afraid to move. What was she hearing? What was she seeing? Oh, my. She had not even had time enough to finish reading about the history of The Grove and here she was, in the same room as the first family who had lived here. These had to be the Hales. Margaret Ingles Saunders Hale and her and John Hale's three children. Lacey felt as if she were about to pass out. She leaned back against the cool wall. The cat stirred. Lacey, gripping the key in her hand, inched towards the front hall, as the family continued to talk about Uncle Jube, their Daddy, the servants, and Stonewall and Anna Jackson!

She pushed herself along the wall until she reached the front door. It was shut tight. The glass panes on either side of the door and the transom above it, which was open and letting fresh air into the room, sparkled as if recently cleaned. Outside, seen through the sidelights, a row of short oaks blocked any view of the rest of the yard. She reached for the knob and turned. The door swung in and she stepped across the wooden sill onto a narrow brick stoop covered above by a huge frame portico. She quickly turned back and locked the front door. In front of her, from the front stoop until the distant oaks, was a level brick walk or carriageway. There was no driveway to the right edged with old Boxwoods. She stepped onto the brick path and started to walk forward when she tripped on a loose brick, stumbled, and dropped the keys.

"May I help you, Miz?" asked a man with a rake. He approached her. "I am Wild Bill Conroy. I work here," he said. "You were showin' the house to people today, right?" He smiled.

"I, uh, yes...I was," Lacey replied, looking back at the house. There was no portico. The front stoop was gone. In its place was the brick entry she had walked on to get into the house minutes before. This was *now*. Nearby were trees, tall trees, not short oaks. Big English Boxwoods framed the front steps and driveway. Holly trees stood in front of the breezeway and the Library wing. None of those had been there a second ago when she had stood under the portico!

"I am Lacey Brew, a new realtor with Glass & Howe," she continued. "And I will be back tomorrow morning to show the place again to the couple from California."

"Ha." laughed Wild Bill. "No people from California but the first Mr. and Mrs. Greer, ever be wantin' to live here. I worked for them nigh forty and more years, good people. The new widow, now, she has kept it for five years since Mr. Greer died, and now she has to sell."

"Oh?" ventured Lacey. She had not had time to read about the seller.

"Well, it sits empty, don't it? Lonely, that's what this house is. I been working here much of my life and I ain't never saw nothing like this empty loneliness." He shook his head. "This kind of house be needin' lots of folks in it, like the olden days."

Lacey had a thought. "How about a calico cat?"

"Dat cat? Sure I seen that cat. Thang's been here as long as I recall. Cats have nine lives. I think this one must have twenty," he chuckled. "Well, ma'am, I be goin' to run. Only work three days a week now, seeing as the fambly is gone and no one around. I check trees, limbs, lights, all that stuff." He gestured to the huge oak tree behind them on the right of the tumbled brick walk. "This here tree been here since the beginning', I reckon. Back from before the War. Gotta watch it. Limbs be fallin' in a wind. Every time."

"The War?"

He looked at her funny. "You know, *the* War, the one set the black folks free," he threw his head back and laughed. "Thank the Lord. Thank the Lord. Not the other war, the one my...um," he seemed to grope for the word, "ancestors be fightin' in, back at the Guilford Courthouse, agin' Cornwallis."

"That War," Lacey mumbled. "The Civil War, of course." She had not heard of Guilford Courthouse.

The rest of the day was sort of a blur to Lacey. She stopped into the office to check for papers for her next showing, tomorrow sometime, a cottage on Coal Street not far from her own place, and then she found a fast food restaurant and huddled in a corner with a big chicken, apple, and cranberry salad and a huge paper cup of coffee. She kept checking her watch, feeling the time lag from her quick drive across country. She was still on Colorado time, she figured. In her old time zone. She had gotten up too early today. But she had had to.

She had brought the booklet along, about the history she needed to know. Sipping her coffee, she opened it and began to read.

"Just as Roanoke across the Blue Ridge Mountains had once been called 'Big Lick' by its earliest English-speaking settlers for its salt licks that attracted game, Rocky Mount's name, once Mount Pleasant, had changed over time when two settled areas merged into one. But both of the names referred to the 1400-foot tall rocky outcropping, also called Bald Knob, a kind

of rounded monadnock, or rounded rock hill, that looms in recent times over the high school.

Rocky Mount and its foothills and mountains are composed of layers and layers of rock, minerals, caves, stories, and history. The essence of each of its eras is captured in the seam of coal on a hillside, the glint of quartz in a cemetery, the twinkle in the eye of a balladeer in overalls at a Dairy Queen surrounded by banjo players, singing traditional songs about mountain men and murder or love, and by the gleam of the glass of thick jars that once held corn liquor. There are also layers of Time, maybe unseen by the everyday person, but felt in the hearts or hands of the history-keepers and artists. The weaver with her loom in Callaway, the painter in her bottomland beneath Cahas Mountain, the songwriter on her way to the Fiddlers' Convention in Galax, the folk artist in Floyd...they understand the layers of Time.

In earlier centuries, great Native American chiefs like Cahas, for whom the mountain beside Boones Mill up the valley is named, supposedly in imitation of the sound of a crow ('ka-hays'), may have stood with their tribes high over the green, rolling, rock-

studded land. They may have planned hunting trips for deer and bison. Later, the Saponi and Monacans, and even later, the Shawnee and Cherokee, and others, certainly stood on Bald Knob to scout out the arrival of the western-moving intrusive English pioneer settlers and soldiers. The first of those settlers had been the family of Robert and Swinfeld Hill, who built the first fort, a blockhouse, in the area, to protect the lives of the English-speaking newcomers. Many forts were built along the western frontier, and some, like Fort Blackwater erected by Captain Nathaniel Terry off what is now Rt. 220, were inspected by George Washington in 1756, well, before Rocky Mount ever existed.

A son of Robert Hill was killed, in fact, by an arrow shot from the bow of an Indian. The young Hill was cut down before his time. Eventually the tribes either emigrated west or were forced to do so as their lands were taken first by the English and later by the Americans or divided up by the earliest settlers of this lovely part of what is today Franklin County, Virginia. Their legacy lasts only in place names and the flints and arrowheads so sought after by treasure hunters. But their sacred places may still remain sacred to their ghosts.

The original settlers brought with them pride, dreams of owning their own land, a complex reverence and disdain for British institutions (church, government, taxation), courage, and the ability to make whisky. Fifth-largest county, in land size, in the whole Commonwealth, Franklin County, settled by Scots, English, and Germans, still has just the one high school, right beneath Bald Knob, and its graduates are as proud and confident as the eagle who is its mascot. The residents of the town today have memories and dreams.

Their ancestors had lost much, especially in the War Between the States, their livelihoods taken, their dignity shaken when the US Government punitively called Virginia, 'Military District No. 1,' after that War's end and imposed punitive revenue taxes on its freight shipped by rail. Their finest young men had been killed or maimed in battles, in a war which was ultimately lost. That war lives on. Not in flags so much, although many a Confederate Flag can still be seen around the county. But in a natural resistance to and wariness towards outsiders coming in from out of the South, and a lingering resistance to anything smacking of control by the Federal Government. Why?

The 'Feds' not only punished Virginia after the 1860's, but by arresting and trying them in the era of Prohibition, the 1920's and 1930's, during the height of the illegal liquor making and transporting in the low, fast cars that put Franklin County on the map as the moonshine capital of the world, beleaguered by Revenuers. The beginnings of car racing could also be traced back to the era of transporting moonshine in fast cars.

A clash of cultures (think Athens and Sparta, the 'Troubles' in Ireland, or Islamic sects in the Middle East) gives rise to danger, courage, excesses of honor and conflict, and intrigues. There is really never a 'victor.' But there are losers. The honorable often stand by honor and lose. The victors get lucky and win. And the causes of the conflicts were serious and complex. In Virginia, plantations needed reliable and cheap labor. Slavery. They had no back-up plan on how to produce crops without slaves. And in the liquor business, they wanted to survive economically without paying taxes to a Government who, in their eyes, had already taken their wealth from them decades earlier.

'Mount Pleasant' was also the name of the

solemn and stately, Boxwood-enclosed Federal-style mansion, the oldest in the Historic District uptown, built by a brother ('Light Horse' Harry) of the famous General Lee known for, among many other things, his horse named Traveller. Still occupied, Mount Pleasant holds its secrets and traditions in stately silence. One other mansion, the Greek Revival Grove, in midtown, has had only three families of owners (Hale, Saunders, Greer) since being built in 1854 as an impressive plantation home for the second wife of widower John Stafford Hale when Hale married into the Saunders clan, who built Bleak Hill out near Callaway. And the old colonial house called The Farm at The Furnace had been the home of early settler James Callaway.

Property, law, courts, and land were to the South what goods, commerce, churches, and busy villages were to the North. Land was wealth for landowners in the South. And money in the bank was wealth to residents of the North. Landed gentry, plantations, and courthouses dotted Virginia just as industrious merchants, village greens, and church steeples dotted New England. Virginia, with its British traditions of landed gentry, gentlemen farmers-turned political philosophers and presidents, great generals, *and slavery...was a rich landscape in which culture and conflict had tugged at the morale and dreams of its citizens for centuries.*

Rocky Mount, tucked in at the far west side of the Piedmont, in 'Southside,' right up against the mountains and cut off from the Great Valley and Shenandoah Valley further north except for the passage through the mountains at Boones Mill, was somewhat isolated culturally. By choice. Proud of its heritage (iron, tobacco, textiles, furniture, liquor, General Jubal A. Early, and Booker T. Washington) and resistant to being shoehorned by necessity into modern life, the Town was a mixture of old and new in a delightful way that attracted visitors and artists and opinions."

Wow. She sat back and savored the history. What details. She had had no idea of the complexity of "The South." Her interest in the region was beginning to grow. She was eager to learn. And what she had seen today, the Hale family dining at The Grove, had been part of this history. Had this happened to anyone else? Did Jim Glass or Coy Howe or Mary See or even young Kim know that it was possible to "see" into the past in that house?

What a day. She leaned forward and put her head in her hands and closed her eyes. The sounds and smells of the restaurant reassured her she was in her *now* time. For a change. She fingered her house keys on the key ring in her pocket. The keys for The Grove were securely back in the lock box at that house. And she had already turned in the keys for the houses she had shown the Fields earlier. What about the actual houses she had shown the Field family? Had she shown them in the present time, or had those been much earlier? She sat up again so suddenly she almost knocked her paper cup over. She glanced around the restaurant but no one seemed to be paying any attention to her at all.

Above her on a big television screen a "breaking news" item streamed across the bottom: "Meth lab found on Coal Street. Husband, wife, two sons, and a neighbor interrogated and taken to the Courthouse. Social Services has been called in to take the boys. Stay tuned for *News at Six* for the whole story."

Meth. She had never even heard of the drug until recently. This part of the country had an awful epidemic of its use. Well, she would have to miss the story since she did not have television yet. In fact, she did not have any modern, up-to-code outlets at all. She would have to get that fixed soon.

After her meal, Lacey headed out to find a grocery store near her own Moonshine Corner part of town. She needed a few basics, and Mary See had told her to drive a mile towards Ferrum and go to the Faire Foods Mart for dairy and fruit and basics. So she had, pleasantly surprised at the low prices. With the bag of groceries in her arms, she walked up her walk between the cheery rows of tulips in the breezy, sunny early evening, happy to be home.

She fitted her key into the door and entered the living room. Having left the windows open for the fresh air, she found the house quite comfortable. It got no direct sun during the day, and the rooms were pleasant. After a brief bath she put a dish of cat food on the back stoop and waited for Callie. But the cat did not come.

Lacey curled up on her sofa by the front window and tried to think through what all she had felt today. And "seen." Had she really seen people from over 150 years ago? Had she really seen someone cooking in the Victorian house? Had she really heard the Hale family talking to each other? Or, were these events linked to what her doctors had warned her about: imagination and hallucinations brought on when very tired, because of the clonk on her head and mini-coma after the car accident? Oh, she wished she knew.

Chapter Three

"Behold, I show you a mystery; We shall not all sleep,
but we shall be changed."

I Corinthians 15:48

Her sleep that second night was deep with no dreams. The neighborhood was so very quiet that the silence almost woke her up. But she stayed asleep all night, one of the first times since the accident.

With a cup of coffee on her front porch early the next day, she saw a tall, slender young man walking briskly up the street with a watering can in one hand and a handful of sticks in the other.

"Good Morning," he called to her. "You are my new neighbor. May I?" And he loped up her walk and stood on her front steps. "Jess Thompson."

"Hello to you," she smiled. "I am Lacey Brew. I started work yesterday at

Glass & Howe Realty in town. I am learning the ropes."

"I bet," he said with a lopsided grin. "I am usually up real early. I work in my gardens most of the day and sometimes wander up into town to the café for coffee and a sandwich, if I can afford it," he added. "I am very frugal. I even make a lot of my own food. Organic, of course. And I will drop some hummus off on the porch for you this afternoon."

"Thank you." Lacey said happily.

"Depends how you look at it, but I feel like the richest person in town," Jess quipped mysteriously. "I know things."

"Ah," she smiled, encouraging him.

"Yes. I have lived here quite a while. I know lots of the town folks. And I know lots of the history of the town."

"I read a very thorough history yesterday, one from the Historical Society. I learned so much. Are you from here?" she asked.

"No. Actually, I was a city boy. But I wanted to have gardens and to invent things. I like to write and publish and have had many articles in all kinds of journals, from science to fantasy to children's book journals. I am really just a child at heart," he smiled. "Truly."

"Well, if I have a chance for a garden,

maybe you would show me how, here in Virginia? I have been out West for many years. So different here," she replied.

"First thing people ask you around here is, 'Who was your Daddy?' Then they ask, 'Where do you go to church?' Then they ask why you are living here," Jess laughed.

"Oh, my. I have not run into that yet." Lacey smiled. "Sure is different than in Colorado."

"Tight hereabouts. Real tight. You can live here for thirty years and still be the new guy, um, gal, on the block. Just ignore it. And since you are working at Glass & Howe, you will soon meet Martha Jo Puntoff and many of the other merchants downtown," Jess said mysteriously with a wink. "And wait until you meet Lee Anne Travis, who is writing a family cookbook and likes to try recipes out on us. Delicious!"

Lacey laughed with him, hoping the people all would all be nice. "Thanks for the advice. By the way, are you the next house up the street?"

"I am right up that hill beyond the huge peony bush and the holly trees. I have raised garden beds in my front yard and use rain barrels that I make for irrigation. And I grow most of my own food. I am a vegetarian, by choice, not by fad. And I am looking forward to a great harvest this summer. I will share," he said shyly. "And I try to respect what might have been sacred grounds for the Native Americans who were here long before the settlers."

"I would love that, having you share your garden. And I want to know more about the Indian culture here, too. I was in Colorado for years and learned what I could about the Native American cultures out there. The Arapahoe, Sioux, Apache. Oh, my." she exclaimed. "I will have to find something to give you in return," Lacey continued. "I draw and paint, so maybe I can make a drawing for you, maybe of your house," she said happily.

"That would be great. Well, I had better be off. Like a rabbit. I will be right up there if you need anything."

"Oh, Jess, before you go, may I ask one quick question? The inside of my house seems really 'vintage,'" she began, and he chimed in to say, "Mine is, too. No dishwasher. I know what you mean."

"So, the houses here are like that? Vintage?" she asked. "I do not have any appliances here at all. I think they were removed instead of being left for me, the new owner. Darn."

"Not all of them, but the few I have

been in here on this street are 'vintage' and then some. You might need an electrician and a plumber to bring you into modern times," he chuckled, starting back up the hill to his house.

Lacey went back inside and tidied up from where she had made coffee. Out the back kitchen window she could see pine trees and thick bushes. Not much out there. There was dust on the windowsills. The glass of the windows was streaked. The air felt heavy, as if holding a secret. She must not let her imagination run her life, she thought, pulling herself back to the moment.

At 8:20 she drove to work and spent the first 20 minutes researching codes and laws in Virginia about assisted care facilities, so she would be ready for her clients at 9:00. Taking her own car, so as not to disturb anyone who had signed up for the company vans, she made her way around a few corners, past the Post Office and Farmers Market with its trestle tables and parking lot, and pulled down the long drive to the historic estate under its canopy of tall trees. She startled a doe and two fawns. Right in the middle of town.

As Lacey parked by the smokehouse covered in ivy at The Grove, Lelia Park jogged by with the three dogs on leashes, coming across the wide lawns to the east of the house. Lelia waved and chugged on, crossing the property in no time, and heading out onto the street that ran from the lower part of town where the shops were to the upper part of town where the courthouse, law offices, and real estate companies were, along with the newspaper, the Rocky Mount *Bugle*. Lacey looked across the vast grounds of The Grove and noticed a line of two-story houses behind a row of trees and overgrown shrubs that marked the eastern side of the property. She wondered who lived over there and if that street or neighborhood had a name like hers did, her Moonshine Corner.

"Good mornin'," called a deep voice from the curve of the driveway. Wild Bill Conroy was pushing a wheelbarrow full of sod and plants and a big shovel. He was dressed in baggy overalls and work boots. He was rugged and solid looking, sort of timeless in his attire.

"Hello," Lacey replied, checking her watch. "My clients said they would be here at 9:00."

"Don't be holdin' your breath," he laughed.

"Oh, I think they are pretty serious potential buyers," she replied.

"Gonna live here as a home?" he asked.

"I am not sure. I think they want it for

a high-end assisted care facility."

"Wow, ma'am, that's quite a mouthful. A what?" He grinned.

"A, um, place for wealthy old folks?"

"Hahahaha," he laughed. "That will be the day. Too funny."

"Why?" Lacey asked, getting irritated. She hoped Mr. Wild Bill would take his wheelbarrow and go off into the woods and not be around when the people arrived.

"Well, no offense," he chuckled. "But I thought I had seen everything here. First nothing but pretty fields full of arrowheads, then the main mansion house for a tobacco planter. Been two widowers, Hale and Greer, and four widows, Hale, two Saunders, and a Greer, at this here house, over the centuries, you see.

" 'Pad' Hale, that being Master John Stafford Hale," Wild Bill went on softly, "had this place built with bricks made right here in a kiln, by slaves," he pointed across the side yard to a brick foundation just visible under two pecan trees, "for his new bride. His other wife, Judith, who had been the older sister of Jubal Early, had died and he remarried a local gal from the Saunders and Ingles families," he continued. "His son by Judith, Major Sam Hale, rode with his Uncle Jube at many battles. His other son,

Dr. Peter, had married Margaret's younger sister Virginia and lived in town here." Wild Bill paused and took a swig of coffee from a thermos and wiped his mouth with the back of his hand.

"But after the War," Wild Bill continued, "and after Pad's death, when Margaret was widowed, she had to take in boarders to survive." He shook his head, sadly, as if he had been there to witness all of this. "They be buried, Pad and Margaret, over yonder," he pointed towards Taliaferro Street across the grounds, "in a family cemetery across that street, which, of course, the street and all them houses there, they had not been there then. All that land," he swung his arms wide, taking in much of the visible town, "belonged to this here property, back then."

"How do you remember all of this?" Lacey asked in wonderment.

"My job," he said briefly. "I be the one to know it. Somebody got to remember. Then later on Ole Miz Margaret's family, cousins, the Saunders, carried on here. A Judge, Senator, and a wise man, Edward Watts Saunders, Sr. He planted that tree," Wild Bill said proudly, pointing to the immense tree with knotty roots on one side of the old brick carriage path. "A Bald Cypress. Not native. But it did good. He added the big Library wing, too," he said, pointing back to the west side of the house. "When he and his wife passed, their son of the same name and his wife Nancy George from Charlottesville, lived here. He was a professor at The University, Dean of the School of Engineering, and they used The Grove in the summers."

"I saw this information in the book on the house's history," Lacey interrupted. "So many names," she sighed.

"No, not really," Wild Bill responded, shaking his head. "Just the three famblies. Hale, Saunders, Greer. In 1959 Widow Nanny Saunders sold The Grove to a lawyer, Thomas K. Greer, a California and Virginia litigator from this county and his wife Dorothy, from out West. They had met in 1942 when he was shipping out as a Marine Officer to the Pacific. After the War and his legal education, he practiced here for about a year and then Roanoke, then out West and here, back and forth, for 45 years.

"They came here and fixed it up startin' in 1959. Part of that time they lived up at the mansion called Mount Pleasant. Mr. Greer told me oncet that was a dark house, heavy. It took five years until they moved in here, in 1964, all five of them."

Wild Bill grinned and chuckled. "One more thing, kind of funny. Odd funny, I mean. Mr. Greer worked for a spell in the late 1940's for the man, great lawyer Carter Lee, who owned that house up yonder, Mount Pleasant. Mr. Greer's very first legal job after law school after the war was with Mr. Lee. And decades later he ended up writing about him in his 'Great Moonshine' book. I heard him tell his son Carter one day when I was out here carrying wood into the wood shed over there," he gestured to a frame building behind the main house, "that when he had worked in Mr. Lee's law office, he had had no idea about any of the moonshining history here. Mr. Greer had been born and raised in McDowell County, West Virginia, see. Because the old Webb home place out by Sontag burned down back when his daddy, Moses Theodrick Greer, was just a boy, and there was no insurance in those days. Family had to leave for the coalfields to find work. But his fambly was from this county. Way back, at the beginnin'. Dat's another story for you, someday. He told me that Carter Lee was the smartest lawyer he ever knew."

"That was way before I was born," Lacey said, adding and subtracting the years, thinking of the 1940's.

Wild Bill kept on; he had the history well memorized. "It was a fancy home again for the Greers, he being a successful lawyer with three children and a pretty wife. Those children played here. Beautiful children, two of them real tall like their parents and dark-haired with brown eyes. And the youngest a tall and beautiful blond with blue eyes like her daddy, and smart as a whip. But just a baby being carried in their arms when they first moved in. And," he added sadly, "died way too young. That makes it twict that a child of the house died, the other being a Saunders son in an epidemic in the early 1900's."

He paused and glanced down at the ground, his face suddenly very sad. "Then the black year of 1989 came along. Miz Dorothy died in Roanoke. And then Miz Celeste died in Norfolk. That park out there on the road, it is named for her: Celeste Park. And Mr. Greer, he remarried a year later, and his new wife, Miz Elizabeth and her little son Master Call came. That young'un was always outside rakin' up the leaves and talking to himself about far off places. They was all here together for near twenty years."

Wild Bill looked right at her and smiled. "During that marriage, Mr. Greer, he wrote that big, big book about moonshining trials. Put it all in there for the world to see. That was a crack in the Code of Silence 'round here, let me tell you. People still be talking about it.

"And," he continued, as if rushing to the end of a tale he had told many times, "When Mr. Greer died, at a motel in Tennessee coming back with his wife from Chicago, she stayed on for five whole years. But it was lonely. And it cost a lot to keep up this place. Then the folks last year, real nice people, wanted it for a hotel kind of place. They was from the city yonder. But it fell through." he said.

"I will be doing my best to get The Grove sold," Lacey said, smiling. "And I appreciate the history lesson!"

He shifted the shovel to his shoulder and started to push the barrow up the drive onto the grass beyond a long row of English Boxwoods that edged the entire driveway. Lacey glanced at her watch and made a quick decision. She wanted to know if she could re-enter the 1864 lives of the Hales by using that old key…and did she have time to do it before the Kellers arrived? Yes!

She made sure Wild Bill could not see her, as she stepped up to the kitchen door this time and used the old key. In 1864 there had not been a kitchen right here. She could even see by looking at the exterior bricks that the modern kitchen had been added later, with other bricks. She took a deep breath and opened the door.

Although it was bright outside where she had just been, the straw-packed earth behind the dining room door where she now stood, was wet. It was raining lightly. Lacey looked around but did not see anyone outside by the smokehouse or the slave cabin. She pushed open the door enough that she could step into the house. The dining room was empty. Walking into the front hall she heard voices...someone crying? Peeking into the parlor, she suddenly realized that the room ended on the far wall with another window. The doorway of the present time, added in 1900, was not yet there. Nor was the library added later on in 1900 by the first Edward Watts Saunders yet built. She walked into the parlor.

"I cannot tell you how grieved we are," said an officer standing beside a chair on which Margaret Hale was seated, weeping softly into a handkerchief. Mrs. Hale lifted her tear-stained face and stared, sightlessly, past the tall man beside her.

"Our runners told us that Major Sam Hale was shot down near the apex of the salient known as the Muleshoe, at the Bloody Angle, they are calling it, riding with General Gordon and General Early; he fell from his horse, mortally wounded, on May 12th. The Battle of Spotsylvania Courthouse

was a bad one for our Army, ma'am, and no one suffers more from his death than his uncle General Early, and his father, Mr. Hale. I so hoped he would be here when I came today, but I fear I must leave and return to our troops. Major Hale's remains will be returned. Further bad news is that General J.E.B. Stuart also died on May 12th after being wounded the day before, at the Battle of Yellow Tavern near Richmond. He was buried at Hollywood Cemetery on May 13th."

"Oh," she sobbed, "how will I ever tell his father? And his wife Elizabeth? They were just recently married," she sobbed. "And his brother, Dr. Peter? And where will he be buried, I wonder? We will have a cemetery here for family, but the Early family and Sam's mother Judith, are buried out by the Homeplace. Oh, I am in such distress," she cried, rising and bravely escorting the officer to the front door. He stepped out into the rain and mounted his horse and rode off up the carriageway between the pines. Margaret returned to the parlor and closed the door.

Lacey found that she, herself, had been brought to tears by this tragic news. She had never seen the wife or brother or Mr. Hale. If she could find a way back later today she hoped she could be privy to more news about this terrible loss for the Hale family, and for the Confederate Army!

Lacey stepped back through the door of the parlor into the hall and then out the front door, and locked it. She found herself back in the present, on a sunny morning, just as the car started down the drive bringing her clients. She wiped her eyes and tried to feel composed.

The big car arrived and the energetic couple spilled out, almost running for the door. "Hi. In a hurry. Sorry. Can we get in right now," the wife asked? "We have to go see Maple Hall in Lexington. Just came on the market."

Lacey had never heard of Maple Hall. She fished the key out of the kitchen door lock box and unlocked the kitchen side door, being extraordinarily careful to use the key to modern times, and they all went in, the man going to the left and his wife to the right. Lacey decided to unlock the other door, to the Wing, a separate house behind the main mansion. She crossed the kitchen floor and went through the laundry room and unlocked a door that opened to a cement carport with the other brick house beyond.

Oh. This was the building that had that old hearth with all the foods cooking on it last night. She tried the same key on that door and it opened. Stepping inside she saw that the rooms were empty. She quickly walked through the rooms and saw how it could be another complete house, these days. There were two large bedrooms and two modern bathrooms and a kitchen with blue counters. And the old hearth was still in the next room, although full of cobwebs, and ancient black iron hooks and pans and pots...Could these be the same, the very same original iron hooks and pots that had been used by "Miz Tiddy" yesterday?

Suddenly the husband, Chip, appeared behind her, smiled and hurried through the rooms. His wife joined him.

"We like this place. It has charm. But if we bought it we would have to change the walls, take down the wallpaper, remove those vintage tile bathrooms, all five. And redo the kitchen. This house here with the old hearth could maybe be a house for the management. But we are not sure. Not sure we want something that needs work to bring it up to the standards we have," Tiffany said, with a pout.

"Those things could all be done," Lacey said.

"Yes, but we need to see some other properties."

"Would you like to put an offer in? A down payment? To hold this in case someone else comes in after you and wants to buy it?" Lacey asked nicely.

They looked at each other. "Aw, I guess not," he said. "I think we can find more of what we really want if we head up towards Lexington or Charlottesville."

As they stood there in the room of the Wing, a gust of wind rattled the old bubble-glass window panes and the reflected colors of the trees, a combination of dark greens and yellows, washed over the glass. It was peaceful. Magical. Quiet. No amount of money, Lacey suddenly realized, could actually "own" this beautiful estate.

They drove off and she locked up, doing what she had done the day before, locking the kitchen door from the inside and walking through the front hall to open the massive front door and locking it from the outside. She stood on the brick porch with its iron railings and looked down the ancient brick path that tumbled over old tree roots to the edge of the property on the north. Wild Bill was up by the cedar trees, pruning. He did not see her.

She turned back and used the other key. She stepped inside the house, holding her breath. Could "it" happen again? Or had these recent "mirages" or "dreams" been nothing more than her over-tired body and mind acting up?

She stood in the front hall. She closed the big door behind her and turned the huge key in its lock. A decorative key, it was an "extra" that could be used from the inside only. Another key opened the other lock. She closed her eyes and took a deep, steadying breath. "Meow."

The calico cat was beside her on the polished floor. The walls were no longer papered in a pale green and cream floral. The ceiling lamp in the parlor was metal. The chandelier of earlier today, with the Kellers, was gone. The egg-and-dart plasterwork circling the beautiful parlor ceiling was intact, nothing snapped off. There was the scent of wood smoke and roses. This was still the house before 1900, probably still during the War. She shivered with excitement and fear. There was an aroma of baked food. A cake?

Lacey tip-toed down the hall and peered into the dining room. It was empty. But there were ashes on the hearth. The windows were covered by damask drapes. She walked to the door that connected the dining room to the modern kitchen, and bravely opened it. And she looked out onto straw-covered dirt, with the Wing and its plantation kitchen across the way.

Smoke was curling up from the solitary chimney of the building with the plantation kitchen. Beyond it stood a taller brick building with a tin roof and one of the frame buildings off to the side in front of it, back then. The smokehouse! She went closer. Someone was humming. Someone was cutting wood. A child was playing with a hoop in the dirt. The aromas of cooking meat and cakes wafted out into the mild day. And across the dirt road, where the modern driveway was in modern time, sat another small brick house, its door wide open. None of the Hales seemed to be home.

Lacey walked over to it and peered in. There was a fireplace and hearth on the far right wall, beams in the ceiling, a packed-dirt floor covered with straw, and some bed pallets along the back wall. It was small, not much bigger than the office she had been given at G & H. This must be the cook's cabin, the house for the plantation cook and her family. Slave quarters? So tiny. She slowly walked back to the main house and entered into the dining room. Slave quarters. This must still be before 1865. The War had one more year to go....

Lacey closed the door and leaned on it. Whatever was happening was scaring her to death. Why was this happening to *her*? She walked back through the main house, locking the outer doors behind her, and out the front door, locking it behind her. No portico. Holly trees to her left and Boxwoods by the door, tumbled brick path no longer is use. She was back in *now*.

There was Wild Bill out there working. He seemed to be digging. Tulips and lilies grew lavishly in the gardens. Cars were going past out on the road. Cardinals and chickadees swooped among the trees. The tall Bald Cypress, not in the yard in the 1860's, planted as a baby tree in 1900 by the first Mr. Saunders, reared hundreds of feet into the sky. And its own offspring, another Bald Cypress in the side yard by the pool, also rose up hundreds of feet over the grounds. It had not been planted until 1959, by Mr. Greer.

Her next appointment was at 11:00 on Coal Street, meeting a young couple over there to check out a bungalow built in 1925. She set her GPS and followed the directions around several corners and up a street she had not yet seen. Like her own street, Cottage Hill Drive, Coal Street had trees along the side of the road, a sidewalk on one side but not on the other, and mostly frame houses with the occasional stucco bungalow or brick four-square sitting beside the others. The neighborhood appeared to be a little run-down. Driveways needed to be patched. Gardens were not well-tended. Lots of bright plastic children's toys were scattered over most of the yards.

Right on time, the couple drove up in a pick-up and came over to stand by her at 35 Coal Street.

"Good morning," Lacey said brightly, holding out her hand. Neither took it. The woman put her hands in her pockets of her jeans and the man crossed his arms over his chest. "Mornin'," he said. "The wife and me are lookin' for something small and we need it quick like. Having us a baby in a few months."

"Well, congratulations." Lacey said, trying to sound friendly. "This house has been on the market for three months and you might be able to offer lower than what they are asking," she said, glancing at the folder for the house. "Let's go in, shall we?"

They went up to the front door and Lacey got a key ring out of the lockbox. Front door, side door, back door. Unlocking the front door, she let them precede her into a dim hall with a room off each side. It was a shallow house. Hall, parlor, dining room at the front and a kitchen and a bedroom with a bathroom in the back. Small.

"I want to walk around," whispered the wife in a little, high voice.

"Go right ahead," Lacey responded. She led the couple down the central hall and pointed out the five basic rooms. "Why don't you take your time, while I check that these other keys work and see if there is anything more in the back yard." Lacey searched for a side door and found it in the kitchen. The couple was still in the front of the house, measuring where furniture might go, as Lacey found the key to the side door and opened it, stepping through onto a dirt yard shaded by trees she did not remember seeing before. There were no other houses nearby, just trees.

"I'm telling you for the last time, Junior Mills, that no way are you going to keep hiding moonshine in our shed. You tell that Clive McCain we won't be taking any more of his moonshine and storing it for him before it gets picked up. Here we are right in the edge of town where anybody could come by anytime to look around, and what would they find? And this being a new house. Don't you be ruining it all. Your Pa worked hard to have this here house for us. And I swear I am not going to stand up for you like I did for your brother. No, sir. You take your own punishment. I want nothing further to do with this," cried a gaunt woman in a print dress that came below her knees under an apron. Then the woman started to cry. The young man, not much more than a tall boy, in overalls, turned around and shuffled

116

off into the shed.

Lacey crept along behind him, unseen and unheard. She peeked inside. A wagon of hay stood in the center of the shed. The boy was lifting jar after jar down onto the ground. He opened a trap door and lifted the jars into it and closed the lid and covered it with straw and moved a big barrel over to cover the trap door. He seemed very nervous. He locked the shed and headed down the street. She could not follow. What was he going to do? She hurried back to the house. If she went through the door, which time would she be in? He was in 1925 if this was a new house then. She drew a deep breath.

Lacey backed up into the doorway and slammed the door and locked it. She leaned against it and closed her eyes. It was *now*. Her head was spinning. Back inside, she tried to pull herself back together. This going in and out of other people's lives was starting to take a toll on her nerves. Could other people see and hear people in other times?

The couple was coming towards her, talking to each other. "We like this place, ma'am," said the man. "But we should prob'ly see a few more before we make us up our minds. And we don't have no more time today. Have to be at the plant soon."

"That is fine," Lacey replied as cheerily as she could. "I can show you. I will look up some more properties in this general neighborhood. Shall we meet this week?"

"We want to stay in this part of town if we can," the wife said. "My great-grandpa and great-grandma lived here on this block. My pa grew up here, too."

"What were their last names?" Lacey asked curiously.

"Mills," she replied. "It don't matter."

They all stepped out near the street and settled on a day and time and got in their car, heading off to work. Children were playing outside. A dog barked. And behind the house they had just left Lacey saw the shed. It was still there. When the couple drove off she walked into the backyard and up to the door, which was propped open or stuck. Slipping between the door and the wall she stepped into the dusty room. There was nothing in there except the barrel. Should she check? Suddenly startled by a bird in the rafters, Lacey hurried back out and drove away.

So, she told herself, trying to be calm, this is *now*. This is *now*. What I saw a moment ago was in the 1920's. What I saw at The Grove today was the 1860's. But I saw it. I have seen it twice. What does that mean? The people back then obviously cannot see me. But the cat can.

Lacey hurried back to the office, knocked on the door of Jim Glass' office and went in when he said to open the door and come in. It was as if he had been expecting her. He gestured to a wing chair in front of an oval coffee table on which was a coffee service with fine bone china cups for two, a creamer full of cream, and a sugar bowl, two little silver spoons, and two linen napkins. What Lacey's mother would have called, "The real thing." Whom had he been expecting?

"Well, Mr. Glass," she began, "I have some questions." She almost immediately wondered if maybe it would be better for her not to tell him what had happened. He might think she was unfit for work, having hallucinations, or something.

"And I may have some answers for you," he admitted, pouring the coffee. "Join me? I just had Nellie bring it in." he smiled. His eyes seemed to be searching hers. "I did not think we would be talking about all of this quite so soon," he whispered.

"All of 'what'?" she asked.

"Keys. And what happens with keys, perhaps? Would you like to talk about that?"

"Ah. So you have had some

experience with keys and locks? Before I came yesterday?" she asked. Her manner, tone, and expression were fairly grim. She was still undecided. Maybe she should just listen. She sipped and waited. "It is an unusual town, for sure," she said.

"There is so much to talk about," he said wearily. 'I know some things might seem odd. Let's just say that there are mysteries." He took a sip. "Maybe," he said with a sigh, "maybe we will save this for another time. All right?" He turned back to his own paperwork. He seemed very tired. She did not know what good it would do to stay and ask more questions. And, a tingly thought gave her goosebumps as she thought it: was he a ghost?

To say that she was just confused would be too simple. Lacey felt like her head was going to explode. Had the conversation she had just had with Jim Glass even taken place? Maybe all this and the weird sightings and feelings of being in other times, were all just part of the healing process from her Post Traumatic Stress. That had to be the explanation. She sighed as she made her way back down the hall to her own niche. She would have to be very diligent not to give credence to these supernatural ideas and events. Just keep on living, one hour at a time, keep on going.

The rest of her day was fairly normal, compared to what she had already, maybe, experienced. Back in her own office, desk piled high with brochures and real estate pamphlets from the town, lake, and general region, Lacey studied the details so she would be able to answer questions when she showed houses. The variety of houses and prices amazed her. Real estate was still a Buyer's Market here. But the big houses at the lake were listed in the millions. She was eager to see some of them. My, a lot were for sale.

She was to show a bungalow across town, in a neighborhood called Forest Heights. She had not even had time to see the other side of town, yet. That was apparently where the big grocery store was, the card shop, the Peebles Department store Carter's Jewelry, Walmart Super Center, Lowe's, and all of those kinds of modern big-box stores, the Eagle Cinema, the fast-food places, some more banks, and the one rental car agency were out on that side of town, where, according to her literature about real estate, the Town expected a new interstate to be built in their lifetime. It would bypass the town. Why would anyone think that would be good for home values or the future?

Groceries. She had been making do,

for the two days she had been in town, with the choices at Faire Foods, up the road towards Ferrum. Without a refrigerator, the house could not hold anything like milk, cheese, ice cream, frozen meals. That reminded her...this would be the perfect time to ask Mary See why there were no appliances in her cottage.

Lacey wandered back up into the main office area looking for her colleague and found her at her desk with sheet music covering it, and one of those silent keyboards musicians use to practice. Her hands were running up and down the keys and her mouth moving as if singing along.

"Oh, hello. You startled me," Mary See cried, shoving her music and keyboard off into a huge bag on the floor.

"Oh, I'm sorry," Lacey smiled. "I did not mean to interrupt. I just had a question about my own new house."

"I was practicing. Might as well reveal the 'real me' to you," the older woman laughed nervously. "I play the organ for most of the funerals here, in all the churches, and it seems like there is one almost daily anymore. Whew. Luckily, most funerals around here, unless they are at Trinity Episcopal Church, use pretty much the same hymns, like 'The Old Rugged Cross.'"

"I am not familiar with many hymns," Lacey admitted. "You must be an excellent musician."

"Ah, I do my best," Mary See said modestly. "The truth is, that I love to play the piano and organ, and I enjoy bringing beautiful music into people's lives, especially when they are mourning. That stone church was started in the 1840's. Very 'British,' you know, in its origins, because the founding families, like the Hairstons, Guerrants, Claibornes, Jubal Early, and Saunders, of The Grove and Bleak Hill, were members. The English ivy that still grows on the church was from Windsor Castle and brought over by some ancient Greer long ago, before they mostly left the church in the 1960's to become Anglicans. Old Prayer Book, and all that. No women, etc.

"Oh, glory be." Mary See frowned. "I have an idea. I can take you around to all the churches and find you the perfect church home," she cried excitedly. "When there is a newcomer, they go all out with the food. And that is really how to pick a church. The ministers and all are one reason, of course," she added, with a wink. "The Methodists uptown have the biggest hall and the most tables, and the covered dishes can be delicious. Nice, nice people. Good food, too.

"Chicken, now," she paused, closing her eyes and removing her glasses as if in a reverie, "the Baptist churches, not counting the Primitives, have great simple country food, you know, where the fried chicken has been prepared by pulling out every single hair before it is cooked...."

"Hair?" Lacey murmured in shock...*chicken had hair?*

But Mary See was on a roll. "The desserts are the biggest at the Baptist churches, and I can tell you which has the best banana puddin'. Sometimes I just skip around in a month of Sundays, and sample a chess pie here, then a fried chicken dinner there, and a pig roast there, or a vegan feast at St. Ezekiel's in the Hills. My, can they do up a weird but filling meal over there. All those teachers from the college. They go to North Carolina for organic foods or grow their own."

"That sounds like a church I want to visit," Lacey said happily.

"Remember, now," Mary See continued kindly, "down here lots of folks still say that 'dinner' is at noon and 'supper' is at night, at least after dusk. Unless you are a fancy transplant, ha ha," she laughed, "from 'Up Nawth' where lunch is mid-day, dinner is the evening meal, and supper is after the opera. Do you know if the men are still here?" Mary See suddenly asked.

"Not sure. I will check. Oh," Lacey suddenly cried, "I keep forgetting to ask you about my house. Do you have a minute?"

"Yes?"

"I wanted to ask you if you knew why my house does not have any appliances. I know that you were the realtor who handled the sale. Dishwasher? Refrigerator? Washer and Dryer? Or did they leave when the house sold?"

"Oh, my. Has there been a theft?" Mary See replied.

"I would not know," Lacey replied. "But there are no disposal, no refrigerator or dish washer, microwave, washer or dryer." Lacey wondered why Mary See's expression was so odd....

"Lawdy, Me. Bless your heart. When I inspected that cottage a week before you came...it was all very sudden, you understand," suggesting, Lacey suspected, that a rush-job may have been done... "I checked off, myself, the following: stainless steel refrigerator, stainless steel dishwasher, stainless steel stove and oven, stainless steel microwave, stainless steel washer and dryer..."

"Good grief. There must have been a theft," Lacey cried, appalled. "There are no appliances at all in there. What should I do?"

"Heavens, girl. Let's lock up and run over there right this instant. I might be blamed for this and I swear on my mother's grave, over at High Street Cemetery, that that kitchen was state-of-the-art when I locked that front door a week ago."

They locked up, checking each door, and exited through the front door, where Mary See paused quickly to wave with a little "Queen Elizabeth" twitch of her right hand, not a full-blown friendly wave, to a large woman in baggy pants and a Hawaiian shirt playing a bongo drum as she walked down the sidewalk.

"Um, Mary See? Who is that?"

"Oh, never no mind about her. That is Belle Thayer, a teacher from the new community college. She is very spiritual and 'counter-culture'…you know, herbal meals, holistic medicine, drums, Native American ceremonies, talks on books," she whispered, as if in awe. "I really admire her. She just does whatever she wants. Refreshing."

Mary See and Lacey got into Mary See's car and headed out of the small lot and curved around the block and down the street, past the Farmers Market and Post Office, to Moonshine Corner. On their way, Mary See waved vigorously to a man with a goatee in a chef's apron and hat who was hurrying along the sidewalk with several large art canvases under his arm. Not too far away the bike tour was going strong, all stopped at the Post Office and listening to their leader. A tall, attractive woman in slacks and a cute jacket was entering the coffee shop.

"That is Lee Anne Travis," Mary See remarked. "Great cook. Probably going to talk to the chef about ingredients in her cookbook. The bike tour must be going in to see our WPA mural," Mary C. said proudly. "Have you seen it yet? The last Mrs. Greer identified the artist, from New England, Roy Hilton, who painted it off site, in Pennsylvania, with Pennsylvania models, where he taught art at a Pittsburgh institute. Now that place is part of Penn State, I think. Anyhow, that's why, she explained in her talk and article, that the mountains look like the Alleghenies and not the Blue Ridge around here and why the people working at machinery all look more Eastern-European than like the Scots and English and Germans who actually founded this area."

She pulled her car up to the curb outside Lacey's cottage. "Okay. Let's tip-toe up to your house and peek in the kitchen window." Mary See whispered.

"No need to tip-toe or whisper. If all those things were stolen, they are long gone and so is the burglar," Lacey said, getting out her keys.

The Willow Oaks were especially resplendent today. They cast shadows on the mown grass and colorful tulips. Squirrels darted along the branches of the oaks and maples across the way. The path to the front porch seemed a bit askew, though, and Lacey stumbled and dropped her keys among the tulips.

"Got them," she said brightly. "Here we are." Lacey inserted a key into the door and opened it for her guest, who stepped right into the living room and sighed. "Ah, just such a perfectly lovely renovation," Mary See murmured. "Just look at those shutters, the café-au-lait-colored walls in here. Look at how beautiful the new hardwood floors are, so dark and rich." Mary See moved into the room admiring everything. "Your furniture is great in here," she added, gesturing to the chenille sofa and wing chairs in their bold geometric patterned-fabric.

Lacey stood still in complete and total shock. Her head felt as if it might just topple right off her neck. *Coffee-colored walls? Dark hardwood floors? Plantation shutters?* She saw modern lights and outlets and a phone cord, cable for a television, and a shower in the bathroom...It was all quite beautiful. And there was her furniture, the sofa under the front window, the chairs across from it, the unpacked boxes up against the walls.

"Come along, dear, this will just take a minute. How on earth could you think there were no appliances. Just look at this." Mary See had already hurried through the dining room and into a kitchen where the Spanish tile floor gleamed and the slate countertops and charming tiled backsplash stood out in sharp contrast to the salmon-coral-colored walls and new windows.

Lacey did not know what to say. There was everything right in place, in a modern kitchen…except, except…She sat in an upholstered booth along the wall, as if she had sat there before. Her favorite mug was on the draining board by the new but vintage-style porcelain "country" sink. *Oh, yeah, she thought. Right.*

"The dishwasher is hidden behind this cabinet. Isn't that just gorgeous?" Mary See said, turning around. "Guess you just did not know to look there. And here, right here, is the stainless steel refrigerator behind another cabinet door. How could you not see this? It is huge."

Trying to make the best of it all without letting Mary See know anything about the times and keys and everything else mysterious she was experiencing, Lacey had the wit to laugh and remark, " Well, at least fingerprints sure will show up well if anyone ever steals anything from this kitchen, won't they?"

But her colleague had finished worrying about the appliances, her attention devoted to a small purring coming from a laundry room just beyond. "Oh, look! How darling, a cute cat!"

At that, Lacey crumpled to the floor.

Chapter Four

"Let your speech be always with grace,
seasoned with salt,
that ye may know how to answer every
man."

Colossians 4:6

Mary See had no idea why her new friend had just fainted, but she assumed it was from exhaustion. Lacey should have had more time to settle in before starting work. The older woman knew a great deal about health and illness, stroke, heart attacks, mini strokes, TIA's, you name it. A healthy young woman of thirty, exhausted from a trip, had just fainted. She was sure, after taking her pulse and checking her skin.

She phoned her family doctor, knowing he would make a house call if she asked, if he were not too busy. What a doctor. He had worked for more than forty years from early morning until closing and then came back in after supper and called in prescriptions until after midnight.

"Yes, this is Mrs. John See…Mary See? I am a long-time patient of…of, of course. Nice to hear your voice, too, Melanie. This is not the kind of emergency for 911 and an ambulance, I am certain, dear. But a young woman who just started work at Glass & Howe just fainted over here at her new house, 33 Cottage Hill Drive. Any chance the doctor might have time to pop over and check her? Thank you so much."

She looked around for a pillow and found the bed made up beautifully in the bedroom. There were three pillows and she took two of them on which to cradle Lacey's head. She checked her pulse. Still out cold. But it did not seem dangerous. She had seen enough fainters in various hot churches over the decades to know if it were "terminal" or just a faint.

While waiting for the doctor, she peeked around. Lots of bookcases and books, a pile of art books on a table, some boxes still unpacked up against the walls in every room. A landscape was propped up against the wall. A Stogner. Rolling hills, forest, cleared fields with a little red clay showing, and an old farmhouse barely visible. Chestnut Mountain in the distance. Nice piece.

It was very still inside and out. The calico cat had curled up almost protectively against Lacey, and was purring. Delicate limbs from trees next to the house tapped on the glass. Cardinals were making their sharp "chirp...chirp" sound out there. Mourning Doves were calling to each other. And the sound of a distant motor burred and buzzed. Maybe just a lawn mower. Maybe Jess Thompson making something for his eclectic yard. Mary See smiled. She was quite fond of Jess.

It was not long at all before she heard the doctor tap on the door and come on in. They greeted each other and he, and a nurse with him, followed her into the modern kitchen. They knelt down beside Lacey and took her pulse, checked her heartbeat, and then all three gently lifted the slender young woman and carried her to her bed and lay her on the comforter.

"When and how did this happen, Mary See?" he asked softly, holding his patient's thin wrist. He smiled warmly at his old friend and neighbor.

"Well, about ten minutes ago or less. We were admiring the kitchen and she sat down. Tired, I would imagine. She just got here night before last and Coy and Jim have had her working since yesterday morning. Showing The Grove, I might add. Nothing like throwing her right into the maelstrom. That is a big responsibility, that house. Well, when the calico cat came in, she looked at it, went white, and toppled over onto the floor."

"Her vitals are fine, sir," the nurse said.

"Thank you, Pat," the doctor said kindly. "I think you can probably go on back. It is under control. Just leave me the smelling salts. See you tomorrow."

The doctor settled back in a chair and glanced around. "You know what? I have not been in this old house for maybe thirty years. Remember when the McCain family and then the Grierson family had this place, ever since, hmmm"…he paused to think, "probably 1915. Mrs. McCain died soon after her husband was put on trial for making liquor. He got a light sentence but their family was never the same. Every generation seemed to live here and then move away. The last one to live here would have been old Miz Ann. She'd married a Grierson back in about 1933 right after her brother Jack ran off. I used to come by and visit with her and Bobby when they were well up in their late 80's. He was a man of few words. Like Ann's father, old McCain.

Wonder what happened to all of their children?"

"I played for some of the weddings of the Grierson children, long time ago. I think they mostly got married in Gladys Creek Baptist. Best organ back then, good minister."

"Oh, yes," the doctor smiled. "I even attended a few times back in the day. That minister, Charlie Webb, could give a rip-roarin' sermon. Then the meals afterwards once a month in their Fellowship Hall were worth it all." He smiled. "Things sure have changed, though, haven't they, Mary See?"

"Oh, my, yes," she said in a melancholy voice. "Our churches are mostly full of old folks," she murmured. "Like us." They both chuckled.

"I remember when there was a little grocery store with a soda fountain next to this house," he reminisced.

"Oh, I remember that, too!" Mary See cried. "I used to go there with my friends Virginny and Matty Ann when we were quite young, and climb up on those stools and drink Grapette! And, as Ginny loved to say, we were like three little white faces in there with all the nice black folks!"

"I cannot remember exactly when that little store was torn down. A shame, really," Dr. Peters continued, "because there is not a grocery over in this part of town anymore, certainly not on Moonshine Corner."

"Well," he continued, shifting back to the present, "she seems to be sleeping. Her breathing is regular and smooth. No distress. Skin is the right temperature. No chills or perspiration. Color is good. Pretty girl, isn't she? What do we know about her?" He looked over at his old friend, who knew just about everything, even before it happened.

"Not a whole lot. Was in a bad car accident a few years ago. A Westerner. Art teacher in Colorado, Denver I think. Soft-spoken, polite, pleasant personality. Hard worker. Quick learner. Bought this house sight-unseen from me, by fax and phone. Drove across country and moved in two days ago. She and I were here today to see why she had no refrigerator. I know there was a perfectly good, large stainless steel one here because I did the walk-through and was here for the Inspection. I do not know how she missed it. "

"Tired, would be my guess," the doctor agreed, pulling on his lip. "I am going to try to awaken her before I leave, just to be sure there are no other problems," he said.

He gently jiggled Lacey's shoulder. She stirred and murmured something that sounded like, "'cat, Jack, cat, door…"

"Come on, Lacey. Let's wake up now. This is Doctor Peters. I am right here."

She opened her eyes. Instead of looking frightened, she smiled. It took her a few seconds, but she struggled to sit up on the bed and speak. "I...I," she paused, drawing in a deep breath, "feel very tired. Where am I?" She looked around. "Where is Jack? What did they do with the supper?"

"You have been dreaming," Dr. Peters assured her, with a grin. "I want you to lift your finger," he pointed to her left hand, "and touch your nose real quickly, right now," he said.

Lacey touched her nose with her left pointer finger perfectly.

"Good. Good. No stroke or seizure. If you can do that with your non-dominant finger, you are not suffering from a mini-stroke. I think you fainted from fatigue."

"I am sure I am fine," Lacey exclaimed, embarrassed to be the focus of attention. Where was she? This room did not seem familiar at all. The walls were a lovely coffee-with-cream color; creamy-colored Plantation shutters were at the window. The floor was dark wood. Crown molding ran around the top of the room. A large closet with its door open was empty and boxes stood near it against the wall. Unpacked. *Her bedroom? Wow.*

"Dear, if you are all right, how about if I run out and get you some supper and bring it back." Mary See spoke cheerily, quickly. Her tone was calm and caring. Lacey relaxed. They were both so incredibly nice.

"I will scoot on back to the office now. If you do not feel 100% tomorrow, please come stop in. I will fit you in," he said.

"I do not even know where your office is," Lacey said in alarm.

"A few blocks away around the corner from the law offices on Main. I am at 121 Cedar. Any time. I hope you feel great soon."

"Oh, thank you both. I feel like a fool. I do not know what happened. I guess I am just tired." She smiled shyly.

Lacey walked them to the front door, trying not to ogle the beautiful rooms and colors. Even the front door was beautiful, dark wood with an oval of beveled glass, almost like stained glass, in the center. Late afternoon light came through it and splintered as if through a prism, into streams of colored light. Magical.

She went out on the porch, expecting it to be bare with the scuffed, uneven planks she had seen since she moved in. Instead, in the warm late afternoon or early evening light…she had no clue what time it was…she saw that the porch was dove grey, with smooth boards and a solid, new railing painted white. Several window boxes were attached to the railings. They were dripping with ivy and pansies. Where there had been cobwebs and chipped paint splinters, now there were freshly-painted walls and shutters, opened and fixed to the wall of the house by antique iron squiggles. And there was a swing hanging from the ceiling. It had cushions. She sat on it and swung gently. On the table out there was a paper box with a note attached: "Hummus. Jess."

Not quite trusting what she had been through and had experienced in the past two days, Lacey closed her eyes and swung gently back and forth. She let her mind roam, deep into colors and scents, deep into textures and voices. This life, she was learning, was not smooth and soft like a cotton sheet. It was more like a wild tapestry of beaded sworls and patterns, sewn and pieced and stitched by changes and events. A paisley shawl but one covered in sequins and beads, like the clothes worn so gracefully by that sweet woman with the long white hair and the baguette whom she had seen on the sidewalk earlier.

She was on a porch swing now. But she knew, also, that this porch was the porch of the family she had heard quarreling about moonshining. She had overheard Dr. Peters talking, as she was waking up, while they thought she was still passed out or deeply asleep. She had heard what he said about the McCains and Griersons. This had been not only their home...now it was her home. Why had Fate placed her here?

Loping by with long strides, her tall, thin young neighbor could be seen hurrying up the street. He had not seen her. He was looking straight ahead and was carrying two bags of something. She had not seen a vehicle at his house. He was energetic and innovative. Passing her house now was an old van with a blond woman of maybe 45 or so leaning over the wheel, music playing, and laughing at something. Her laugh twisted and turned in its merriment all the way to Lacey's ears. Like quicksilver, beautiful, fast, elusive.

Who were her neighbors coming home from work to have dinner. Whoops! Supper! With their families on Cottage Hill Drive in Moonshine Corner? Startled by her interest in this, she had to laugh at herself. She had never before had the slightest interest in neighbors. Was she changing? The thought shocked her...in a pleasant way. It had not taken much time, to change!

Time was a funny thing. Invisible but ever-present, like air. Something you took for granted like a translucent curtain against a dusty window. Time, like a curtain, changed the view. It wavered and back and forth, back and forth as if moved by a gust of wind that changed the terrain from rough tall grass to a smooth lawn and wildflowers. Time and chance, she recalled from somewhere, "happeneth to them all."

It was not long at all before Mary See arrived with a hot supper of chicken and rice and a small salad. "I will leave you now, dear, if you feel perfectly all right. I am so glad it was nothing serious. And I am glad we solved the mystery of the beautiful appliances," she added happily. "I am going to tell the men that they or Kim can take over for you tomorrow, okay? You really need one good day to rest up. Don't try to get everything done too soon. I will see you Thursday."

"Thank you so very much," Lacey said, taking her new friend's hand in hers. "You have been a life saver. Oh, by the way, that young couple I showed the bungalow to on Coal Street today would like to see some similar houses in the same neighborhood. If I am not in tomorrow...."

Mary See jumped right in and told her Kim would be able to take care of it all. She would have Kim contact them by email tonight and set it up.

"Do you have your cable television and internet set up yet, Lacey? I need to get the email for us at the office."

"I just have not had time," Lacey fibbed, as there was no way on earth she could say her vintage 1930's outlets of a few hours ago had not been up to anything modern. But they would be now. If she remembered which key she had used to get in tonight.

After her meal, Lacey pottered around inside the *now* version of her new home and was very happy with the modern amenities. The bathroom was perfect as was the kitchen. The laundry room, clearly the old mud room expanded and with a nice back deck added, held new appliances and a closet. The back deck was above a fairly long back yard planted with a profusion of flowers that were starting to bloom. A row of trees separated her property from that behind her. And an empty lot still stood between her house and the corner of Cottage Hill Drive and Autumn Street. She owned that lot. What fun she could have with it. A garden? Paths and bushes? Trees? Thank goodness, she found herself thinking, that empty lot did not have a key to unlock different time periods. Ah, she would remember that thought soon.

She heard a knock on her door. It was barely dark out. Who would it be?

"Lacey, forgive me for coming over unannounced," Jim Glass said, "but I got a call from our dear Mary See about, um, your fainting spell, and she told me you needed tomorrow off to rest and get settled, and I came by to apologize for rushing you right into the job, and all…" his voice petered off.

"Oh! Come on in. Have a seat," she pointed to the pretty couch and chairs in the living room.

"I wanted to get this over with, as soon as possible," he said mysteriously, "before anything else happens." He settled onto the sofa and continued where they had left off at the office earlier that afternoon.

"To get back to what I was starting to explain to you," he began abruptly, "I cannot remember if I told you the beginning. But I had been at an event at The Grove, when we first took it on to help sell it. I thought I saw Ned Ruter. I would have dismissed it all as my being tired…except that when I looked at this person again, he raised his finger to his lips as if to tell me to stay quiet! Then he went into the hall. I did not see him again." Jim Glass stood and paced. "It may have been someone else entirely, though.

"When I came to work the day after being at The Grove and thinking maybe I had seen my old, deceased, friend Ned, there he was, right there in a chair in my office. He asked me if I could see him. I told him I could barely make him out. He seemed almost translucent, like a mist." Jim Glass closed his eyes, as if to gather strength. He took a deep breath.

"But," he whispered, "it was Ned Ruter. He was dressed in a tweed jacket, bowtie, grey flannel trousers, shiny wingtip shoes. Always the dresser. He looked like a dandy from the 1920's. He told me that he had been trying to find a way 'back' since his death in that plane crash, and that one day he just found himself at The Grove."

Lacey was far too scared now to ask any questions. She sat rigidly in her chair, unable to take her eyes off Jim Glass's face as he continued.

"He could not figure it out, either. But he remembered being in a park with winding paths and a lovely fountain and, get this, a castle, just before he 'appeared' in the parlor of The Grove. Believe me, it is an awful lot to take in all at once." Jim Glass sighed, sat back down, and leaned forward, as if afraid to meet her stare.

"Ned Ruter tried to explain to me that

he thought he had 'arrived' here in Rocky Mount, his hometown by the way, so there may have been some kind of pull…? Anyhow, that he arrived by means of a landscape painting that is now hanging in your office. He actually thinks he stumbled out of that painted park into the parlor at The Grove, where the painting had been for the Open House." Jim Glass smiled, but it was a crooked, unsure smile, as if he thought she might think him unbalanced.

"He said he slept for a long time after he stepped out of the piece of art. He could not imagine what had happened. You see," Jim Glass leaned towards her conspiratorially, "He never knew he had died, of course. One wouldn't, would one? He remembered being on a plane in a storm. That was where his memory stopped. Never a religious person at all, not one who, shall we say, 'believed' in life after death or the Great Beyond, or even in God, he explained to me in detail, he thinks he was in a kind of death state that wore off, letting him come back. He has no idea how that oil painting fits into anything, unless it acted as a kind of 'back door' back into this world."

"You are telling me," Lacey asked, "he is a man who died in a plane crash over forty years ago and suddenly reappeared and ended up right here in the town he lived in before the crash, and has no idea what happened?"

"That seems to be it." Jim Glass replied softly. "And he also told me that he is not alone. No, no, he does not know the others, but he sees them. Everywhere. But," he admonished, "Ordinary people, live people, cannot see these *returned souls* at all. I hesitate to call them 'ghosts.' But there are people who can see them. Can you see, um, *returned souls*, Lacey? You seem to be one of them, as am I."

She just stared at him, unwilling, as of yet, to let him know what all she had been experiencing! *One of them! No way!*

Jim Glass went on, "He says that there are parallel universes, different Times, happening simultaneously. Always have been. Like onion layers? But the only people who know about that are the ones who died too early, people who died in accidents or tragedies, wars, that kind of thing, people who did not get to live out their allotted lifetime, and people who do not have a strong belief in God or a 'Great Beyond.' His life was cut off by a plane crash when he was about to retire.

"The family you met today, Field wasn't it, died together in a boating accident on a ferry crossing over near the Eastern Shore of Virginia. They were on their first vacation, having come from Endicott. A tragedy. I remember reading about it. The daughter, Brenda Field Marks, had a husband, Trevor Marks. He was serving in the military. And, unknown to her, of course, he died soon after she and her parents did. He may be out there somewhere, too."

"Even if I try to accept all of this," Lacey said softly, "how on earth do I fit in? I am a normal person. And I am only thirty. Why am I here? Why could I *see* the whole Field family, if they were not alive? And how about the people out on the street who waved at us?"

"Clearly, my dear, you must also be," he coughed delicately, "dead."

"I am NOT dead," she said loudly, causing him to wince.

"Well, you have to be. That is why Ned told me to hire you."

"I would know."

"Ned Ruter has ways of knowing things. He is not here in Rocky Mount all the time," chuckled Jim Glass. "He lives in a parallel world, and he told me that his world is the late 1930's, post-Depression. I guess he got to choose, through a painting, and he chose to be younger again, but to skip the Great Depression. Told me he came in through a Marsha Paulekas painting of an abandoned frame house in a pretty field. He showed me a key ring he has. It was on a table inside. Each key unlocks the same house, but unlocks it in different eras. Right now, he has chosen to be in 1938. The house, he says, is lovely and comfortable. He has 'moved in' and made it his home. There is a family living there in our time, but they cannot see him and he cannot see them. However, he has confided in me that their dog seems to sense something, and often barks when he enters. A watch dog. If only the people knew. Ha ha ha," he laughed.

"That is impossible. The whole thing." But she knew in her heart it was quite possible....

"No. Not. It happens. He has shared with me that other 'deceased' people from Rocky Mount, long gone from here of course, buried, many of them in their own family cemeteries, are here again. They bump into each other in 1938. Or if he uses another key, his world is even later, 1960, which he remembers well because of Kennedy's election. When he uses a 1960 key, he himself is older, but the world has more conveniences, especially modern bathrooms with showers, telephone service, color television, etc. He is quite content."

"And he has come back to G & H?"

she asked.

"Yes. That is what amazes me. He wants someone here at G & H to be available to help other *returned souls* find proper housing. And he had your, um, addition, built on."

"The Fields? Ghosts?"

"My dear," he clapped his hands. "I do so hate to use that word, but, yes, *returned souls*, and they seem to be the very first clients to arrive looking for a new home. They came because of you."

"I still do not understand. I am not a ghost."

"Forgive my intruding into your personal life, Lacey, but weren't you in a car crash and hospitalized?"

For a moment, Lacey was frozen in shock. *Could she be dead?*

"Lacey, Lacey?"

"Yes, I mean no. A few years ago, actually. I was taken to the hospital, presumed dead. But I was in a deep coma and they told me later that for about one minute I was technically 'dead,' no signs of life on the machines. I do not remember that. I did not see a light or anything. If it was a near-death experience, I do not remember it at all."

"Well, forgive me again. But were you, are you, what people call a 'believer,' someone with such a strong faith and belief in God and a spiritual afterlife that you might have wished or believed you would pass right into that new stage at death, someday?" He gently cleared his throat. "The 'light'?"

"No. That was one thing my parents and I argued and bickered about quite a lot, actually," Lacey admitted. "I think that they had such a strong belief in God and the afterlife that they worried and worried that I would not be protected, spiritually, at death someday."

"Well, from what Ned has tried to explain from what he knows, those folks with belief are lifted right into the next spiritual stage, never to turn back. But the rest, the ones with serious doubts or who never had a belief system or notions of religion or spirituality, and the ones whose lives were cut short by a tragedy---much of the world, actually---they have a choice: start to believe or be stuck, here. Forever."

"Forever?"

"Your momentary death, however brief in real time, must somehow have 'counted' in your being here as a real person and one able to commune easily with the others, the *returned souls*."

"I am finding all of this almost impossible to believe," she murmured.

"Tell me, as I am new at this, as well. Have you noticed anything at all unusual since you came in yesterday?"

"Not really," she fibbed, in a scared voice.

"Have you felt like you were walking through a curtain or a wall or anything that separated you from, shall I say, two worlds?"

She thought about it. The feeling last night on the sidewalk outside her porch. The feeling in the back hall where the new office had been added on here at G & H, the cobwebs she kept walking through? The odd feeling when she had opened front doors at several houses...including her own, right here! Could they be barriers?

"Maybe," she admitted. "I have sensed that I was 'breaking through' soft barriers. And I have seemed to be in other times," she added, deciding to drop the real bomb-shell on him. She and Ned Ruter....

But Jim Glass may not have heard that comment, and replied wistfully, "Ah. I have not experienced any of that. Ned asked me to ask."

"Did you die, too?" she asked suddenly.

"Heart bypass last year. They say I 'died' for about 30 seconds. I have no recollection. And, nor do I have any spiritual or religious beliefs. I was brought up by Bible-thumping parents who grew up in the 1930's, back when moonshining was a way of life here, and some families stayed away from church. But my parents were devout. My grandparents all were involved secretly in money laundering and transporting in the late 1920's and on. The Mills. Heck, almost all families were in one way or another. Making shine, transporting it, selling it, and so on."

He stood up. "My grandpa had been a deputy. Got paid $1 a year for that job. He collected the 'granny fees' in his part of town, for the Big Man. Can you believe? My parents grew up in a Code of Silence hereabouts. Then they married and moved away, returning in the 1950's when I was a boy. They died years ago." He paused. "They do not seem to have stayed behind. They have both gone on, I suppose," he said sadly. "I should be happy for them," he mumbled. "I had not really believed they truly were 'people of faith,' as some folks call it. I struggle with faith, myself."

"All of this weirdness should make a believer out of you, "Lacey announced. "And of me." She looked at him, smiled, and wondered if she should ask... "Tell me, did you have, let's see, I guess it might have been an uncle, called Junior Mills?"

He just stared at her, open-mouthed. "Um...no one, no one knows about him and his brother," he finally blurted out in a hoarse whisper. "My mother was their younger sister."

"Well," she smiled sadly, "thanks to all this hocus pocus you have put me in, I do. I even saw Junior and his mother."

"This is astounding." Jim Glass cried. "Astounding. Oh, how I wish I could see my granny again. They had a daughter, my mother, after they moved from that house."

"Well, maybe come with me on one of these outings," Lacey suggested.

Jim Glass stared up at the ceiling, silently, as if deep in thought. He continued, "All I know is what Ned has shared. I am the only one he has talked to about all of this. I guess it has been going on forever, but how would anyone know?"

Lacey thought about it and then said, "Whenever anyone has said they have seen a ghost, this must have been what happened. They may have seen a *returned soul.* Also, some people might be able to 'see' into another world, however briefly. But most people cannot. And seeing people in an earlier time, live people living in their own era, is something else altogether. I now have experienced both. As has Ned Ruter."

She lowered her voice and whispered,

"In fact, when I was at that 1880's Victorian yesterday, I saw a woman in a long dress cooking bacon in the kitchen. It was just a flash. She was not a *returned soul*; she was living in her house in her Time. We were in her Time. No electricity. I was alone in there. None of the Field family was with me. I wonder if they would have seen her? "

"You may have seen someone from the late 1800's! That house was built in 1885. It is a true Victorian house. I have no idea if the Fields would have been able to see her. We, you, Ned, and I, just do not know enough about this yet!" said Jim Glass. He leaned forward, hands on his knees. "It actually is very exciting! This may never have happened before, this whole 'seeing' *returned souls* and being in other Times! They seem to be two quite different phenomena. Being able to see people in other times involves keys! You had the old keys."

"I wondered if it had something to do with keys," she mused, amazing herself that she was accepting this outrageously odd situation. "Every time a key is involved, it seems I suddenly have access to a different period in Time. Keys! Who has lots and lots of keys? Realtors!" She clapped her hands.

"And locksmiths," Jim Glass said quietly, with an odd look on his face.

"Lacey, as far as I know, only Ned Ruter, you, and I know anything at all about this, about this…condition or ability. No one else at G & H has a clue."

"Except Nellie?" she asked, smiling. "Is Nellie part of this? The young woman who brought coffee for the Fields yesterday and for us? She appeared out of nowhere."

"Nellie. I had forgotten. Well, yes, I guess she knows. She apparently was one of the young victims of a terrible, terrible fire in a factory on the main street through town long ago, 1889, I believe, when a fire destroyed over twenty buildings near the Courthouse. Perhaps the very site of our building. Quite a few young factory workers, all women, died tragically in that fire," he said sadly. "The Historical Society re-enacts it as part of their annual, sold-out, and very popular 'Ghost Tour' in October."

"And I am the new realtor for our ghost clients? Do I often get to be with non-ghost clients?" Lacey asked.

"Of course you will often, and maybe usually, have real clients. We had you scheduled for some today. Do you remember Mary See mentioning that at our morning meeting? You were to have two sets of clients. They would be real people."

"I have met with one 'set' twice. Real Californians as far as I could tell. And one young local couple on Coal Street. Also alive." She realized how very odd that must sound! "The young woman said her family had been the Mills, also. Mr. Glass, um, Jim, the Fields seemed real to me. So did Nellie. What if I cannot tell them apart?" Her eyes were huge.

"I am guessing that no one can see the *returned souls* except you when you are out with them. It may be that no one can even see *you* when you are with them. And maybe even the *returned souls* cannot see into other time periods...although it would seem that our Ned can. Hmmm. But that might just be the keys."

"That would explain the newspaper vehicle almost running into us here yesterday when I backed the van out. The driver did not see me in that van because I had the Fields with me."

"Being with *returned souls* might make you all invisible to the rest of the people around." Jim Glass stared up at her paintings. "At least that is what Ned has shared with me. I have to believe him, I suppose. I find it amusing in a way that Ned has insisted we not use the word 'ghost.' Politically incorrect, you see. Too scary."

"Well, I think he is wrong about being seen or not seen. People waved at me when I was with the Fields. But why me?" Lacey looked frightened. "The people who waved looked real. One lady with dogs, one walking with shopping bags, bikers."

"I have no clue," he admitted. "I know so little of all of 'this,'" he admitted. "My question is how and why did Ned find you? Somehow Ned heard about you looking for a job in real estate. Online? Or maybe he met you somewhere."

"I was in Colorado for years. I was an art teacher, high school level. I collect regional art, landscapes. I put a notice up online for a real estate job anywhere in the country and this is what I received: a letter and then two calls from Glass & Howe, here in Virginia. Maybe I am here because I am an outsider."

"Ah. Landscapes."

"You could not think…"

"Maybe Ned found you because of your paintings."

"I had ordered a painting of the Blue Ridge Mountains when I thought I might move to Virginia, it is true," Lacey explained. "It was an oil, a rural scene with an old house tucked into a field with some red clay and pines." She got up and looked for the painting, which was still propped against the wall in the dining room. She brought it to him.

"Ah, a homestead near Chestnut

Mountain," he exclaimed. "A Stogner." He handled the landscape almost reverently, perhaps worried that Ned Ruter or someone else might suddenly step out into the room. They both studied the painting for a few seconds and then she placed it back in the other room. "Her husband Joe makes beautiful wooden bowls."

"Ask Ned, next time Ned is in touch," Jim Glass suggested. "If he has been in any other paintings or if that is the way, the portal. I am curious. The collection of art in the office was his. A real art connoisseur. We need to get on top of all the mystery."

He grabbed a piece of paper from his pocket and a pen. "N-E-D R-U-T-E-R. Mean a thing to you? Just a name. Of course not!" He handed her the paper on which he had written the same thing backwards.

"Now, Lacey Brew, look at this! I am good at word puzzles. What does it spell, backwards?"

"R-E-T-U-R D-E-N! Or, switch Ned around: RETURNED; you have got to be kidding!" she said.

"He is Ned Ruter now! *A returned soul*," Jim Glass said quietly. "Oh, my Lord. Amazing. His name foretold it. Bless his heart."

Jim Glass said goodnight and headed home, assuring her that she could take tomorrow off.

After he left, she wanted to keep busy, to get her mind off the amazing things he had shared with her. Lacey looked at her bookcases. She hooked her television up in the study. And she hesitated only briefly, with a tiny qualm of fear, when she started to hang her large collection of original art. How on earth was it possible that someone, especially a deceased someone, could pop out into *now* through a painting? Even in the *Harry Potter* books and films, people in the paintings just moved around between paintings. They did not emerge into a room. Thinking such a reasonable thought, Lacey went ahead and placed paintings of the Rocky Mountains alongside some of Virginia, alongside some of European cities. Her collection was eclectic, and she was proud of it.

When she started to wear down, she made a cup of herbal tea and got out some of her dusty religious books, a Bible, some concordances, hymnals, and other religious volumes she had inherited from her parents but had never really studied. Her parents had died almost as soon as Lacey had received her graduate degree in art history about seven years ago. She missed them both terribly. They had died far younger than their own parents had.

Their lives had been cut short before their time! Talking with Jim Glass about the intriguing notion that people who "believed" in God went right on to a "light" in the Great Beyond, while doubters did not, and people whose lives were cut short too early, did not, had made her decide to do a little research and study. Her dear parents apparently, had "gone on." My. So complex.

It would seem several things possibly were out there: people who had died too early, people who died with no faith in God...and these were the *returned souls* who could come back, perhaps through the portal of a painting, and continue on in a world few could see into. Then, there were the people she had seen who were living in another time altogether, like the slaves and Hales in 1864 at The Grove, in 1933 the McCains and Griersons right here at 33 Cottage Hill Drive, and in 1925 the Mills over on Coal Street. They were not *returned souls*! She had entered their Time periods. Somehow, she, Lacey Brew, age 30 and losing her marbles, apparently, was able to "visit" other time periods because of keys that opened into other years. But those people she saw were not *returned souls* or supernatural. She was literally standing in their lives like an invisible guest in an earlier time. Lacey was going to assume that Jim

Glass had never had the experience of visiting other times. And Ned Ruter had been able to and even had keys that gave him access to different time periods. Keys!

She curled up under her soft sheets and coverlet, with a bedroom window cracked to let in the breeze. Before she had read more than two psalms, her eyes closed and she drifted off to a deep sleep.

Chapter Five

"For a thousand years in thy sight are but as yesterday when it is past, and as a watch in the night."

Psalm 90:4

The morning was bright, the curtain wafting in a mild breeze. Lacey felt refreshed, the first time she had since her arrival. And she had today off. She badly wanted to get her house in order. Pictures hung, clothes put away, boxes of kitchen things sorted and placed, books organized. But first of all, she wanted to be on her front porch to savor her new life on her *now* porch, alone. She made some coffee in her coffee pot and went out, dressed in her jogging clothes.

The first thing she saw was her new acquaintance, Leila Park, running by with three dogs on leashes. At first Leila did not glance over her way, but when she did, when one of the dogs stopped to sniff around a tree, she saw Lacey.

"Good morning. Is this your new home?" Leila called cheerfully, coming a little closer, as the dogs tugged at her to keep running with them.

"Yes, hi." Lacey called back. "Just taking today off to get unpacked. Seems like it will be a great day."

"This is a neat house," Leila said. She was on the front walk now. "I knew the family who used to live here. My friend was Kelly Grierson, a really fun person. But she moved out of town. This house was on the market for years! I did not know who had bought it."

"I am glad you knew the family," Lacey replied, happily. "I wondered who they were."

"Oh, they were a real old family here. Back in the day, I think some of them ran moonshine out of this neighborhood. But, then again, lots of people did in the 1930's."

"I am eager to read more of the history about this town, the moonshining era, the Civil War, this neighborhood, and all," Lacey said with a smile. *Oh, if you only knew*, she was thinking.

"Plenty out there to read! Great library on Franklin, before J & J Fashions, and across from Haywood Jewelers and Angle Hardware. See you later," Leila waved, heading back up the street towards Jess's house.

Lacey sat on her porch enjoying the window boxes and early sunshine and her coffee, and started to wonder, hmmm... what did the *big* key with the tassel open? Was she brave enough or stupid enough to open another "Pandora's Box" and try to find out? Or might she get stuck in the past? Could that happen? Or, what if the house reverted to the 1930's. No more appliances, no more television. But she had to know. What had happened to young Jack?

A van started up Cottage Hill Drive and turned left at the corner of Lacey's property onto Autumn Street. A pretty young brunette with a cloud of hair was at the wheel, driving very slowly. Looking.

As she daydreamed and rested, Lacy noticed out of the side of her eye that the young woman was walking across the empty lot towards the porch.

"Hello." she said, with a beautiful smile. "I think I am Locked out. I have a Key to the House next Door but it Will not work and I am Renting it for several Months. I do not Think the Realtors left me the Right set of Keys."

Lacey actually heard herself moan. *Keys. Not again.* She could barely believe it.

"Hi! How may I help you? I am brand-new here, myself. This is my third day. I am Lacey Brew," she introduced herself as the young woman came up on the porch, asking, "May I?" very politely before doing so.

"Of course. Have a chair. Coffee?"

"Oh, Yes! Thank You. I am Bianca Rose Harriman. I know, Crazy Name. Lots of History in my Name, I have been told," she laughed. Her laugh was silvery and unusual. Lacey went inside for a cup of organic Red Rooster Roast, from Floyd.

Bianca Rose sipped and handed over a piece of paper. "My Notes for how to get Here," she said. "Maybe you can tell me Where to go to get a Key that Works?"

Lacey glanced over the piece of paper. It was printed like this: "Pass Grove, Turn right at Bootlegger's, left at Bank across from Post Office, left onto Autumn. There Will be a gorgeous Lamppost on the Corner of Cottage Hill and Autumn. House is on Right." Lots of the words were capitalized. Odd.

"Well it seems you had the correct streets and house," Lacey commented, glancing across the lawns to the house in question. "Um, do you mind me asking...but so many of your words are capitalized. Did you have a German-speaking parent, by chance? I don't mean to intrude...."

Bianca Rose clapped her hands in surprise. "You are the first Person ever to ask Me that! Oh, my! Well, Yes! My Mother was from Wiesbaden! How did you know?"

"I studied German. And it is the language where nouns are capitalized," said Lacey, happily, smiling at her neighbor. "It was simply a guess. And when you talk, it is as if the nouns and some other words get extra emphasis. Kind of neat," Lacey continued.

"Oh, I love That," Bianca Rose cried. "I feel at Home Here already!"

"But, let me warn you, I am so new I hardly know where the grocery stores are," Lacey laughed. "Will you be staying at that house over there very long?"

"A Month at least," Bianca Rose said cheerily. "Depends on What I find."

"Find? Oh, I did not mean to intrude! Just listen to me," Lacey added sheepishly.

"Oh, I am searching for Treasure! And I love Cats," Bianca Rose added, seeing the calico dart by. "More than just about anything except Jewels and Roses and Poetry. I tell Fortunes, too," she giggled. "I always wanted to be a Gypsy. My Family came from Here, way back in the 1860's. After the War the Ones who were left mostly moved to Missouri. I grew Up out There but Something kept pulling Me back to Virginia so I finally decided to come Here. I asked a real estate Company if There were any Rentals Here, and Mary See rented me This. I dropped by over There for the Keys and they had been left for Me in a Box with a Note. It was too Early for them to be Open. I took the Keys and here I am."

"And you are sure that none of them fits?"

"I admit," Bianca Rose said, "I only tried the Front Door."

"Well, let's go. I have today to unpack, but this will not take long, right?" Lacey said more cheerily than she was feeling.

Bianca Rose headed back to her van up the street and Lacey locked up and followed, cutting across the grass...her first time to walk out in the empty lot that was part of her property. She saw a terrapin under some grasses and butterflies winging their way across the landscape. The land was not as level as it looked from a window. Were those the remnants of a brick foundation? She found herself walking up and down small, almost unnoticeable, slopes.   What might be out here, she wondered, if I used the 1930's key to the house and came out here some night when no one was watching? Or, she thought, what if I had a key to the 1860's for my house and this land?

When the two young women had both reached the front door of the house Bianca Rose had rented, Lacey took the key ring from her. She decided to take a chance and said in a light tone, "Bianca Rose, let me try the back door first with these. You stay here and if I get in I will come through the house and unlock the front door for you. Okay?" Lacey smiled as nice a smile as she could, considering the secret plan up her sleeve.

Lacey stepped off the shallow porch and made her way excitedly through overgrown Boxwoods---had there maybe been a Maze here once, she guessed— around to the small backyard. It was bordered on all sides by Leland Cypress trees, very tall. They hid this property almost completely from the back windows of her own.

She studied the key ring, with an anticipation and wisdom she had gained in the few days since her own arrival on Moonshine Corner. She would never take keys for granted, ever again! Three keys. If a "normal" person in *now* saw these and used them, would the keys open into the present time, with nothing else happening? Did it take someone like herself, using old keys, to have a time-warp occur? This would be a test. Lacey drew a deep breath and tried the oldest, largest key in the lock on the old backdoor.

The key stuck. But with a little jostling and jiggling, the key caught and the tumblers turned. Lacey pushed on the door. Like the ones at The Grove, it was one of the very old "no-nails-construction" doors, held together by many wooden pegs and not a single nail.

A cool, soft, darkness enveloped her as soon as the door opened. The air smelled like cornbread and smoke. Like the plantation hearth at The Grove, in 1864. No point in reaching for a light switch, she reasoned. Feeling her way into the room, she saw several people huddled around a hearth, in rocking chairs. A small fire burned. A pot hung over the fire. A wooden table held a plate containing a circle of cornbread with several pieces missing. A candle in a pewter holder and a lantern shed the only other light in the room. It was not until Lacey crept a few steps further into the quiet room that she saw that the residents were black. She could faintly hear their conversation.

"But I'se not sure, Papa, if'n Tiddy would leave The Grove, not now with Miz Margaret and her hands full of those three young'uns, with Master Hale gone on bidness," said an older woman, a quilt on her lap, to an older man. "And with Mas' Sam dead and his wife gone home. Poor young widow Hale, all in black, leavin' in a carriage t'other day. My oh, my. It be sad."

"Mama, we's got to give a home to Tiddy purt soon. When this Wah is done wit, she may not haff a home no more. That cabin is not hers. It is the Hale's." So spoke a younger black man.

As they spoke there was a knock on the door. The older man opened it. Lacey stepped back against the wall. It was the Hale son, John! He had a piece of paper.

"Good day," he said politely. "My mother sent me to share this news with you, Jim and Hally and Jimmy," the boy said quietly, acting very mature, perhaps because he had been entrusted with an important mission.

"You may have heard," he said sadly, "that my half brother, Major Samuel Hale,

was killed in battle on May 12th." They nodded soberly, sadly. "And my father, who has been away on business, received a newspaper today that has very important news in it for freemen and freed black slaves." He looked at each of them. "My father is an honorable gentleman, and he wanted to warn you of this. Allow me to read it. Please stop me if you have a question," said the boy solemnly.

He held the newspaper up in the light from the fire and the lantern.

"From the Conscript Office of the Confederate War Department in Richmond. Written by Lieutenant Colonel J. C. Shields. June 1, 1864." He paused. "It calls for the 'immediate impressment of five thousand free Negroes and Slaves to work on the defences of Richmond and Danville... and...Negroes impressed into service should be those not engaged in agricultural operations and can be spared without too great a sacrifice to the community.'"

The boy swallowed and paused before reading the rest of the page. "President Lincoln has issued The Emancipation Proclamation to free slaves. It takes effect now, in June. Already, in some parts of Virginia, around Richmond and Winchester, freed slaves are being impressed into work, for the Army and for building things like train tracks. Any freed slave, young men between 18 and 52, could be called up by the Court and picked up by the Sheriff, and taken away. This is called 'impressment.' They would have to go and work for the military for 180 days and then they could come back. They might have to work hard labor, like building railroad tracks. Or they might have to serve in the Army, for the Confederate States of America."

John finished reading from the paper. "We know that your family, the McGhees, is free, one of the only families here that is. My family thinks you should know that this could happen. Tiddy and her family at The Grove are not affected by this," John added. "And we are not going to tell Tiddy yet. But my parents wanted you to be safe, so they sent me to warn you. My father has already sent nine of his servants to work for the Confederacy."

John stepped back towards the door, but the older woman reached out for his arm and gave him a gentle squeeze. He gave her a hug, again the young boy more than the messenger.

"Let me send some cake home with you, Master John," she said kindly, "for thinking on us folks over here. We are mighty thankful. And we be sorry and sad

171

about Major Hale. He was a fine gennelman," she said softly.

John thanked her and hurried on home, walking through the trees and open lands that separated his home from this neighborhood.

After young John Hale had left, Mama Hally McGhee spoke to her family, seriously. "We'se 'bout the only folks like us who be free. 'Member dat lawyer Mr. Early, who is a Gen'ral now in the Wah, and that boy's uncle, 'stablished I were not a slave, in a court over ten years ago. So you be free, too. Bless the Lawd," she said. "My friend Jane out at the Burroughs plantation, she done tole me Booker, her son, is so hopin' to get away when the Wah is done! He be younger than you, son. In case, though, we gots to keep you from being 'pressed, Jimmy, gots to keep the Sheriff from knowing you is here. Done good so far. We knowed somting like this was happening. Now it is here."

The woman called Mama tipped back and let herself chuckle. "Don't know how much longer we's gots to do this, but no way is your Pa or me going to let them take you off to work for the Army of the Confederacy," she said. "And Tiddy may have troubles but Tiddy don't be knowing you is still here and if'n we bring her over, she might let it out. She is awful loyal to them folks. But no one," the old woman said emphatically, "is gonna be takin' my boy and im'pressin' him into work. No sir."

"Mama," said the son in question, "can I have the rest of this pone?"

The fire flickered. The woman handed her son the plate of cornbread. She wiped the three-legged skillet quickly with bacon grease and set it back on the fire. She poured some raw cornmeal into a bowl and added bacon grease. She worked it with her hands and stirred in some water from a pail. Shoes scraped on the brick hearth. When the skillet started to smoke she poured the new mixture in and smoothed the top with a spoon and covered it all with ashes. She washed her hands from a small pitcher and a cloth.

"That be awful nice of the Hales to let us know, to warn us," said old Mr. McGhee, staring into the fire. "They be good folks."

Mama McGhee sat back down and continued quilting and started to hum. Lacey thought she recognized the melody... "Ezekial saw a wheel..."

Wow! *Pone? Free* black people? An old Spiritual. Lacey started to back out of the room but wanted to get to the front door. She turned and started over to what should be the front of the small house when she tripped and dropped the keys. She stood totally still. Frozen. Her instincts told her the people could hear the noise. But no one moved or even turned around. A calico cat, though, came right up to her and meowed loudly, as if recognizing her. Lacy grabbed the keys and dashed to the front door with them in her hand. She grasped the doorknob and turned it. It was stiff. No way to use a key.

The door suddenly opened toward her. "Lacey," cried a sweet voice happily, "You did It. We are In." With that, Bianca Rose stepped over the threshold into the room. "Let's find the Lights." She reached next to the door and flipped a switch and the small front room was flooded with light from a ceiling fixture above them.

"How pretty!" Bianca Rose cried, as she walked around the room admiring the details. Lacey blinked and looked around. The room was beautifully furnished in an English-cottage style, as if right out of "Country Life" magazine! There were overstuffed chintz chairs and a sofa, a coffee table with a porcelain vase of fresh-cut flowers. Table and floor lamps, an area rug on gleaming hardwood floors! Art on the walls. One painting was of a gypsy caravan and children playing around a campfire. The windows were covered with ruffled drapes, which had been in style twenty or more years ago, she thought.

"I love it. It is Just what I Hoped for," Bianca Rose said, jumping up and down. "Here, let Me take the Keys. I will try each One in each Door now and make sure I can get in and out. Oh, thank you so much." Bianca Rose gave her new friend and neighbor a quick hug and danced off out the front door to get things from her overflowing van.

Lacey quickly dashed back into the kitchen. The floor was hardwood. The windows were shuttered. The appliances were black. There was a kitchen work island. And there was the boarded-up fireplace with a brick hearth. No rockers. Nothing at all to hint at the black family and their secrets. On impulse, Lacey bent down and touched the bricks. They were warm. Oh, my Lord. She hurriedly left by the back door and ran home, waving to Bianca Rose as she saw her in the distance.

The morning mood was changing as the weather changed. Clouds had moved in, hanging low over the trees along Cottage Hill Drive. No cars were out. No dogs barked. A wind picked up and started through the highest treetops, pushing the trees one way and then the other. No birds sang. Lacey felt suspended in Time, part of her in the deepest 1860's wartime, a time of losses and secrets and dreams dashed and dreams coming true. Part of her was in Prohibition and the early 1930's, watching people try to survive by making and selling illegal whiskey. Part of her was in the present. Totally exhausted. Keys *were* the key.

She could spend her day off getting her house in order. Or she could get in the car and explore. Or maybe she could think about the keys. She had used both of the smaller keys to her house. She had not found a use yet for the big key with a tassel. A complicated and scary decision needed to be made, if she were stay here and live.

If she deliberately used a key that opened into another time period, so far she had always been able to "leave" and come back to *now*. There were some questions she had, now that she had "seen" into other times here in town. Everyone knew the South had lost the War. But what had happened to the McGhees, the Hales, and General Jubal Early? Wild Bill Conroy had filled her in on most of the history of who all had lived at The Grove since their era. But what about Tiddy? Jane and Booker? That must be Booker T. Washington, she realized, putting her hand on her heart in shock!

What about the son, Jimmy McGhee, who was worried that the Court and Sheriff would grab him and impress him, as a freeman, into military service or labor for 180 days? Had he avoided that? And what about the Mills family of the 1920's and the McCains and Griersons…and young Jack McCain, of the 1930's? Her head was swimming. She sat on her porch swing and watched the clouds and treetops and tried to think her way through a maze of situations she could never even have dreamed of just a few days earlier. And, she asked herself, why had she been "brought" here? Was there some plan?

How was it possible that someone could come and go between time periods? Surely, in all of the whole world, Mr. Ned Ruter of Rocky Mount could not be the first *returned soul* to "appear" after having died and having to remain behind. But, even if he were one of millions, why was nothing known of this kind of thing? Why had she been brought to this little town to witness it? For Mr. Ruter had got her here! Was she supposed to do something for someone? Was her knowledge of art and artists somehow helpful? Were her paintings going to allow other people to come and go into the current time, right here? And what about all the identical calico cats? Or one cat.

Lacey went back inside. As she stood in her own living room a melody began to run through her mind, as if it had just sailed in through the window. *"Swing low, sweet chariot...coming for to carry me home; swing low, sweet chariot..."* All she knew of that song was that it had been a Negro spiritual sung in the cotton fields by slaves hoping for release into a Heaven after this hard life. *"I looked over Jordan, and what did I see? Coming for to carry me home..."*

Lacey curled up on her sofa with some of the religious books left by her parents. A King James Bible, an Episcopal Hymnal, some scholarly booklets and serious pamphlets on theology. She had hardly ever looked at these, so wrapped up in her former Colorado life and relationship and her job, that Lacey realized she had been living more on the surface of life than looking deeper, for "meaning."

She had been here less than a week and her entire way of seeing existence had been turned upside-down. She was no longer certain about anything. Even Callie, her adopted cat, might not be what she seemed! Why did a calico cat keep appearing in different places and times? How old would Callie be if she were a kitten in 1864?

Arithmetic! Lacey hunted for a pen and paper and worked it out. Nine lives? All these wives' tales…but it sure seemed that the same cat kept coming up to her no matter which era she found she was in! Okay: if Callie had been a kitten in 1864, she would be 150 now! And 150 divided by 9…would be a little more than 16 years per "life." The Civil War years, Restoration, the Victorian era, WWI, Prohibition, the Great Depression, WWII, all the decades since, right up to present time. So many blocks of about 16 years added up. Callie was very old.

Cats lived about that long sometimes. Callie might be in her 9th life! Was something coming to an end now? Was that why Lacey had been lured into this complex place? Was she to witness it all, share it?

"A band of angels comin' after me, comin' for to carry me home. Swing low, sweet chariot…."

She could try harder to build a spiritual view of life and go forward with belief and hope, and faith. She made a row on her coffee table of some of her inherited religious books, and studied some of them for the rest of the morning. She wanted to find whatever it was that her parents had found in Christianity. Why had she always been so reluctant to try? She needed to focus. This was life or death out here.

Chapter Six

"Lead me to the rock that is higher than I."

Psalm 61:2

In her reading *"The New Testament in Modern English,"* by J. B. Phillips, one section in "Letters to Young Churches," said, "…whatever we may have to go through now is less than nothing compared with the magnificent future God has planned for us. The whole creation is on tiptoe to see the wonderful sight of the sons of God coming into their own."

Her parents had believed. If God wanted someone to come to him, he drew them to him. Christ Jesus, the Son would draw people to God. Not everyone would be drawn to him. Not that it was at all predestined, just that each person's life and choices determined the steps of belief, faith, understanding, and salvation. Interesting. One had to try. How about non-Christians?

After studying some of the Bible and more scholarly Christian commentaries, Lacey spent the early part of her afternoon unpacking while listening to Aaron Copland's "Quiet City." Then she drove over to the grocery store and got basics for her refrigerator, now that she had such a beautiful new one. She bought a glass bottle of Homestead Creamery strawberry milk! She put everything in the kitchen away, emptied her kitchen boxes and made some custard, one of her favorite comfort foods.

She finished reading the history of the town, that she had picked up at work, and made a list of places she wanted to see. There were so very many historical places to see: Cemeteries. Graves. Ruins. The Booker T. Washington National Park. The Jubal A. Early Homeplace. The original Callaway home, The Farm, at the Furnace. The Iron Furnace. Fort Hill. The Blue Ridge Institute at Ferrum College with its collections of rural life in earlier times. The Old Chapel Church in Sontag. The Stonewall Jackson Home! The Museum of the Confederacy. Appomattox Court House. The Historical Society of Western Virginia. The Virginia Museum of Natural History. The Virginia Museum of Transportation. The WPA Mural. Fairystone Park. The O. Winston Link Museum. The Science Museum at

Center in the Square. The Crab Orchard Museum. The Museum of Frontier Culture.

Lacey saved a shelf in a bookcase in the living room for books and booklets about Virginia. Shopping for some of these books, which she had already heard about from Wild Bill Conroy and Jim Glass, would be like a treasure hunt!

She tried to stop thinking about her recent experiences. Was it just her brain? Was she having moments of hallucinations and dreams, due to her head injuries? When she started to think that was it, she asked herself how her brain could possibly know details of this town in different times. She had not read much detailed history about the town before some of the experiences had swept her into other times. If, on the other hand, the experiences of being in a room in the 1860's, 1880's, 1920's, and 1930's had actually happened...then she needed to be informed. And she needed someone to confide in! Her Colorado friends, whom she had hardly heard from since her move, would surely think she were crazy. Ah, now that she had internet service and phone service, maybe they could get in touch.

How she wished her parents were here to share these thoughts with. Her parents would have tucked her into bed with a lap tray and soup and crackers and tea and a great movie to watch. Her boyfriend would have held her in his arms and assured her everything would be all right. Just as he had done countless times during their brief years together. Yet, things had turned out not to be all right. Lacey knew well that she could either let bitterness and depression fill her thoughts, about what had happened in her life already---losing both parents and then him because of accidents. Or she could face the facts that they were gone and that her own life had just taken a very odd turn!

Or...she started to think... Oh, so hard to do, so hard. A thought started to make its way into her consciousness: could her parents be *returned souls*? Had they had religious doubts, but had not discussed them with her because of her lack of interest? If they were *returned* would she ever find them or would they find her? How would they know where to look? Yet their faith had seemed so strong.

Restless to get out for a drive, Lacey chose a pamphlet about colonial Rocky Mount and headed up the street in her car to find Fort Hill on the grounds of Christian Heritage Academy, not far away. She needed to see the remains of Fort Hill, an 18th century stone blockhouse built by Robert Hill to protect this part of the frontier from Indian attacks. It was believed to be the earliest structure here. She wanted to start at the beginning of settlement here in town.

She drove down Main Street beyond the Courthouse and turned up the fairly steep Scuffling Hill and followed it around, passing the adobe stucco Catholic Church and a neighborhood of attractive, newer homes, until she found the entrance to the school. She took the curved road down past the buildings and parked near the stone ruins. No one seemed to be around. There were two cars parked near a school building.

The wind rustled the small forest of old trees on the steep hillside. After all she had experienced so far, Lacey was not sure what she might encounter here, at this stone blockhouse built before the Revolutionary War. No keys were involved! In a funny way, she almost wished she had some keys right now. My, what was happening to her? What might she see and learn?

The ruins sat on top of the hill down a bit from the campus buildings. At one time, she mused, this spot might have been a strategic place from which to look out over the area, and to protect it from raids. But today, aside from the brief history played on a tape, and the ruins themselves, little else seemed to be there. No ghost sidled up to her with a tale of woe. No Hill stood in the doorway, where a son was said to have been killed by an arrow. No Robert Hill walked toward her demanding to know why she was there.

Could this perhaps have been a sacred place for the Native Americans before the English-speaking pioneers came? There was nothing on the historical marker about that earlier era. A high place from which to look out over the countryside. Perfect. A place sacred to the Saponi? A gathering place for the Monacans? A lookout for the Cherokee? Or just a tall rocky hill. And, what was Scuffling Hill named for? Who had scuffled, fought, up and down the steep hill long ago? Frontiersmen and Indians? Slaves?

How very amazing, she told herself as she stared over the treetops into the sky, that she should even be hoping for another encounter in another time period. Why was she changing like this? Was she supposed to be learning something profound here in this place, in this county, in this town?

Looking at the plaques set up for visitors, she read that Robert Hill had been born in Dublin, Ireland, came to this country and married his wife Violet Linus in Chester, Pennsylvania, in 1741, and that he fought at the Battle of Point Pleasant in the French and Indian War, built this fort in the mid-1700's, and died in 1778. "Defender of the Frontier," it said. Wow. She wrapped her arms around herself and stood mute.

Pulling a small grey book, which she had found in her office at G & H, out of her bag, Lacey looked up Robert Hill and his blockhouse/fort. "Of his five sons, two were killed by Indians, one tomahawked and scalped near Bald Knob, the other shot by an arrow in the very door of the blockhouse. Still a third was killed by a panther. The story of this one family is sufficient comment on the dangers of the early Frontier." So historian and lawyer T. K. Greer had written in his *"Genesis of a Virginia Frontier, The Origins of Franklin County, Virginia, 1740-1785."*

Lacey strolled past the ruins and a few yards down the hillside, covered with mature trees that blocked a view anyone, Native American or member of the Hill family, might have had in the 1700's. Just trees now, trees swaying in a breeze. Birds singing. She leaned up against a large tree and shut her eyes, trying to imagine being here in the 1770's and either, as an Indian, having to give it up to settlers, or, as a pioneer, to try to keep it safe from Indian raids. How tragic for the Hills that a son had been killed right here in the doorway! And another tomahawked. And a third son killed by a panther? She would have to read up on wildlife in these mountains. All she had ever encountered in the Rockies, on walks in the foothills, had been a stag running through the forest.

Everything back here felt so different from the West, where she had been raised, first in Arizona and later in Colorado. The vast dry spaces out there, often edged by mountains like the Sangre de Cristo range, the Dragoons, the Chiricahuas, or the Rockies, had been the hunting grounds of many Indian nations, like the Chiricahua Apache. Cochise and Geronimo had belonged to that nation. Cochise's hideaway had been in those red mountains. Forts had been built out there, also, to protect western-moving pioneers and to protect the borders of a growing country. She had seen Fort Concho in San Angelo, Texas, and other forts in Arizona, like Fort Huachuca, and in Colorado, like Fort Carson. But the feeling out there was different. Here, closed in by blue mountains and forests, verdure and tranquil farmland, it was harder for her to imagine the bloodshed and terror of the early pioneer years.

A crazy idea suddenly came to her. Keys had been the way into the different time periods, so far. What if she stepped through the doorway of the renovated fort, even though most of it still was a ruin?

Would anything happen? Without keys? *Should she try it? Was she losing her mind?*

No one was around. She walked back over to the fort and touched the stones. Could some of these have been part of the original fort, or were these mostly newer, put here in the reconstruction? She stood very still and tried to feel the odd sensation of walking through a barrier, a cobweb, anything…as she had in the past few days, to find herself in another time.

Nothing. Just a breeze. Just the birdsong. She took another step. One foot was inside the stone wall. Her leg tingled. Was it that *she* had some special gift? Or was it that she had used the keys? Had this happened to others?

She stepped totally into the inside. Both legs now tingled. It was very cold in here. Dead cold. Like a tomb. Not warm and pleasant as it had been just inches away. She had never realized how brave she was until this week. Or crazy. Or both.

"Who are you?" a man's voice asked, startling her badly. "You do not belong here. Go away."

Lacey looked around frantically. Where was he?

"I am behind you. I followed you here. You are prying into things you should not know."

His voice trailed away. The cold dissipated. She stepped back out into the sun. There was no one there. Up in the parking area nearby a car was parked, that had not been there earlier. But she had not looked back there for at least ten minutes. Maybe a tourist?

Then Wild Bill Conroy walked up to the car. "Miz Brew. Hello." He stood next to the blue car and waved. "I am out visiting the sights," he called, smiling. He started walking towards Lacey. They met by the information panel with its video and buttons from which to hear the history of Fort Hill.

"Well." said Lacey, caught off guard. "This is my first time here. Quite interesting."

"Yes. Creepy, too, don't you think? Pioneer history gives me the creeps," he said. "But I have come up here often."

"I am doing much the same thing," Lacey admitted, trying to smile. "Do you have someone with you in the car?" Lacey suddenly asked, seeing movement.

"Oh, no. Just my dog."

"Well, I have to head on. I have been up here awhile," Lacey said, glancing at her watch.

"We got here about ten minutes ago, ourselves. I have been wandering around."

She headed back down to town. Who was the voice who had spoken to her? A ghost. A real person? An Indian? A Hill? She needed to hit the coffee shop and have a big latte and calm down. Wild Bill Conroy had just happened to be on the grounds when she was in the Fort? *Right....*

Lacey drove into town and cruised around until she found the coffee shop downtown in the Arts District between The Harvester Music Venue and the Train Depot Community Center. She sat at a corner table and ordered her Latte. Leaning back in the comfortable leather chair, Lacey "people-watched" while she tried to make sense out of the weird things happening to her in Rocky Mount.

The large room was decorated in old photographs and business signs made into posters, advertising canned foods, like tomatoes and peaches. The posters were colorful: "Smith River Brand Pie Peaches," Prilliman & Co. Henry, VA.; "Roaring Run Brand Tomatoes," Jack Garst, Boones Mill, VA.; "Algoma Apples," Callaway, VA.; Lacey was enchanted by the signs. Given all that had happened in the past two days, Lacey giddily wondered if a farmer might step out of the tomato canning picture and approach her. Did the phenomenon of *returning souls* appearing require actual paintings, or would old posters serve the purpose? How would she know? She caught herself thinking of all of this and laughed aloud. She needed some long sleep!

On the music system in the coffee shop, Joan Baez's was singing the famous ballad by The Band in 1969, "The Night They Drove Old Dixie Down." She heard, "They should never have taken the very best." Instantly, Lacey thought of Sam Hale, Jubal Early, J.E.B. Stuart, Stonewall Jackson, Jimmy, and all the people she had heard of or seen from 1864. For the first time in her life, the words rang home to her heart. She was living right in the heart of Dixie and that huge time of conflict and despair. Danville, where the song took place, was very near Rocky Mount. She would have to visit it.

Across the room was an older couple, dressed in crisp sporty clothes. The man's back was to her. But the wife, with a cute "bob" haircut framing her thin face, seemed to have Parkinson's. Her arm and hand shook whenever she lifted them to take a sip of her drink. Lacey looked away. Age.

Aging. It scared her. She had lost her most beloved family before they ever got old. Would she ever get old? Would she look like that lady someday? She had short hair, nice clothes, a handsome husband, a sweet smile. Jim Glass and Coy Howe were not exactly "old," she thought, but they were the oldest people she had talked to in a long time. Where she had worked in Aurora, she had spent most of her time with colleagues her own age. Now she felt that she wanted to know more people of all ages. This was definitely a new idea!

In another corner of the room sat a table of friends cheerily chatting and laughing. They all had red hats on. The Red Hat Society. Even though it might, someday, be a fun thing to do, to go on excursions with ladies her own age…when much older…Lacey did not really like to join groups. She was not much into what she called "mass fun." But these women were having a good time. She could tell.

Seated by himself by a window whose wide sill was covered with potted flowers, was her neighbor Jess. He had not seen her. He was busy reading while he sipped tea. There was a large teapot on his small table. Interesting young man. And in yet another nook in the room, sort of an upholstered booth, sat the lady with the pretty white hair and long batik skirt. She was reading a book. On her left arm were at least five bracelets. Her feet were in leather sandals decorated in silver and turquoise. She also looked very interesting. Lacey hoped they would meet. She looked like an artist, maybe a writer.

She withdrew into her thoughts, able to do that in a coffee shop. That was the best thing about a coffee shop! It was a haven. Being in a coffee shop never failed her. And there was a great deal to think about. The drive up to Fort Hill had been fascinating and scary. Meeting Bianca Rose earlier today had also been odd and scary in its own way, because of what Lacey now knew about that other house's 1864 "world." Needless to say, thinking that her own house at 33 Cottage Hill Drive had been the McCain house in 1933, also made her catch her breath! Had young Jack McCain ever come home? How would she find out? Newspaper records? Real estate records? Obituaries? She had her work cut out for her. Lacey sipped her coffee and crumbled another corner off her orange scone. She liked this place. She liked this little town. Just a few days already and her world had changed utterly!

Bianca Rose would be in the neighborhood for at least a month, so maybe Lacey should have her over. How about asking her, Jess, Leila Park and her husband, her colleagues at work, and maybe the new woman with white hair, after she had introduced herself, which she might do today. All of a sudden, Lacey paused in her thoughts and smiled. A few life-altering days in a new town and she had changed THAT much already! Thinking of having strangers over to her home? This was new. In Colorado she almost never had anyone over, even when James had been there. Everyone had been too busy. Well, she decided, I am not too busy anymore!

Lacey walked across the room to where the woman was reading, with a pile of James Michener books beside her coffee.

"Excuse me," she interrupted quietly, as the woman glanced up with a pleasant smile, "I am brand new to Rocky Mount, and wanted to introduce myself. I am Lacey Brew. Just moved here from Denver, to work at Glass & Howe Realty. I saw you yesterday when I was showing a house. Besides hoping to meet you, I wanted to ask where you got your baguette," Lacey said cheerily.

"Why, I am delighted to meet you! I am Teri Prater, and I have not lived here too terribly long, either. My husband and I moved here after Hurricane Katrina destroyed our home in Louisiana. We are settling in here, far from the Gulf, and enjoying the quiet. Oh," Teri added, reaching for a piece of paper, "here is my address and phone, and the name of the bread shop. It is called 'Kneaded,' and is new! It has its main bakery in Salem and they truck fresh items over here and to the Lake and Christiansburg daily. Great bread!"

"Thank you, so much, Mrs. Prater," Lacey said...just as her new acquaintance laughed and said to call her Teri. "I know I have my white hair, but I do not think of aging! Just 'Teri' to everyone," she smiled.

"Let's meet here sometime for coffee, would that work for you? I can take some time, they have told me, as I learn the ropes here," Lacey asked. "And I am still moving into my home on Cottage Hill Drive. Not quite finished yet!"

"Oh, my, Moonshine Corner!" Teri exclaimed excitedly. "We have read about its history. So interesting!"

"Where do I find the history?"

"The Gertrude Mann Collection in our Library and The Historical Society on Main Street, just past the hospital," Teri explained, "pretty much have everything. And they have special tours for the public that we have taken. Really informative. There is a Ghost Tour around Halloween and a Moonshine Tour in the spring. Both of those tours, by the way, feature The Grove. And, I have heard," Teri lowered her voice, "that they are working on the very first Native American Tour!" she said excitedly. "We can't wait!"

"I would really enjoy those," Lacey responded, thinking of all the secret knowledge she could contribute. "Well, I had better get back to my list," she pointed to her table. "I am keeping track of whom I meet and some of the places I have already visited, like Fort Hill."

"That is a place we have not yet visited, ourselves," Teri replied. "I am the history nut in our family. My husband is the gardener. He spends most of his time outside or finding new plants."

"I will have to introduce you to my gardening neighbor sometime," Lacey said, looking over to where Jess had been seated. But he had left.

"I look forward to hearing from you. Thank you so much for coming over! I could tell," Teri dropped her voice to a whisper, "as soon as you came over and spoke that you had to be from somewhere else! The local or native women rarely will go up to a stranger to speak. Kind of keep to themselves, I have found. And, of course," Teri wiggled her bracelet-bedecked arm, "my style does not quite fit some of their notions of what a lady my age should wear." She laughed and Lacey joined in.

Lacey sat back down and pulled out a notebook given her by a pal when she had decided to move to Virginia. She started to make another list: linking cause and effect for all that had been happening to her so far.

Art collection	portals
Non-believers	returned souls
People dead too soon	returned souls
Callie	ninth life?
Back office at G & H	an entry for ghosts/returned souls
Ned Ruter	lead ghost and Returned Soul
Jim Glass	? facilitator?
Mary See	Town Grapevine
Dr. Peters	historian
33 Cottage Hill Dr.	McCains 1933 Griersons
35 Coal Street	Mills 1925?
Bianca Rose house	freed slaves, freemen, McGhees 1864
The Grove	1864, portico, slaves, Hales, Saunders, Early
Empty lot 33 C H Dr	?

| Fort Hill | mystery man |
| Wild Bill Conroy | ? |

Lacey took her list and headed back out into town. She would give some thought to the biggest, tasseled key. And she would walk around her empty lot, maybe at dusk this evening, to see if anything odd happened. She might also use the 1930's key to her house, before dark, to try to overhear more from the McCains!

Bianca Rose's van was still parked in front of the house on Autumn Street. Callie was wandering among grasses on the empty lot. Her own house looked peaceful as the sun was about to set. The Willow Oaks stood guard and the flowering bushes and trees in her neighbors' yards gleamed in the last of the sun. Somewhere up the street children were playing, their happy voices carrying on the breeze down to Lacey as she stood on her sidewalk with the key ring in her hand. The tasseled key was inside, in her dresser drawer. No door on the house fit it. It had fit in the front door that first day, but did not work, so maybe it had belonged to a door that was no longer on the 1930's house. Lacey planned to find out. But right now, while no one was paying any attention, and no one was nearby, she walked up to her house and used the older key and stepped in.

Her sofa was under the window. The walls were papered in a pale floral print. The light hardwood floor was bare. She tiptoed toward the kitchen, from where voices were coming.

"Hand me the flour, child," Mrs. *McCain asked a young girl Lacey had not seen before. "I will be making hoe cakes tomorrow and am not sure I have all I need here. Prilly, if'n I give you a dollar, please run next door to the store and bring me back a box of baking soda and a jar of Algoma Orchard apple sauce. We ran out of ours. They are open. I saw lights on a bit ago."*

The kitchen was mellow. A small ceiling light illumined the yellow walls. The little girl had blond braids. She took the dollar and ran into another room. Lacey quickly followed. The bedroom Lacey was using as hers, was the girl's room. The child reached into a small jar on a dresser and shook out some coins. Clutching the coins and the paper dollar in her hand she darted out the front door and started to run...next door! Lacey followed.

In less than a minute she found herself following the child into a small one-room store with a soda fountain. Prilly hopped up on a stool. An older black man came over, wiping his hands on an apron and asked her what she would like.

"Bakin' soda and Algoma Orchard Apple Sauce for Mama, please. And a Grapette for me!" He turned and came back with a bottle of grape soda and a glass. Then he rummaged around on a shelf and found the Baking Soda and apple sauce and dropped them into a small paper bag.

"Forty cents, all told, Missy," he said with a smile, and she handed him the dollar and some of the change. "I am paying for my own soda separate, from my coins," she told him proudly. "And I want to hear a story, please?"

He laughed. There were no other customers in the little store, so he leaned back on the wall behind the soda fountain and thought for a minute. "How's about the one about the calico cat, Celia, who came to live with my family after the Civil Wah?"

"I love that story!" Prilly cried, sipping her Grapette. And he proceeded to tell the story about the skinny, scared cat who had wandered into a yard in 1870, and had won the hearts of the family who lived there in the house right behind this store, Jimmy McGhee had started this very store some years later. Celia had loved the store.

Prilly listened raptly and hopped off the stool and hurried home just as the sun was setting. Lacey followed, conscious of the calico cat following them across the yard to the McCain home.

"Here, Mama," the child called, putting the bag and the change on the wooden table.

Lacey noticed this time that the countertops in the kitchen were wooden. White dishes were drying on the porcelain, ridged part of the sink. Mrs. McCain had pulled supper out of the small white oven and was starting to place plates on a table. What was Lacey's dining room seemed to be a bedroom in this time. A kitchen table in the big kitchen was set for three. Lacey was eager to see if Jack would be there for supper!

"Mama," Prilly asked, "Is it just you and Ann and me for supper? Is Pa not here?"

"Your Pa is out, child. Don't you pay no mind to what he is doing. You know we cannot talk about it."

"I know," she said sulkily, toying with her fork. "But I saw Bobby and Papa by the truck last night, putting bottles in and I was scared."

"They will be fine, honey," her mother said. *"Bobby's Pa and your Pa have talked and it looks like they have worked out something new. They do not want us to know, but how can we not know? And I think it is safer for us to know than not to know. What if the Law comes by and we do not know what to be quiet about? Besides, I told your Pa that my brothers both got jobs with the Civilian Conservation Corps and they will be working to make a National Park at Fairystone! Isn't that something? A real nice park not too far from here. Remember when Pa and I took you children there once to hunt the little fairystones? Mr. Fishburne of the Roanoke newspaper gave them the land. Wasn't that grand of him?"* Mrs. McCain smiled as she pushed a straggle of hair off her forehead and sat down.

Ann came in from the other room and seated herself. She looked very pretty in a dotted dress.

"Mama," Ann began, *"Thank you again for helping me and Bobby. The wedding was so nice. Thank you for using so many of your eggs for our wedding cake and for having ham and butter. And real coffee. Wherever did you get that? It was delicious. I doubt my Bobby had ever had a meal that tasty! And thank you for letting us stay in the extra room for now,"* she added. *"I just*

wish Jack would come home! Whatever happened to him? It has been months."

"I have to reckon our Jack ran away to keep from the beatings his Pa kept giving him. I imagine he is safe somewhere, maybe at my parents' over in Christiansburg. But no one has told me. I cry about it most every night, I am so worried," Mrs. McCain admitted. *"But your Pa is so stubborn. He will not let me go find out."* They all started to eat.

Looking at their plates, Lacey remembered it was the Depression! They were eating vegetables and hard boiled eggs, probably from their own chickens. Each also had a baked apple at her place. Sugar and coffee were scarce. People raised their own foods when they could.

As she stood there watching…her very longest visit into another era, the cat pounced on her and grabbed her leg, sinking her claws into Lacey's pants and hanging on! Lacey stifled a yell. It hurt!

"Mama, mama, look! Cleo is in the air, just hanging in the air! It is magic!"

Prilly started to come over and Lacey pried the little claws off her clothes and the calico cat dropped back to the floor and hissed. Lacey ran out through the front

203

rooms and leaped off the porch and stumbled and dropped the key.

When she got back to her feet, she immediately looked behind her, hoping not to find Prilly or her family coming outside! She was relieved to see her own new front porch with the window boxes. She was back in *now.* But she had had such a long time in the other era! And she had learned that a small store and soda fountain had stood in her empty lot in the 1930's and that Fairystone Park was being built just then. She walked over to the tall grasses and remains of a brick foundation in the center of the field. She stooped down and touched the bricks, the remnants of the store. A faint scent of grape pop wafted towards her and a butterfly swooped down and lit nearby.

The sun set. The breeze picked up. The limbs of the towering Willow Oaks, which were so much shorter in the 1930's, wavered and swung like arms. Lights started to come on up the street. Jess's lights were on. On Autumn Street, the other direction, lights came on in Bianca Rose's house. A streetlight beyond where the colorful van was parked came on. It all looked so innocent, so peaceful. Through the open windows music wafted out.

Tomorrow, during her lunch break, Lacey would scoot over to the Historical

Society and start to research Moonshine Corner. Were there records about the McCain's? The little store? Had the McCains and Griersons ever been caught for making white lightning? Had the Griersons and Mills been caught for transporting it?

Chapter Seven

"Be not forgetful to entertain strangers: For thereby some have entertained angels unawares."

Hebrews 13:2

First thing the next morning on her way to work, Lacey stopped in briefly at the Post Office around the corner from her neighborhood and signed up for a P.O. Box. She took a moment to study the Roy Hilton WPA mural. The woman on the left looked a lot, in her dress and hair, like Mrs. McCain, of the 1930's. Getting her Post Office box keys, two of them, which looked identical, gave her a thrill of anticipation. What if one of those keys worked in another era? Now, that would really be something! Wouldn't it have been amazing if the Northern artist had painted people making moonshine, instead of furniture and textiles, in his mural! She laughed.

"Good morning, young lady," Jim Glass greeted her as she settled into her office at the back of the building. "You will be showing some clients two houses over in Callaway today. The houses are quite different from each other. One is old and one is new. The clients are from California. They told us they wanted to get away from the traffic and earthquakes...and taxes! There was just a 6.0 in Napa Valley! Lots of damage. I told them this was the place to be! They are coming," he winked at her, "through the *front* door at 10:00. Their name is Preston."

"I will be ready," Lacey replied. "Do I have a van for today? And does it have a GPS?"

"Yes, you do have a van. Its tag is 'GH3 VA' and it has a GPS. Type in the exact address and it will take you there. It is about a ten to twelve minute drive, through some beautiful country. And for these first two or three weeks or so, young lady," he continued, "you can take time off for yourself each day until you are ready to work full-time. We do not want to overdo it," he said kindly.

Mr. Glass consulted a list which he then handed to Lacey to keep after he read it to her. "You have probably read enough about the town or seen a variety of houses by now to know that here in town there are many kinds: Bungalows, American Foursquare, Colonial-Revival, Federal, Queen Anne style, Greek Revival, neo-Colonial Revival, Gothic Revival, Gothic Revival/Queen Anne, Tudor Revival, 'Worker's Cottages' of the original Bald Knob Furniture Factory era, and modern ranches."

"I am learning as I go," she laughed. "I saw that you had included this list in your own booklet and I am glad. The application for a Historic District was very thorough," she added. "I am studying a little of it daily. And as I drive by a house on the list, I am checking it off so I know which style is which. I showed a Worker's Cottage already!"

"Good for you," he exclaimed happily.

Lacey set up a new file for the Prestons and checked all the houses in the Callaway area, especially the two she would be showing first. She had been reading about Callaway, a tiny crossroads west of town, named for one of the early settlers, James Callaway, who had owned hundreds of acres long ago. The Callaway area was now mostly farmland but had been full of apple orchards in the last century. And…it had been one of the busiest areas for the transporters of illegal moonshine to drive through on their way out of this county and up into Floyd County or beyond. The area also had many farms owned and operated by the industrious German Baptist families who had started settling there long, long ago.

As she sat at her desk she spent some time studying the three paintings on her wall. One was a watercolor of a park-like estate, presumably in England. The little bit of mansion visible in the background resembled the one in one of her favorite films, "Brideshead Revisited." That novel, by Evelyn Waugh, had been a retrospective memoir story of a houseguest at the mansion who had occasion to visit it decades later when it was used for billeting officers in WWI. It was one of her favorite films because of the soundtrack and the characters, all unique. But it was a heavy, sad story. This artist was not British, as she had thought. Looking at the signature she saw that it was by Suzanne Ross. Maybe this was a Virginia estate over on the James! Was this the one that Ned Ruter supposedly stepped out of?

One of the other paintings was of a mountain creek surrounded by autumn trees. Leaves floated in the rushing water and a child was playing on the bank. Tucked into the rocks on the right were the remains of a moonshine still, its copper parts broken up and mixed in with limbs and rocks. The artist was Karen Sewell.

The third painting was smaller. Also an oil, it had the fanciest frame. It was a picture of two women reading in a bright room. Its artist was Tricia Scott. Lacey admired all three paintings and was intrigued by the supposed "arrival" of deceased Ned Ruter, through the painting of the estate and old mansion. If paintings were "portals" for all that was happening, then maybe something would happen with these other two, as well!

At 10:00 the Preston couple arrived through the front door of G & H and sat down with Lacey at her desk in the front to review what they were looking for in a house.

"I only want to look at houses built in the past ten years," said Carly Preston, eagerly studying the pages of houses near Callaway. "I do not like old things that much."

"I hope we can find something with a combination of new and old," said her husband, Tim Preston with a rueful smile. "I have Preston ancestry in Virginia and have been looking forward to something historic.

I have done much of my Virginia genealogy, and think this county has a perfect location from which to visit Blacksburg, Roanoke, Botetourt County, and other areas where the Prestons were active long ago."

"I think we might be able to find something new and something old," Lacey said cheerily, thinking to herself how ironic it was that she, of all people, with no known ties to this state, had "access" to old and very old....

They all got in the van and headed out of town towards Bethlehem Road, up past some crossroads that may have been communities long ago and past a place called Gogginsville. She had read that Captain Moses Greer, of Revolutionary War fame and who had served on the first County Court with Swinfeld Hill, was buried with his wife on top of a forested hill in Gogginsville. There were many closed-up buildings every few miles that had once been country stores or gas stations. Some of these little buildings had been "drops" for the moonshining folks. She turned left at the Franklin County Speedway sign. Much of the land was taken up with farms. The rolling fields held crops or cattle. There was an occasional dairy farm. A string of ordinary brick ranch houses bordered the road for awhile. The occasional country church stood alone. Many had Church of the Brethren on their signs, a church not yet familiar to Lacey. Callaway was about eight or so miles west of town, and she knew it would be an easy trip.

"I refuse to live in an old place," Carly said from the back seat. "No ghosts. No mice. No insects. Just a nice modern place with an open-concept and maybe a Great Room with a view of the mountains."

Tim chuckled. "Most of the new houses will cost a lot more, honey. We have a budget to think of."

"This is our first house together, and I want it to be so perfect that we will not have to move for years," she said.

"We will start with some two-story houses that were built in the past twenty years," Lacey interjected. "They each have acreage, if that matters to you. And the lack of zoning here means you can have horses, llamas, goats, chickens, dogs…" she laughed, trying to lighten the mood in the car.

They pulled into a driveway of a two-story house, a Colonial, with wooden siding and a split-rail fence decoratively sur-rounding two acres of lawns and gardens. The young couple wandered inside and checked out the rooms after Lacey had opened the front door with the one key in the realtors' lockbox.

They wanted to see as many houses as possible today, so they went to the next one about a mile further to the west. The view from the second house of the Blue Ridge Parkway in the distance was breathtaking. Lacey, who had never been out in this part of the county before, was enthralled. The view was as majestic as her views of the distant Rockies had been when she lived in Boulder before she had lived in Denver with James. Here, the ridges were just as close, and were a dark blue and thickly covered with trees, unlike so much of the Rockies, which were above tree-line.

"This house has a huge master suite and en-suite bath," Carly admitted. "But," she pouted, "the kitchen is not up to my standards at all. There are unstained brown cabinets, a tile backsplash, white Formica countertops, and white appliances. Ugh. And," she added disgustedly, "those floors are laminate! I really, really have to have hardwoods and stainless steel. I mean," she paused dramatically, "what if we entertain a lot and people saw our outdated kitchen?" Tim rolled his eyes so Lacey could see him, but did not say anything aloud

"You could easily get the kitchen updated," Lacey said. "There are many cabinet shops here, as this was once a very big furniture-making part of the world. Just down 220, in fact, in the tiny town of Bassett, there was what was the biggest and richest furniture company in the world!"

"I have heard of Bassett Furniture," exclaimed Tim. "I really had no idea that it had been nearby."

"I have been reading up on things about the whole region," Lacey admitted. "Vaughan-Bassett still makes wooden bed frames and dressers and wooden furniture over in Galax. And I read that a brand-new book is out, called *"Factory Man,"* by Beth Macy, all about Mr. John Bassett, III, keeping production here instead of letting it go to China!"

"I have heard of Galax!" Carly cried. "The Old Fiddlers' Convention! Every August! I can't wait to go!"

"I have not read all about the music world here yet," Lacey said. "But Rocky Mount has lots of live music. The Harvester Performance Center has acts almost every week. Rocky Mount is the end or the beginning, depending on how you look at it, of what is known as The Crooked Road Music Trail."

"I hope to travel the whole Road," Carly said, hugging Tim.

"We will!" he said. "But let's find a house. Are there some older ones on your list?"

"I don't want 'old'," his wife started to complain, but he put his finger on her lips. "Just let's look at some older ones."

They drove even closer to the stunning, serrated ridge of mountains. Hawks could be seen floating high in the air. "Right over there, you can just barely see the tent, event center, and log home of Mysterious Ridge," Lacey pointed. "It is a wedding and event venue."

"How nice!" Carly said.

They pulled up in front of a brick, Italianate house with a small front porch and a brick chimney. The house was old, lots older than Carly wanted. But Tim's face lit up when the van was parked in the neat driveway to the right of the stately house.

"Now, this is what I mean," he said, almost running up to the door, with Lacey hurrying behind, hoping there would be only one key for this place! Carly hung back.

As Lacey worked on the lockbox and Tim waited patiently, Carly walked around the house, out of sight. It was a clear, warm day. It was perfectly beautiful out here in Callaway.

She pulled out three keys. One was old and bent. One was large and shiny. And the third was brand-new and small. She took a breath and tried the small new key and the door opened into an empty foyer with a straight hall cutting the first floor into two parts. They walked up the hall. To the right was a parlor which opened into a dining room. On the other side of the hall were a kitchen in the back and what looked like a bedroom in the front. The stairs led straight up to a similar layout. There was a central hall with two bedrooms on each side and a bathroom on the left.

"Carly will hate this," Tim said, as he smiled his way through each old room admiring the crown molding, hardwood floors, and old sash windows. "The bathrooms up and down are 'vintage tile' and she will have a fit," he sighed.

"Is there a reason she does not want an old home?" Lacey asked.

"Oh, yes! When she was a child and used to visit her grandparents in their old home, in Maryland, she says she saw a ghost. It walked through a wall right in front of her. She ran to tell her family and they were silent. Finally her grandfather asked her not to talk about it to anyone else. And that was it. They apparently believed her! So there must have been a ghost. It really put her off old houses, for life," he ended.

Yes, I understand, Lacey thought! "Well, is there any point in even having your wife come inside then?"

"Probably not. I just really wanted to see something old. You know, when you are dating someone, it just does not occur to you to ask your date, or your fiancée, if she has had an experience with ghosts or is afraid of old houses! My mistake." He laughed. They stepped back outside.

"Why don't the two of you take some time, with the brochures, and pick out a few more to see today, while I run in and check that all is ok inside. I will be gone only a few minutes," she added, hurrying back up to the front door as if to replace all three keys.

While they made themselves comfortable on a stone bench next to an English Boxwood and began to look through more listings, Lacey inserted the oldest key into the lock. She had noticed that there were two locks on the house.

Stepping into the foyer and hall, she stopped to close the door and to listen. Voices were coming from the dining room. She crept down the hall.

"It is shocking. It is horrible what they did to that poor minister on June 15th," said a woman. She was probably in her

sixties and dressed in a long dress with ribbons on the bodice. She was setting the table for supper.

"This is the end of June already," a man replied, "and here we are trying to live through this war that I did not want anyhow. I have no sons to send to the Army. I served long ago and I thought we were finished with wars. I do not have slaves! Your father did not have slaves. I understand the reasons for the war, to separate from the Union, the need to protect our right to send goods to England, Virginia's determination to keep slavery, even though I think it is wrong. But what has happened to Elder John Kline out near Linville is horrid."

"I heard that the militarists shot him dead for advocating his pacifist views. Poor man," said the woman sadly. "Our own soldiers shot him."

"The Brethren are pacifists. People know that. There is room for both: people who fight and people who object to fighting. They have buried him at Linville Creek Church of the Brethren. So sad, such a waste," he said.

His wife continued, "Look what happened to those young cadets from the Virginia Military Institute last month! Two hundred and seventy four young men, just boys, sent in to battle. Nine killed, forty eight wounded. And our General John Breckinridge won the day. Then that Yankee general, Hunter, burned VMI to the ground on June 11th because it had sent the cadets to the Battle of New Market in May! Then he burned down our own Governor Letcher's house in Lexington in retaliation for our generals asking everyone to help drive the Yankees away! But our Jubal Early defeated Hunter at Lynchburg on June 19th."

Her husband walked to the window and gazed out onto the beautiful dark purple hills. He was standing right next to Lacey! She held her breath, even though she knew he could not detect her presence.

"Supper will be ready when I get the Brunswick Stew in the porringers," his wife said, adjusting a pewter fork. "And they are fighting all over eastern Virginia. You heard that Major Sam Hale, John's son by his first wife Judith, was killed in battle? He was Early's Inspector General. I heard that in town the other day, at church, I believe, after we had stepped out to chat. Poor Margaret. Poor young Elizabeth Hairston Hale, Sam's widow. Only married one month! And did you know, Thomas, that he was killed on May 12th, the same day as his father's and stepmother's' anniversary? How tragic."

"War is tragic, Helen," he replied softly.

Lacey was thrilled to hear more news about 1864! But it was horrible news! *Brunswick Stew? Militarists?* She had been inside long enough. She would have to research who had owned this pretty home back in the 1860's. It was fairly far from Rocky Mount, or would have been, by carriage, back then.

Back in the van with her clients, Lacey pretended to listen to their discussion about the pros and cons of kinds of houses. They visited one more fairly modern one before she drove them back to town.

The scalloped ridges of the Blue Ridge Mountains edged the county in dark blue. High up on the top she could make out what looked like a castle. She would have to ask someone what that was. As they drove back through some other clusters of newer houses, Lacey chose a road that curved past the crossroads of Callaway. There was a weaving studio and a small grocery store and a post office. Then there were farms and farmhouses, rolling hills, trees. Quiet. The Prestons were chatting with each other about the views. When they curved around a bend and passed some hilly fields with stones in them and a few large horses grazing, Tim asked if she knew where Bleak Hill was, at the headwaters of the Pigg River.

"I am afraid I am so new here," Lacey began, "that while I have heard the name, I have not yet been there."

"It is privately owned now," he said, "but it was the Saunders farm and plantation in the 19th century. My ancestors were friends of theirs. I hope we drive by it. It is very near an Episcopal church." As they wound along past the pretty fields, Lacey saw a sign for the church.

"Look," Tim said excitedly, "please slow down for a minute. That," he pointed to a very small cabin behind an ordinary small white house set back from the road on the right, "is the childhood home of Jeff Richards, one of the men killed during the 1930's! He was going to tell all about who was running the granny fees and protection rackets, but he was killed to shut him up before he could testify. It is all in Mr. Greer's *The Great Moonshine Conspiracy Trial of 1935.*" "We now know that he was set up by his partner, Edgar Beckett, who managed not to be in the car that night." They slowed to look and Tim got out for a minute to take a quick photo of the cabin. Carly acted bored, paying no attention to the houses.

Lacey took the next left, across from the imposing conference center called Phoebe Needles, a stone building beyond the Richards property. They passed an old Episcopal Church. She followed the road, seeing a large house up on a hill on the right.

"Bleak Hill," exclaimed Tim Preston! "Now I know where we are. I studied the maps but there are so many curves and turns and crossroads that I do not think I could have found this without help."

Lacey pulled up into the long, steep drive so Tim could better see the house. There were no cars around. He wanted to step out and take some photos. Carly sat in the car, apparently uninterested in the house. Lacey sat there, wondering what on earth she might find if she had keys to Bleak Hill! No such luck, though. She would have to content herself with its written history. It was privately owned.

When Tim returned they headed back to Rocky Mount.

Tim Preston suddenly said, "I have my notes on all of this. He read from some papers, "Pioneer Peter Saunders built a house and it later burned and was rebuilt and burned again. It was frame, not brick. And the same Peter Saunders had a son, Fleming, a Judge, who married Alice Watts. They had sons Samuel, Fleming, and Peter. Samuel married Mary Ingles, and two of their many children were their daughters Margaret Ingles Saunders and Virginia Alice Saunders.

"Mary Ingles had been the daughter of John Ingles, the son born after his mother Mary Draper Ingles' Shawnee captivity in 1755, who made her way back to Draper's Meadow on foot by following the river, what is now called the New River.

"Both Margaret and her sister Virginia, great-granddaughters of the famed Mary Draper Ingles, married the Hales, father and son, of The Grove.

"Fleming's son Peter married Elizabeth Dabney and built Bleak Hill (named by his wife for the Dickens' novel). Their son, Edward Watts Saunders, Sr., was the second owner of The Grove after Margaret and John S. Hale. And his son of the same name was the next owner. All these families were tied together in so many ways," he commented while Carly fidgeted, bored.

"I find it interesting," Lacey commented, "that Peter's grandsons Peter and Samuel were brothers whose offspring both ended up as owners of The Grove. I have been showing The Grove," she said. "It is on the market for the first time since it was last bought by the Greers in 1959. Interested?"

"This is so, so, so boring," Carly almost cried, acting like a tired and spoiled child having a tantrum. "I hate all this talk about who lived where and who married who and who built what," she whined.

Tim turned to her, where she was in the back seat, and replied, "If you cannot bear to hear about family history and Virginia history, sweetheart, then maybe we should house hunt somewhere like south Florida or Hawaii!"

"I would like Florida," she exclaimed.

The rest of the drive was in silence, tense silence. Lacey pretended not to notice the tension. But she really wanted a chance, soon, to talk to Tim privately about some of the history. It was so much easier for her to learn history from people and not pamphlets and booklets.

"We are staying at Claiborne House," he remarked. "I would like to come by tomorrow, if you are free," he asked Lacey, "to look at some printouts of more modern homes."

"Certainly! Some of them will be at Smith Mountain Lake. If you decide to look at any out there, our realtor Mary See handles the Lake," Lacey replied.

"Sounds like a plan!" Tim Preston said, gripping her hand in a firm shake. Carly sneered and walked off. She was so unfriendly.

Lacey hurried inside and plunked herself down behind her closed door and took a big breath. Was being a realtor any fun, she wondered? Not yet!

Chapter Eight

"Flee as a bird to your mountain."

Psalm 11:1

The early evening of the day Lacey had spent with the Prestons found her driving up Scuffling Hill to Fort Hill. She found the hilltop magic and mysterious, and maybe secretly hoped something else supernatural might take place! And she had brought along a quilt to sit on while she enjoyed the quiet. It was light enough and warm enough to enjoy the air. She curled up not far from the stone fort and pulled a Bible out of her bag. Reading the Psalms was becoming a favorite pastime, and she skipped around, recognizing passages she had heard all her life.

Then she heard an odd sound. As if someone were digging. She looked around but saw no one. The sound stopped. A hawk flew over, settling in an oak. She glanced over at the doorway in the fort, where she had had a scary moment when a man's voice had startled her and told her to leave. She had finally convinced herself that it all had been her imagination, and one more leftover effect of her head injury. It looked as if a tree had recently toppled over, dislodging some very old stones.

"Ms. Brew, what a surprise," called a man from behind her.

"Mr. Howe!" Lacey stood up, prepared to be polite to her older employer by standing.

"I am surprised to find you here," he said with a smile.

"This is only my second visit, to sit awhile," Lacey responded. "I find it mysterious and peaceful up here. Sort of a magic hill."

"I come up every now and then, myself. Did you hear me digging?'

"Digging?' Lacey repeated. "Why, I did hear something, but could not figure out what it was," she answered.

"Ah, yes. Well, it seems my little secret is out," he admitted. "I come here about once a month to dig for treasure."

"Treasure?" Lacey cried, excitedly.

"Yes, ma'am. Some of us old-timers think this hill may be where the Beale Treasure was buried. Not around Bedford. But here, on this famous hill...a hill most people have forgotten all about," he chuckled. "It seems to be famous only to a handful of historians and to the Hill descendants. Some show up every now and then for a ceremony put on by the Daughters of the American Revolution, The Virginia's Old Carolina Road Chapter, or by our Historical Society."

"I know nothing about a Beale Treasure," Lacey said happily.

"Well, my dear, I do not have the energy this evening to share the tale, but, in a nutshell, gold was brought back East to be buried for safekeeping, long ago, in 1819 and 1821, buried twice. Lost."

"Why do you think it is up here?" Lacey asked, looking around at the forests and hill and old stone fort ruins.

"Because I have a hunch. I think this was a quiet but known spot. It was known in the 18th and 19th century. It was safe here. The school was not here then. And it just feels to me," he added sheepishly, "like a place where there are secrets."

"Mr. Howe, I never would have imagined you to be a treasure hunter or to have imaginative hunches," Lacey said excitedly. "But I agree with you that there is 'something' unusual up here. I feel that, myself. I guess I associate it with the tragic history of the Hill family. The ruins, and all of that," she let her sentence die away. The breeze caught her last words and carried them into the treetops.

"Please do not tell anyone, dear," he asked her kindly. "It is a hobby of mine that no one knows about, now that my sweet Laura is gone, bless her soul."

"I will keep it a secret," she promised. "I wondered, actually, if there might be a sacred place hereabouts associated with the Native Americans before they scattered when settlement seemed inevitable."

"I, too," he said, looking straight into her eyes. "I have been digging a little here and little there for many years. Never been discovered until tonight! But in my wanderings up on this hillside, I have seen long hills upon hills, deep in the forest now, what might be mounds, sacred burial places that the Saponi or Monacans may have created long before white men took these lands."

"Mounds!" Lacey cried. "I will have to read about mounds. I have heard of them in Ohio and Indiana."

"You know a lot, for someone as young as you are," he said nicely.

"I grew up in Arizona and Colorado," Lacey explained. "Our Native American history was well known and interesting to trace. And in my studies I ran across the famous Mounds of Indiana and Ohio. My knowledge of the many Virginia Indians is rudimentary. I have had to start from the beginning. And I know all about the Trail of Tears," she added, sadly. "Horrible.""

"Interesting that we both find something special or mysterious up here, don't you think?" Coy Howe asked her, starting to walk back to the school area. Lacey followed, her hour of study and isolation having prematurely ended. Neither of them noticed another person standing behind the stone ruins, listening.

By the time she got back to her cottage on Moonshine Corner, a mist had started to settle on the ridges. It swirled around the lamppost at the corner of Autumn and Cottage Hill. The sky was darkening.

Inside her cozy new home, *now,* Lacey put the lights on and pulled her shutters on some windows and the drapes on others. She took all the keys out of where she had hidden them in her dresser and a drawer in a flip-top antique table that had been her parents'. She lay the four keys down on a coffee table and stared at them, as if by staring she might discover their secrets. She had kept the 1864 key to Bianca Rose's house. She knew that one key opened this house to 1933. One key was in the current time. The fourth, and largest key, with the tassel, could be anything. It could be a door key. Or it might open a box or a chest. This was the town associated with Lane Cedar Chests! Perhaps there was a chest here. A 1930's chest? That would mean she would have to use the 1933 key and poke around. But she was not up to it tonight.

Lacey listened again to "The Night They Drove Old Dixie Down" and stretched out on her couch with an apple and some cheese. Tomorrow she was to meet the Prestons. Most of the modern or recent homes were out beyond Westlake in the eastern part of the county by the lake. If they saw anything they liked, Mary See would take over.

Lacey wanted to go back to The Grove tomorrow to learn more about 1864. She had last seen Margaret Hale grieving. Then there was the McGhee family where Bianca Rose was living! Lacey was very curious about the lives of Jimmy McGhee and his parents in 1864. She had not known that any freed slaves, or "freemen," had lived in the South!

Would the keys work much longer for her? Was all this some kind of test or something, for her alone? Was she supposed to solve some mysteries? Were other people involved, who maybe did not even know that they were? Like Jess, Bianca, Wild Bill, or Coy Howe? How about Callie-Cleo-Celia-Celine!

Mr. Howe was digging for an early Western 19th century treasure, the Beale Treasure, buried in Virginia and never found. She would have to look that up! And several families, the McCains, the Griersons, and the Mills were all involved with moonshine in the Prohibition Era. What about Jack? And hadn't Bianca Rose mentioned a treasure? Could *she* be looking for the Beale Treasure, as well?

Tomorrow, or the next day if she had time, Lacey hoped to stop into the art gallery in town, where members of Bald Knob Artists displayed. It was time to buy some more local art! Some of their work was upstairs in the Public Library a few blocks away. There was an exhibit there right now of portraits and she had seen a vibrant one of what looked to Lacey like a tormented Abraham Lincoln by Suzanne Verde Paddock. The artist had an entire series of

Lincoln paintings. Lacey wondered what the local people thought of them. She knew that Judge Park would find them of interest.

Lacey hoped fervently that President Lincoln was safe in Heaven or somewhere and not a *returned soul*, since his life had been cut short by assassination! If Lincoln suddenly showed up in Rocky Mount, all hell might break loose! The way things had been going so far, in her new life here, just about anything could happen.

Chapter Nine

"How excellent is thy loving-kindness, O God! Therefore the children of men put their trust under the shadow of the wings."

Psalm 36:7

The rest of the week was fairly uneventful, for Lacey, as she became more familiar with the town and county. Showing four new houses to clients was "ho-hum" after showing old houses. The new houses were in sub-divisions that had been farmland. Only one key per house. Nothing unusual at all.

Mary See had actually "clucked" in disapproval when Lacey had mentioned having a few people over for dinner at Lacey's home. "But you are new here, dear! That just is not *done!*"

Lacey had smiled in reply and told her that she was from out in the Wild West and it was done all the time. But Mary See declined the invitation, claiming a prior engagement. Lacey invited Teri Prater and her husband, Bianca Rose, Jess Thomspon, Lee Anne Travis, the Parks, and her colleagues from work. She had bumped into Lee Anne twice at the Coal Car Café, and they had enjoyed talking. Bianca Rose had not been visible for a few days, and Lacey had left her invitation on the door. As she stood there, she worried and wondered about how the McGhee family had fared. Maybe she would never know. She hesitated to use her old key. 1864 was getting so bad, and, of course, Lacey knew the South had lost that war. She'd never thought about this war so much.

Summer was becoming hot. Lacey could not help but think of the women 150 years ago in their long dresses, or the men in wool uniforms, and how very uncomfortable they had to have been. Even the people in the 1920's and 1930's had only fans to keep the hot air circulating in the stuffy houses in town. G & H was comfortable, and she enjoyed her job. Nothing else unusual had happened. She had not even seen Nellie for over a week. If anything, both Jim Glass and Coy Howe seemed to be avoiding her. Lots of secrets there.

And had anyone seen or heard from Ned Ruter, the original catalyst behind all these mysterious happenings? Perhaps he was on a summer cruise on a lovely liner in the Mediterranean! Or was he, maybe, visiting Australia? Or London? That man got around. He should come home and help!

One day Lacey drove down to the crossroads of Ferrum to eat at the Paradise Sports Grille by the railroad tracks. She had seen an ad for it on FaceBook. She had brought along two books and a map to study about moonshining in Franklin County.

Seated across the room from her were a blonde with light blue eyes and sparkly eye shadow and blue nail polish, with rows of crystal necklaces and a petite dark-haired woman in black with a big camera. Neither sounded local. They were deep into conversation. Lacey ordered a salad and devilled eggs and read about the past.

The row of buildings had once been the site of the Ferrum Mercantile Company, the place in the 1920's and 1930's where literally tons of sugar and yeast had arrived weekly by train car. Ingredients for making liquor by local families struggling to make a living then.

She did not judge them, now that she understood more about the poverty, ever since the end of the Civil War. And the freed slaves, many who stayed on the land, had their own small farms but no money at all.

Until 1946 when it had been repealed, presumably after the Federal Government had lifted the economic sanctions on the South because the Southerners had been such a huge part of the successful winning of WWII and the country needed Southern industry, the "Pittsburgh Plus" act that had punished Southern industrialists since Restoration for shipping goods by rail, by charging them what it cost to ship from A to B, plus what it cost to ship from A to Pittsburgh, had kept the old iron and steel industries, and all the others, from flourishing.

And while there had been a few men or even groups of men who had controlled the making and distribution of the illegal liquor, and had sometimes orchestrated the removal of people who might talk too much to the wrong authorities...most of the moonshiners, transporters, and "law" had been ordinary folks. The few who had sent men off to the asylum at Marion, VA, or who had had people killed, were just a handful in the overall picture of that era.

An old book, "*An Old Virginia Court*," by Sherman Wingfield, as well as Mr. Greer's legal history on the 1935 trials of moonshiners, both quoted the vast, unimaginable amounts of sugar and other things purchased by the moonshiners in a four-year period leading up to the trials: 70,448 lbs. of Standard Brand yeast; 33,839,109 lbs. of sugar; 13,307,477 lbs. of corn meal; 2,408,308 lbs. of rye meal; 1,018,420 lbs. of malt; 30,366 lbs. of hops; 15,276,071 lbs. of grain products; 600,000 "non-gurgling five-gallon tin cans." During a trial, according to the Wingfield book, "One of the lawyers pleading with the jury for his client, said, 'Men, send him back where he came from: send him back to his mountain home.' The judge interrupted: 'You mean, send him back to keep making the same kind of mean whiskey he was making.'"

Mr. Wingfield wrote that a woman transporter, Willie May Carter Sharpe, on trial had said, "It was the excitement that got me...and most other rum-runners employed by the big shots. They were mostly kids who liked the thrill of it. There were women of aristocratic families who wanted to go along with me on a night run just for the kick of it." Lacey suddenly wondered if young Jack had hitched a ride with a transporter, like Willie May, and had gone far away.

One of the men on trial admitted under questioning, as reported in Mr. Greer's book, that "...they sold three or four carloads a week of sugar...four hundred bags in a car...and maybe meal, they would sell a carload in two weeks."

She sat in the restaurant, with its tropical décor of palm trees and umbrellas and beach balls, ate her delicious salad, and thought of what all had happened right in this row of buildings when the Ferrum Mercantile Company had been selling goods for illegal liquor to be produced. What might happen if the owner of this place, Robb Hart, who had introduced himself to her when she entered, had an old key to the building? Would she dare ask him? Would she see Clive McCain picking up bags of sugar? Would she see one of the Mills boys from Coal Street talking to people about distribution? Would Deputy Mills be hanging around? Edgar Beckett?

She had looked through the current phone books for the area and had checked off the surnames of the families of the people who had been put on trial and indicted or let go. They were: Rakes, Ferguson, Abshire, Nolen, Beckett,

236

Priliman, Shively, Shiveley, Cooper, Cundiff, DeHart, Wimmer, Easter, Fralin, Guilliams, Griffith, Greer, Hodges, Hatcher, Jones, Lee, Maxey, Martin, Nicholson, Smith, Turner, Wray, Bondurant, Dixon, Richards, Daniels, Davis, Foster, Mason, Radford, Webb, Sigmon, Burnett, and others. Their families were here now, many of them. She could add Mills, McCain, and Grierson!

Intrigued by the little she had seen in the 1925 and 1933 encounters with moonshiners and transporters, Lacey had recently started to ask if some people would talk to her about the past. The slim and dapper local journalist, Stephen Morrison, had given her a tip on where to ask and she had. Most said they knew nothing about it. Or they admitted they had been told fibs and fables, so they would not know the actual truth, and thus, could not be harmed if anyone learned of it. They had been told untruths to protect them and to uphold the Code of Silence. Some denied it all.

One who responded to her request was a very elderly man who wanted to meet Lacey at a fast-food restaurant. So she had gone there for breakfast and met him. She asked him if he had known things about the moonshine era that had not been made public. He took her to a corner table and had told her a very interesting tale.

He said that when he was a young child, up the road, he and his brothers had been sent to bed and told to stay absolutely quiet because someone was coming to talk to their dad that night. So, naturally, he stayed awake and strained to hear every word. And he had heard them talking about an ambush that would take place the next night in which Deputy Jeff Richards would be traveling, with a black prisoner, Jim Smith, from Callaway to Rocky Mount. The man said that Richards had asked Carter Lee if he could not wait til the next day to bring Smith in, and Lee had insisted it be that following night. Years later as an adult, the old man told Lacey, he learned what had happened. And he never said a thing.

The next night, the night in question, Deputy Edgar Beckett, who was usually with Jeff Richards so much that they were known as "Mutt and Jeff," said he felt ill, and begged off riding with Richards when Jeff went to get Jim Smith to bring him to Rocky Mount to jail, on Lee's orders.

Richards had to be eliminated, as Richards had bragged that he was going to tell all to the Feds and at the Trial. Richards and Smith were ambushed and shot to death near the Church of the Brethren. Beckett had known ahead of time and had not been along on the ride. The old man said he had never before, ever, told this story of what he had heard except to Mr. Keister Greer, whom he trusted. And Mr. Greer had made notes and said he would not reveal this story in his legal history, because even though it was true, according to the man who had recounted his childhood story to him, it was still hearsay. And his moonshine history was going to be only documented facts.

The other person to get in touch was Mrs. Greer herself. She recounted a car trip she and her late husband had made to get a story after her husband had asked around. They drove out into the woods of Back Creek and went into an elderly man's cabin, which was really just a shack. The man was very old and very nervous, as if someone might still find out about what he knew and eliminate him. This man had told Mr. Greer and his wife, during that clandestine visit on Back Creek in Roanoke County, that back before the Grand Jury Trial in Harrisonburg in 1935, he had seen a car's headlights coming right towards his cabin.

There was no road coming towards the creek, so the car clearly had run off the road, as if the car were out of control. He saw it crash into the creek, near his cabin and had gone out to look before the police arrived. He said there was a dead man in the car who had been killed by a gunshot, not by the crash. He hid. And when he heard about it later, in the news, it was ruled an accident, death by crashing into the creek. Totally hushed up. It had been a murder. But the police who came to get the car and the body were clearly on the payroll of the men in charge, and covered up the crime. Forever.

There had been some very powerful men in charge of running the moonshining back then. No one messed with them and lived. And, again, Mr. Greer had said that, while fascinating and doubtless true since it had been seen by an eye-witness who had seen the bullet hole in the windshield and the bullet in the dead man, and he'd no reason to fabricate such a story, that he could not use it in his legal history because it was also hearsay.

So those two actual events, the child overhearing the plot to kill Richards, and the eye witness to a murder of a man involved in the racket, never were told. Until now. Now she knew.

Lacey suspected the Code of Silence was still operating. Maybe she was here to help end it. What good did it do her to learn more facts about that era if she could not learn the fates of the McCains, Griersons, and Mills? Maybe if she could gain access one more time to the 1930's in her own house, she could discover things not in either of these two authoritative books!

Walking outside after lunch, Lacey saw two families pull up in cars full of children. A sprightly little girl in a batik skirt and top and sparkly shoes and flyaway blond hair, like a pixie, danced around the car while her quiet, smiling brother waited for their mother to get out. Lacey had not seen any of them before. The family in the other car seemed to be two women and four boys. All the boys were dressed for soccer.

"HI!" called the woman with the girl and boy.

"Hi!" Lacey called back, pleased to be spoken to. She walked closer.

"We eat here after soccer practice," she explained. She had multiple earrings and necklaces on, all glittering with stones. Her hands were covered in rings. "I make jewelry. I am Ellie Sorensen," the woman laughed, holding up her hands. "I do not usually wear them all to soccer practice! I forgot to take them off! My kids, Lewis and Calla." She had a bright laugh and her eyes were blue, twinkly and crescent-shaped. The other women came over with their boys; one mom was a redhead and everyone was very friendly.

"Good to see someone new," the redhead said. "I am Linnie Weeks-Shaw, and this is Kate Weeks-Shaw," she smiled. Kate and Linnie shook hands with Lacey and smiled. "And our four boys." The four attractive and polite boys shook her hand.

"I am Lacey Brew, new to town, a realtor at Glass & Howe. I am trying to become familiar with every piece of history! Today I am doing old Ferrum."

"Ah, wonderful. Be sure to check out the college and all of its programs and the Blue Ridge Institute!" Linnie said, herding the children into Paradise Sports Grille. "Live here?"

"No, I have a bungalow on Cottage Hill Drive in town," Lacey replied.

It was a good day to check out the Blue Ridge Institute, so she went over and spent a few hours looking at the current exhibits of old canning labels. There was one for Algoma Orchards! She had seen a real jar with a real label in the McCain kitchen! Lacey leaned over to study the label. How many, many answers to her questions probably lay right here in this building!

On a wall was a framed newspaper article from 1933 about young runaway Jack McCain! Lacey read it. He had never been found and was presumed dead. Some people had thought he had run off with a circus! Oh, how Lacey wanted to solve that mystery. But she would have to use the old key. And with each use, she was becoming fearful that she might "stick" in another Time and not be able to return. What would that mean for her? She was just a visitor, herself, into their era. She was not a ghost; they were not ghosts. But was she, in some way, a *returned soul*...on a quest?

Learning that the Blue Ridge Institute had archives, she asked permission to come back sometime and look through old articles and photos. In one room there was a real copper still set up. Lacey walked around it, studying its complexity. A lot of work had gone into making corn liquor. Had it been worth it?

On her drive home she passed a little cement structure she'd not noticed on her way to Ferrum. It was packed with cars. Bowling's Hot Dogs. She pulled up and looked in. It was not too early for a small, early supper, she convinced herself. She got a stool at the counter and ordered what everyone else was eating: pinto beans, a very pink hot dog, a wedge of cheese, and a small bottled coke. A little dish of chopped onions was placed on the side. Mostly blue-collar workers in here, she saw. Men of all ages. No women at all except for the busy waitresses. So, this must be "Southern food," she thought, enjoying her pinto beans. She had never even heard of pinto beans before today. They were good!

What might this building have been in the 1920's and 1930's? Perhaps a place where liquor was dropped off to be picked up secretly by transporters in fast, low-slung cars loaded with whiskey to head up to Woolwine and Endicott by the Parkway, to the west? Or just an old building?

Chapter Ten

"Faith is the substance of things hoped for, the evidence of things not seen."

Hebrews 11:1

"It has been so long since we were invited to a real dinner party," Teri Prater exclaimed, giving Lacey a quick hug as she introduced her to her husband Don.

"I like having people over, even if I am new here," Lacey replied with a smile. She showed them where she had beverages put out in the dining room. Virginia wines from Albemarle County, Château Morrisette, and Brooks Mill Winery in Franklin

County, Virginia "Virginia Lightning" made by Belmont Farm in Culpeper, some dessert wines, some lagers made in Lexington and Roanoke, and several kinds of bottled water and soft drinks. Her glasses were some she had inherited from her parents, and she was happy to be able to use them tonight.

"Lacey! I am Here!" called Bianca Rose from the porch where she was holding the door for Lee Anne Travis who had a basket of desserts to carry in. Behind them were Lelia Park and her husband, Judge Park, who stood almost seven feet tall! He ducked to enter and gave her a big and friendly handshake. "Great to meet you! My mother is from Estes Park!" They chatted for a minute about Colorado and then the Parks went on into the living room and greeted Mary See, an old friend.

"Lee Anne, meet Bianca Rose, and please just go around the room as people arrive and introduce yourselves, although I imagine you all know each other," Lacey said happily, as her brand-new friends came up the steps. She had expanded her guest list to include Jim Glass, Coy Howe, Kim Hull, and Mary See. To her surprise, they all came, even Mary See, who had called and explained her plans had changed and she could come, after all. Kitty Glass could not make it, being out of town with a grandchild. It was a big crowd for her little house.

There was some "Enya" playing in the background and candles around the room. Her art collection was on the walls in every room, and she was tickled to see Jim Glass walking around with a glass of wine and staring warily and carefully at each one. Coy Howe had made himself comfortable on the couch next to Teri Prater and her husband and they were chatting about rural development in the county.

Lacey had asked Lee Anne Travis to bring some desserts that would be in her *"Family Memoir Cookbook,"* so they could be sampled tonight. A Kansas native with lots of good recipes from her family back there and other places she had lived, Lee Anne had brought a cobbler, a pie, a cake, and brownies. Kim and Lee Anne were talking together. Jess was wandering around looking at her books and paintings.

When Lacey went into the kitchen for a minute to check on the foods in the oven, she saw an older man in there, someone she did not know. He was standing with his back to the room, looking at one of her Virginia oil paintings by Karen Sewell of a copper still by a creek and a boy playing in the sparkling water.

"Ah, hello," Lacey said. "And, excuse me, but are you with one of the other guests? I am not sure we have met."

"Good evening," he replied politely. "I came with your neighbor," he said vaguely, almost as if he were not certain.

"Well, please come on into the other room," she answered hospitably, while wondering if he had come with Jess, or perhaps with Bianca Rose?

"Very nice house you have here," the man said, looking intently at the modern appliances and floor.

Lacey asked him if he had ever visited this house before, but Mary See interrupted them before he could reply and the older man slipped past them into the dining room. Callie had come out of Lacey's bedroom and was purring at the man's feet and he was talking to her softly.

Mary See said, "Such a nice group of people, mostly new to me, dear, except for Jess, the Parks, and our office! However did you manage? You have been here just over one month! Let me help. What needs to be done out here?"

"I am pleased, I must admit," Lacey laughed. "There is only one guest I am not sure of, that older man who just left and walked into the dining room. Not sure whom he came with."

"Oh, a mystery! Let me try to find out," said Mary See, taking a plate of shrimp with her as she hurried into the next room.

"Poor, poor man," Lacey laughed to herself. "He does not have a chance!" But when she glanced in, he was coming back to the kitchen and Mary See was talking to Teri and Don.

Across the hall by her country landscape by Penny Simmons, Coy Howe and Lelia Park were engaged in a conversation about a new minister at one of the old churches. They both were congregants.

Jim Glass had made his way past every painting visible and was standing alone, as if deep in thought. When he caught Lacey's eye he subtly gestured for her to join him by one of the paintings of an old house and orchard near Cahas Mountain, by Beth Garst, of the apple orchard Garsts.

"Lacey," he whispered, "has anyone emerged from one of your paintings since our," he coughed gently, "discussion of returned souls?"

"I have been so busy with work and exploring the region, frankly, Jim, that I would not know. But if someone had come through, the way you said Ned Ruter did, I guess that person would also be able to open a door and walk away from here."

"I just have a hunch. I get hunches. I do not like to get hunches!" he said.

Lacey smiled and patted his arm. "Look around. All these good people are as real as, well, as real as Mary See!"

She shepherded them all into the dining room to get plates and to start to circle the table beautifully covered with a cut-lace tablecloth and her Wedgwood "Hunting Scene" china. There were platters of baked chicken, boiled shrimp, sliced roast beef, salmon, sushi, a pasta salad, cole slaw, a vegetable lasagna, artisan breads, a green salad, cubes of cheese covered with a honey sauce and fresh raspberries, wedges and slices of Gouda and Havarti and Cheddar, bunches of grapes, a bowl of Bing cherries, and slices of prosciutto. Everyone, except the mystery man, helped themselves and found chairs in the living room, dining room, kitchen or front porch. Only the older man remained, standing at the table.

Lacey approached him. "Sir, may I ask you if you feel well? Are you all right?"

He looked at her, tears in his eyes, and smiled. "I have never been better, young lady. I am just disoriented this evening. I, um," he paused, "have been here before. Very long ago. But it all has changed so very much. It is so beautiful here now.

Happy. No sadness. No fear. No grief," he murmured. "No anger, no hiding anymore."

Lacey looked at him. She looked at her Callie clinging to his leg. Without warning, she suddenly said to him, "Watch out! Cleo is going to rip your trousers!" And he jumped and paled. "Cleo! Cleo?" he cried, picking up the calico cat.

"I know who you are," she whispered kindly. "Do not be afraid. Jack McCain, no one knows. But I know."

"How could you? I have been trying to get 'home' for over 80 years, my dear."

"And you just found yourself here, didn't you? You came through the painting, from the creek bed, on a sunny day in 1933." She took his arm and hugged it, overcome by the realization that runaway Jack McCain was standing in her kitchen! A *returned soul*.

"I do not know how you could know," he said. "I ran away when I was 13. I ran into the hills near Woolwine, a long way by foot back then. And I hid out there near some still that had been abandoned. The men who used to run it all were arrested by Colonel Bailey in 1934, when he came to look for moonshiners."

"I have read about it," Lacey said quietly.

"They did not betray me. I stayed a year or so, living off the land and in an abandoned hut. They did not know who I was, anyhow. They had not known my Pa. And I must have died in the winter, of 1935. I fell asleep. It snowed. That is the last I remember. I guess I froze out there. I was too proud to come home...."

"And your life was cut short," Lacey said, almost to herself. "And you have been trying to get home ever since. And you are here! But you are older and your family is gone. I am so sorry."

Jack McCain looked right into Lacey's eyes and said, "I have no idea what is happening. I have been wandering, in places I had never been, and all of a sudden out by a creek in Floyd County, where there were ruins of an old copper still, I found myself taking a step. I thought I was crossing the creek. It is a creek up there that is a special creek. Water flows from it to the west and to the east, a kind of dividing creek, by the Two Rivers Church. And then I was stepping into this kitchen! The creek was gone! But when I looked up, there on the wall, was an exact picture of where I had just stood. And here I am!"

"I do not understand this, either, Mr. McCain, but I think I have been brought to Rocky Mount to help people like you.

251

Another man, who died in 1969, recently appeared here, through a painting. He said you all are called *returned souls*. You are here because your life was cut short before its time or because when you died, you did not have faith enough or belief in God, that might have taken you straight on, to the next stage, or the light, or God. So you are here. And you can stay or you can try to believe in God and pass on. You are only the second one I know of...oh, I am wrong! I met a family a few weeks ago who were back, looking for housing! Do you need a place to live? I can help. I can show you places you can live and no one from our current time will know about you. But you can meet people like you. It is a lot to take in."

"Do you suppose, is it possible, that my family might be here, too? *Returned souls*, like me?" He looked so eager that Lacey did not know what to say. She needed to get Jim Glass and Jack McCain together. Could she do that tonight? How about on the back porch?

"I will be right back!" Lacey said, hurrying into the living room to find Jim Glass.

"Come with me a minute, Jim," she called, as if to ask him to open a bottle of wine or something. Everyone looked comfortable eating and talking. Lacey took

Jim Glass's arm and brought him back to the kitchen and closed the door.

"Jim Glass, I would like to introduce you to someone…someone like Ned Ruter," she said quietly, watching his face to see if he understood.

"Really?" Jim looked around eagerly. He saw the older man standing by the door to the laundry room, with a calico cat in his arms. The cat was purring and licking his hand.

"Please do not raise your voices," she warned both men. "We cannot cope if the other guests flood in here!"

"Jack, meet Jim. Jim, meet Jack." She let the men shake hands, warily.

"Jim, this is young runaway Jack McCain who has miraculously come 'home' to his childhood kitchen. He is a *returned soul*. We must help him."

The look on Jim Glass's face was one of shock and joy.

"I have read all my life about your disappearance! Your mother and sister and her husband never stopped searching for you! Your father went to jail and your mother died around WWII, alas. I have read so many articles about it!"

"Well," Lacey interrupted, "we have not discussed this yet, Jim, but I have had access to 1933 right here in this house, because of one of the old keys on the key ring you all left for me on the porch beneath the cushions."

Both of the men, one in his sixties and one in his mid-nineties, just stared at her in shock. The cat looked right into her eyes.

"The key had let me 'see' and 'hear' part of some days in 1933: I saw Cleo, Mr. and Mrs. McCain, Ann, Bobby Grierson, you run out the door, and, later, on another visit, your little sister Prilly. And your cat, Cleo twice. I call her Callie. Let me just say that you were very much loved and missed. And, chances are, with the grief your mother felt after you ran away, she may have lost her faith in God, if she had had any. And for all we know, your mother may also be a *returned soul* trying to get 'home.'"

With that, Lacey went back into the party, letting the two men chat on the back porch, each with a plate heaped with food.

It was very hard for Lacey to focus on the conversations and compliments on her party while her mind and heart were so full of the McCain miracle. But she made a special point to get the guests to tell Lee Anne about the desserts and how they would make them in Virginia, so their maker could hear how they liked everything. Her family recipes for the cakes and pies were just different enough from the Southern ones, that a lively discussion took place. Lacey was delighted. The cookbook, which would contain family recipes from Kansas, Louisiana, Virginia, Ohio, Utah, North Carolina, and other places Lee Anne had lived, would be a great project for the community and Lee Anne just needed a boost to get her to sit down and write it.

Judge Dave, as he liked to be called, had a passion for history, it turned out, and was a huge fan, being from California himself and not Virginia, of President Lincoln. Lacey asked if he had seen the portraits by Suzanne Verde Paddock at the Library and he had not. She felt good, sharing information with people who lived here! He also was familiar with the house and the old McCain tragedy: arrest, death of wife, runaway son. He had been Mr. Greer's protégé years ago, and a very close friend of his. He missed visiting The Grove.

As the evening went on and people started to leave, a breeze came up that blew the curtains back and forth against the windows cracked open for the fresh air. The sharp noises of frogs and cicadas filled the night outside. Lacey was pleased to see that Bianca Rose and Teri Prater seemed to have had a good time together. And Teri's husband and Jess had been discussing plants and gardening, and Jess was handing Don a plant! He must have brought some along.

Teri and Bianca Rose both had lots of dangling jewelry on, and both women had a flair for mixing and matching eclectic fashions. Mary See might have been flirting with Coy Howe...Lacey was not positive, but both had their heads together and were chuckling. Kim had gravitated towards Jess. They were about the same age, after all.

Jim Glass came back into the party alone and when Lacey raised her eyebrows, he simply said, "I told our visitor I would look around for some old keys. I think one of us will be showing houses, from the back door, tomorrow," he said gleefully. "It works! It works!" Then he put his finger on his lips. Whispering, he said, "It was that Sewell oil in the kitchen!" He looked warily at other paintings nearby.

Lacey tidied up the plates and platters after the last guest had left. She was filled with peace. And with joy. Whatever was happening, however odd, however unique, she seemed to be pivotal to the events. Just imagine Jack McCain arriving in his childhood home tonight. How beautiful.

When she curled up in her bed, she pulled a Bible off the table nearby and opened to Hebrews 11. "Through faith we understand that the worlds were framed by the word of God, so that things which are seen were not made of things which do appear."

Lacey turned off the light. Like a star in the dark sky far above her home, a light was starting to twinkle in her soul. A light of belief. A new understanding of Christianity. It felt brilliant, comforting, colossal. What had happened in her kitchen tonight was a turning-point in Lacey's life. She was moving from despair and confusion and loss towards joy.

Chapter Eleven

"But as it is written, Eye hath not seen, nor ear heard, neither have entered into the heart of man, the things which God hath prepared for them that love him."

I Corinthians 1: 9

The weeks after the party were filled with all kinds of new experiences for Lacey. She was invited over to her new friends' homes. She met Teri and Lee Anne and Bianca Rose at Coal Car Café regularly, to talk about music and books and food. Mary See took her to several churches, and the wonderful meals and fellowship times afterwards, and Lacey found herself gravitating to the Episcopal church out by Phoebe Needles in Callaway. She took her own copy of *The Book of Common Prayer* along and even joined in a drumming circle out there once a week. At a business lunch in town, she met a lively alumna of Salem College in North Carolina who was willing to talk to her about Anna Jackson, and also about some marketing ideas for the realty firm. Her life was filling up with good things.

Jim Glass had her showing all new houses, after he learned about how keys took her into earlier time periods. And she wondered if he, himself, might be showing the old houses so he could try to get into an earlier time! But he would not answer her when she asked!

Quite a few *returned souls* came to her room at the back of G & H, to look for suitable housing, and she found most of them nice places on or near Coal Street, one of the streets with the most empty homes. They were empty partly because even in the current time, people had moved away because of foreclosure or had been arrested for drugs. It was not considered a "nice" neighborhood, so it was more empty than not. But that was perfect for housing for *returned souls*, who were invisible to the modern world, but comfortable in decent houses in a tree-lined neighborhood.

There was to be an Open House on Coal Street, for one of the homes that had been put up for auction by a Trust. G & H had asked Lacey to manage it, using Paragon Estate Sales owned by Flip Paragon. She had met once with Flip and had given him a key to the house, an L-shaped Italianate brick house on a corner. But before she had given him a key she had gone over on her own, on a late afternoon, to make sure the key she gave Flip would be for *now*.

Trying the front door, having it stick for a second, and then swing open into a dark hallway, Lacey stepped into a musty hall and shut the heavy door behind her. The walls were covered with flocked wallpaper. Harpsichord music was coming from a parlor nearby. And there was the aroma of tea. Lacey did not know what Time she had stepped into, but was actually happy to be going back into another era. She had missed it!

She walked down the hardwood floor covered with a faded needlepoint, floral runner. There was a streaked mirror on the wall to her right. And when Lacey passed by it and glanced over, she almost fainted!

She backed up and looked again. This was the first time she had seen herself in a mirror in an earlier time, and she had to assume this was an earlier time, because Coy Howe had told her this house had been updated with painted walls. Where and when was she? Or was it someone else?

In the mirror, looking right back at her, was a face she did not recognize! The face was heart-shaped. The woman's eyes were blue, like her own. The hair was brown and in ringlets. Where had she seen that face before? Where?

Leaving the intriguing face behind, Lacey found the parlor and saw another, older, lady playing the harpsichord. On the beautiful piece of furniture sat a gold box with a tasseled key in its lock. Her key? It looked the same. When the musician turned her face towards the door, Lacey saw that she looked like the woman in the mirror, but much older. Mother and daughter, perhaps?

"Penelope Rose? Is the tea ready, dear? I have finished playing for today." The lady rose and crossed the room and sat on a silk loveseat. A minute later the younger woman came in with a silver tea tray and set it on the oval table by the loveseat.

"Here, Mama," she said, pouring her mother a cup from the silver pot into a fine bone china cup.

"Is there news today? Has the stage come in with the news?" The mother sipped her tea and held the saucer and cup and closed her eyes.

"I have heard that our General Lee has taken a position at Washington College in Lexington, to be the President. And he wants us all to move on. And our General Early is going to live in Lynchburg, and he is writing about 'The Lost Cause.' We are being called 'Military District Number One,' and Federal troops will be staying in Virginia for some time to come. As if we all were criminals," cried the daughter.

"You know, dear, that your father thinks we should move. We cannot take everything with us. But he would like us to leave Virginia and start fresh, out West, in St. Louis."

"St. Louis! But that is ever so far away," said the daughter, standing and walking to the window. "Do we have to, Mama?"

"I think it might be best, dear. Your uncle is out there and we could stay with him until we got settled. Select a few pieces you want to take. I will do the same. Alas, I cannot take the harpsichord. But I will take

our silver, since the Union troops never found it in our well! You heard, didn't you, that they did not find the Hale silver, either? Margaret had hidden theirs in their well, also, right between the main house and the plantation kitchen. But the jewelry seems to have been taken."

"I will comply, of course, with your and Papa's wishes about our moving. Alas, so very many fine young men from here died in the War. The one I had put my heart on is gone. And another I also liked so very much died in prison at Camp Douglas near Chicago. I will never find another like them, here. Oh, Mama," she cried, leaving the room in tears.

"Poor little Penelope Rose," the mother whispered. "My poor little ivory rose."

As Lacey listened, she started to wonder if the young woman, who must have been looking into the hall mirror just as she had, might look an awful lot like Bianca Rose? Could it be that these were her Virginia ancestors, who had gone to Missouri after the War? Oh, my!

Lacey did not stay another minute, but let herself out, put the 1860's key in her pocket, and made sure the current key would be the one Flip would use to set up the estate sale later today.

When she and Flip met at the house after dinner, she used the *now* key and stepped into a fresh, painted hallway. No runner on the floor. The mirror was still on the wall. There were couches and chairs, the harpsichord, a dining room table, lamps, books, china. The loveseat was missing.

"Oh, Lawdy! Bless my heart!" Flip almost danced through the downstairs, pad and pen in hand, looking at the treasures. "This house has only been lived in a few years on and off for the last 150 years since the family left in 1865? Are you kidding me? Who has kept it in such perfect shape? A relative who stayed here? I have rarely seen anything so perfect. Just look at these pieces! They will bring a fortune. Did Mr. Howe know exactly who will get the money?"

"I think it is going into a fund, until the heir is located," Lacey replied, wondering again if Bianca Rose had any ties at all to this house. She would have to ask!

Flip went back out to van. He had locked himself out of it! Lacey called the local locksmith and the nice man said he would be right over. And he was there within a few minutes. After he got Flip's car open, he took some keys from Lacey that she wanted copies of. Each had a label on it: The Grove 64, McGhee 64, Mills 25, Callaway 64. She did not give him the 1933 key to her own home. It was at home in a box, safe. The locksmith made no comments at all about the odd labels, and said he would return the old and new keys tomorrow. Both Flip and Lacey were impressed that the locksmith would work at night.

Lacey stayed to watch as Flip and his helper made lists and decided where to put the smaller items, for display, and for sale for the Paragon Estate Sale on Sunday. She stood at the harpsichord and ran her fingers over the keys, sadly. She sat on the silk loveseat and thought of the family who had had to leave such beautiful treasures behind so they could afford to travel to Missouri after the War, to start over, and for their beautiful daughter Penelope Rose to have a future.

"Mercy!" Flip cried, running in from the dining room. "I have never! This is a museum!" And he dashed off, carrying a lamp under one arm and a box...

"Flip, stop! Please," Lacey called after him. "Please, let me buy that box right now. Please? It would mean so much to me!"

Flip handed her the box. Key missing. "You may have it, dear," he said, rushing on. "It is missing its key. And no one can open this kind of secret box without its key, so no one will want it. Bless your heart."

Lacey hurried home. She threw open her door and ran to her bedroom, where the key with its red tassel was buried under some nightclothes in a drawer.

She sat down at her desk and took a deep breath. If the key opened this...

It did. It slid in and the locks tumbled and the top lifted up. Lacey was afraid to look. She closed her eyes. How had that family left such a lovely box behind? Maybe it had been by accident.

Opening the top with her eyes open, Lacey saw that the box was filled with papers, folded and tied with a pink ribbon. She untied the ribbon. She unfolded the top papers. It was a letter.

Dear Samuel,   *April 14, 1864*

I have written you so many letters these past years, while you were away with your Uncle Jubal in all of the Battles. But I never mailed any, and now I know that was the right thing to do, after I learned of your marriage.

I did not want to admit to myself that you had found another to be your true love. Elizabeth McElmore Hairston is lovely and I wish you both much happiness. I read about your engagement. And, honestly, dear one, I could not bring myself to attend your wedding, so I pretended to be ill. My heart was yours for a time, and your heart is now hers. I wish both of you nothing but happiness and long lives.

Yours Forever in Friendship, and in Christ,

Penelope Rose Ferguson of Rose Hall

Lacey was stunned. This lovely young woman had been in love with Sam Hale. He married someone else and died a month later in battle, after this letter had been written. She had never mailed it. And here she was, Lacey Brew, a no one, holding a love letter that had never reached Sam, her beloved. And Penelope Rose had moved to Missouri. Had she found a new love, a new life out there?

There were more letters in the box. Lacey skimmed them. They were all older than the one on top. All were love letters from Penelope Rose to Sam, written in 1862, 1863, and 1864. Never mailed, Never seen. She put them back into the box and lay the key inside on top, and closed the lid.

When she had recovered enough from an emotional day, Lacey walked outside under the tossing trees in the night wind. She walked right across the empty field where once a little shop had sold apple sauce and baking soda and Grapette in the last century. She walked up to the house on Autumn Street. She knocked on the door and Bianca Rose answered right away.

"I am sorry to come over so late without calling first," Lacey began, but Bianca Rose hushed her, and pulled her into the room. There were candles burning and violin music on in the background.

"What is It?" Bianca Rose asked, anxiously.

"I have to ask, forgive me," Lacey began, "If you are searching for a box of letters. Is that the treasure?"

"How Could you Know," Bianca Rose cried, putting her hand over her mouth. But her eyes were sparkling and happy, not angry. "However Could you Know?"

"I am helping Flip Paragon and Paragon Estates get a house on Coal Street ready for an estate sale," she said. "It is by far the prettiest house there. But it has sat empty for a long time. Coy Howe, of my real estate firm, is handling everything. There apparently is some kind of Trust that was set up after WWII, for the upkeep of the house. It is called Rose Hall, by the way," she added, smiling, watching Bianca Rose's expression change from curious to joy.

"Without giving too many secrets away," Lacey continued, "I believe the family, the Ferguson family, father, mother, and daughter, moved in 1865 from that house to St. Louis. They left behind many of their pieces, like a harpsichord, a loveseat, a dining room table and chairs, a buffet, books, things like that. They probably took with them smaller things, like their silver flat-wear, their china, some books, linens, clothes, pictures. But they left behind a beautiful wooden box. And the key to that box was on a key-ring for the house I bought. I have no idea how it got there, but I had put it safely in a drawer, hoping someday to figure out what it was. Well, today, I did."

"Oh! I do not Know What to Say," Bianca Rose cried, taking both of Lacey's hands in her own. "Yes. Yes, That is my Family. Let me get the Chart!" Bianca Rose dashed from the room and returned with a piece of paper with a family tree on it. I did all this on ancestry.com," she said proudly.

"Look," she said. "Here is the Penelope Rose Ferguson you are talking about, here: 1845-1890. She married Henry Stevens. Their daughter, Helen, 1869-1936, married George Harriman. Their son John Harriman, 1886-1970, married Else Siderits from Vienna. Their son Andrew Harriman, 1918-2003. My father, Quinn Ferguson Harriman, 1950-2013. Then, here I am, 1984-. Bianca Rose Ferguson Harriman.

"Young Rose was my Third Great-grandmother. She was born Here in 1845. They left when She was 20. She married in St. Louis and had my Second Great grandmother, Helen, in 1869. Helen died in 1936. See? It is All right Here? I did not know Where to start. I had the Names and the Town, but no Address. And I had the name Rose Hall, but no One here knows about Rose Hall. No one!"

"No one was left to remember. Well, they will now," Lacey smiled, giving her neighbor a hug. "You may well be the only heir to the estate. And you and I need to go over there first thing tomorrow to see it all."

"If it is Mine," Bianca Rose hesitated, "do I have to Sell it? Do I have to have an Estate Sale?"

"Heavens! I have no idea," cried Lacey, reaching for her cell phone. "Let me call Coy Howe."

"Mr. Howe? I am sorry to bother you at home," Lacey said. "But I have something of a miraculous surprise here for us all at G & H. I have located an heir to the Rose Hall estate. Yes! Bianca Rose Harriman from St. Louis! Oh, could you? Thank you so much!"

"He is calling the firm's attorney right now and then will call Flip Paragon to halt the work over there before he gets too much done at the house for the sale this Sunday."

"I am in Shock," Bianca Rose said, crying. "I have never Been So Happy!"

"Come by my house in the morning. We will make copies at the office of your family tree and you will probably have to meet our lawyer and maybe make a few calls. I really do not know! If there had been a Will somewhere along the way, leaving the house to you, that should help."

"Oh, please, let there be a Will somewhere!" Bianca Rose said happily.

Lacey walked home, across the empty lot, stopping briefly to imagine life in the former shop 80 years ago. She was eager to get the copies of the keys from the locksmith. She never wanted to lose her special keys.

If her neighbor were able to inherit Rose Hall, and perhaps even live in there, would Lacey ever reveal to her that she had seen her ancestors in their parlor on the day they decided to move to St. Louis?

How much of this "insider" know-ledge that she had seen and heard could she ever share with anyone? All of a sudden,

Lacey felt alone and isolated. Her being able to visit other Times was a blessing and a curse. She knew too much. And everyone she had seen or heard, from the McCain family her first night in town, to the Fergusons in their parlor at Rose Hall today, had gone on to live out their lives. She needed to stop worrying about all of them. She needed to stop wanting to know more. And, most of all, she needed a friend she could talk about it all with.

Chapter Twelve

"Thou shalt not be afraid of the terror by night; nor for the arrow that flieth by day."

Psalm 91:5

Lacey picked up the copied keys and the originals and put them safely away. Now that she was not showing The Grove, she missed seeing Wild Bill! Every now and then she drove through the grounds looking for him. But he was not there. Then she would drive up to Fort Hill hoping to find him there, and he was not there, either. Had he left town? Whom could she ask?

Lacey got Jack McCain to come with her one day and stood with him on the front porch of her home, of his home. She explained that she was going to unlock the door with the 1933 key. Was he up to being in there with her? Would the family "see" him? Would Jack be able to see them?

She unlocked the door and stepped into the dim living room, with its pale walls and old light fixtures. There was a scent of peach pie. Cleo bounded over and jumped into Jack's arms! And when Lacey turned to see that, she saw that Jack was 13 again! And radiant with a smile so bright it filled the room.

"I do not want to leave," Jack said. "How can I stay?"

Lacey looked around but did not see Mrs. McCain or Ann or Prilly.

"I don't know!" Lacey cried. "What if I leave and lock up and you stand there, all right? And if you are able to stay, then stay and lead a good life of good things, sweet Jack," she said, hugging the boy. "And if it does not work, you may find yourself back out on the porch *now* with me, and with Callie. By the way, Jack, Callie was here long before you McCains had her at your home! I saw her in 1864. She was called Celine by the Hale family at The Grove. And after the Civil War, she was Celia, for the McGhee family in the house behind ours, over there, where Bianca Rose is now. I figure that our dear cat is about at the end of her nine lives."

Mrs. McCain and Prilly came into the room from outside. They set peaches on a table. They did not seem to see Jack, who was standing in the center of the room! He coughed. They did not turn to look. They could not see him…just as they could not see her.

Jack came closer to Lacey and threw his arms around her and sobbed. "They cannot tell I am here!" She held him. "We had better go," she said. "I have an idea."

When she and Jack were back outside, *now,* he was once again a man of 94. He was crying. "I saw my mama and my little sister," he sobbed. "They could not see me!"

"That is their time. That is 1933," Lacey replied, giving him a hug. "Their lives went on. I do not know when they died. But I know how to find out. Dr. Peters knows the history. He knew Ann and Bobby Grierson when they were old. Let's try to find out when your mother died. Maybe we could find her, if she did not go on…if she is another *returned soul.*"

"Mama was not much into religion," Jack said. "Pa made liquor and she was always worried. She used to talk to us about

273

it, even though he had told her not to. He said the men in charge of granny fees, that means the money moonshiners had to pay for protection from the law, meaning the sheriffs and deputies," he explained, "and getting the sugar and meal from the train every week, would harm anyone who talked. The Government was sending someone down to look around, hearing that this county had so many people making moonshine. But that is right when I ran away. I do not know what happened."

"I am just really starting to know all the history, as fast as I can," Lacey responded. "I have some books that detail the entire era. Who came, who talked, who got killed, who went to trial, who got indicted, who got off."

They were on the new porch now and they went back inside, to the present home, with its modern appliances. Lacey found the books by Wingfield and Greer and had Jack McCain sit in a comfortable chair in the living room so he could read about life in the 1930's after he ran away.

"I have an idea!" she cried. "I will paint a picture of this house, as it looked when you lived here. I have been in it enough times to remember the details of the porch and door. And I will hang the painting in here! Maybe your family will emerge, just as you did? We can try!"

Lacey disappeared into her study and rummaged through boxes in her closet in there, returning with oil paints and a canvas. "I have not had time since I got here," she explained, "to paint."

Going out into the front yard with a small table and folding chair, she sketched the house, with the older details. Then she started to paint. In a few hours she had a decent painting of the house. It showed the entire house, porch, and calico cat. She had put a pie on a window sill. The rag rug she had seen in the kitchen in 1933 was on the porch, a multi-colored braided rug. When it was done, Lacey brought it inside to show Jack, and then propped it up against a window in the kitchen, to dry.

Leaving Jack to read, Lacey took a drive, to try to sort things out. She drove up to Fort Hill and sat on a bench while a wind tossed the trees and clouds scudded across the blue summer sky.

She felt as if things were coming to a close. She had been busy again at the office, especially with *returned souls* looking for houses. Jim Glass and Coy Howe had helped, now that they understood the enormity of the situation of G & H being a kind of portal for people living on, invisible to the world. Coy Howe had been seeing Mary See quite a lot, for business lunches, and apparently he had shared with her his passion for finding the Beale Treasure, because they went together sometimes, shovels in the car, to the forest behind Fort Hill.

But today, with Coy Howe and Mary See at work, Lacey thought she had the hilltop to herself, until she heard singing, and saw Wild Bill emerge from the ruins themselves! He seemed younger.

"Oh, you startled me," Lacey cried. "I thought I was here alone."

"Hi! I come up here a lot," Wild Bill admitted.

"Are you looking for treasure?" she kidded him, laughing.

""Not treasure so much, actually," he said. "But arrowheads."

"You think there might still be some around after all this time and all the visitors?" Lacey asked.

"Just one. I just want one." He came over and sat next to her on the bench. "I like you, Ms. Brew. I think you are a good person. I have seen you around town, showing houses, greeting folks at the coffee shop. You have a kind and loving spirit. I like that. And everything here is new to you."

"Well, thanks," she said, blushing. "I am happy here. I did not know if I would be, but there is so much more to life here than I expected," she added. "I have had some amazing experiences already. I would love to share what all I have been through, but I do not know if I should." She sighed.

"You mean, like meeting Callie back when Callie was Celine, and Celia, and Cleo?"

Lacey jumped up from the bench. "How did you know about the cat?"

Wild Bill just smiled. "Maybe you are not the only one, who...."

"Who can be in different places at the same time?" Lacey finished his thought.

"Yes, and in more than one Time." Wild Bill replied softly, patting his chest by the pocket. "Different times in one place."

Lacey looked at him. He seemed sad. How could he know about the cat? *How could he?*

"I think I know," he began, "who you are. You are here to bring things together. You will literally 'lace' up the loose ends and bring closure to this community, this place so peaceful on the surface but so filled with loss. You can see me."

"Of course I can see you," Lacey said.

"Ah, but no one else ever has been able to. No one. Except Keister Greer, because he was so passionate about history. And one artist, in 1858."

Lacey was stunned into silence.

"Let me share something with you," Wild Bill continued. "I have been here," he swept his arm to include the hilltop and the surrounding area, "since this fort was new. I have been unable to move on. I have been unable to heal." Again, he put his hand on the pocket of his shirt, over his heart. "I was gone for awhile, searching for my way home. I found it."

Lacey was staring into his face. What did he mean? How could he have been here so long...centuries!

"Follow me," Wild Bill said, rising and offering her his hand, which she took. It was the first time they had touched and he felt like a real person! Just as when she had hugged Jack McCain and he had felt solid and real.

They walked over to the doorway of the restored fort and he began to talk. "When the Historical Society tried to restore these ruins, these 18th century stones, they did not get it quite right. But who was there to tell them?" He laughed. "The actual original doorway was on the other side, the side facing down the hillside, so Robert Hill could see approaching strangers. The restoration has the doorway up here," he pointed, "as if the Hills wanted to look up towards where the school is now." He laughed.

"How do you know?" Lacey asked timidly, afraid she already knew.

Just then a Red Tailed Hawk flew over, quite low, and dropped a feather at Wild Bill's feet. He stooped to pick it up. "I get a feather most times I come up here," he said reverently. "I think it is meant to be a sign of peace, of sorrow, of regret, of healing, perhaps of apology."

"For what?" Lacey asked, holding her breath.

"For that warrior having shot me in the chest with his arrow."

Lacey almost fell over. He held her up. They leaned on the warm stones. "You had better tell me everything, Wild Bill," Lacey whispered, holding the hawk feather.

"Well, it began when I was shot by an Indian and the arrow went into my heart. It really hurt but the shock of it all killed me as much as that arrow did. I fell down, right there," he pointed to the land just outside the back wall of the restored ruin. "There had been a doorway right there. My father, Robert Hill, ran over but it was too late. My mother fell to her knees and put my head on her lap and cried and patted my hair. I will never forget. Never. They must have buried me beneath a tree here. With the arrowhead in me."

"I read," Lacey said, "right over there on the marker, that your father was from Dublin, Ireland, and married your mother, Violet, in Pennsylvania. Your way of talking seems to be an unusual medley of accents and dialects. That must be why!"

"Aye," he laughed! "My Da was from Dublin and he talked with a brogue. Mama and he both were educated and could read and write real well. They educated us all best they could, given the turmoil of my childhood. I have picked up lots of lingo over Time, from the people I have been around."

"Sometimes your dialect sounds black, or 'country,' Irish, or stilted British," she laughed, the reality of his story almost choking her up.

"I can speak the King's English, complete with the 18th century words, if I have a mind to, my lady," he chortled.

"Tell me more!"

"Well, after I died, very young, I seemed to wander. I do not know where, exactly. This land was still a frontier. I think I was in a forest. No one could see me. I remember that. I could sneak up on Saponi and Cherokee villages and watch. I learned so much, things none of us Hills or other frontier folks knew, except maybe the early Spanish, and French Jesuit trappers and missionaries knew some of it. I learned about the Indian cultures. They were not all alike, either. But they farmed. They had marriages and women were treated really well, much better, truly, than a lot of frontier white women of European extraction. I also saw a lot of horrible things, like massacres and later, the early slavery hereabouts. And one day I was standing under a huge stone land bridge and a man was painting! He painted me standing there. I walked over to see. He could not see me. But he had been staring right at me when he painted. Anyhow, when I stood by his shoulder and looked at his canvas, I saw two men standing under the enormous arch of stone."

"Who was it?" Lacey asked excitedly.

"It was the famous German painter from Bremen, who traveled all around the continent from Niagara Falls to Georgia, painting in the 1800's. He spent a long time in Virginia. And in 1858, the year I was standing under the rock, he painted 'Natural Bridge, Rockbridge County'! Edward Beyer!"

"I have seen that print," Lacey cried! "He did so many of Virginia. White Sulphur Springs, Salem, Yellow Springs. Many others! They are glorious!"

"Well, there was no one standing there but me. And he may or may not have been able to see me. But I am in the painting!"

"What happened next?"

"Soon after the painting was displayed and prints were made, I found myself stepping out of that very scene into a room, a fancy room, in the Harshbarger house, in what is now Roanoke. It was Big Lick before that. And when I figured out that it was the 19th century and I was in this part of Virginia, I headed over here, looking for Fort Hill."

"And you found it, and stayed."

"Yes. I stayed. I was here for that entire terrible War. I saw such tragedy, on both sides. And when the Union troops came through in June of 1865 to read the Emancipation Proclamation to the slaves, at every plantation, a funeral for Mr. Plybon out in the county had to be stopped while all the troops rode through. Those Yankees did not give a hoot for a funeral. I watched it all.

"I have been out here so very long, looking for closure or meaning or something, and the arrowhead that killed me, so I can 'move on.'"

"I guess you were not seriously religious, a believer, when you were killed?"

"No. I was not. I was raised a

Protestant, my parents were Quakers, back in the 1700's. But I never found it very helpful."

Lacey looked at him closely. "You are older than you were when you were killed."

"I think I am aging a little by little. I have been around since about 1750. I think I have forgotten when I was born," he said. "But in life now, I am 35."

"Why do you spend so much time at The Grove?" she asked softly.

"I know things. I know the history of the place, the town, the slaves, the plantations, the government, what happened to whom in the War Between the States, crimes, the moonshining, the conspiracies, liquor trials. Secrets. Mr. Greer used to share legal and trial and conspiracy secrets with me, things people had told him, because he knew I could not tell anyone, and he could not, either. It is an awful lot to know," he said wearily.

"What about The Grove?" she asked again. "I have seen into the house in 1864 several times."

He looked at her in amazement. "I had no idea," he said. "So you saw Jannie and John and Mary, Margaret Hale. Did you see John S. Hale?"

"I never saw John S. Hale. But I was there the day the messenger came to report that Major Sam Hale had been killed at Spotsylvania Courthouse! It was awful."

"Aye, it were," Wild Bill commented, lapsing back into older English.

"Well, since ye be asking me," he chuckled, "I saw where Margaret buried the family jewelry. Right out by the brick carriage path. I do not know why the lady chose such an open and vulnerable place! She had lowered the Hale silver into that well, and the Union troops never found it. But they raided the smokehouse, took all the meats. They were looking for General Early. But he were off having supper with someone over at The Farm, not too far away. When he heard he was being hunted...mind you, this was directly after the Treaty at Appomattox...he fled to Canada. He went to Florida and Mexico. He was all over before he came back and settled in Lynchburg."

"Why Lynchburg instead of here, where he was from?" she asked.

"He saved Lynchburg from General David Hunter, that's why. After the War Lynchburg asked him to come back as a hero, and he did! He is not even buried in the old Confederate Cemetery, with the famous rose garden, over there, did you know? He is buried in Spring Hill. Fell down the stairs when he was 77 and died of his injuries in 1893. Later on, the famous

Carter Glass, who helped create the Federal Reserve, served as Secretary of the Treasury under President Wilson, and co-sponsored the Glass-Steagall Act, to help control banking, in 1933, was buried next to him!"

"So you know where the Hale jewelry is? Have you looked at it?" she asked.

"Oh, yes! I moved it before the Union troops ever came, for its safety. I was right there but they could not see me. I buried the box beneath a Boxwood that was near a stone bench in the front yard."

"Is it still there?" Lacey asked breathlessly.

"Yes, and I will take you to it, this evening. You can act like you are checking on the house, which has not sold yet, right? And then I will give you the jewelry!"

"I cannot keep it," Lacey said. "But I could give it to the lady, Mrs. Greer, who still owns the estate and it might help her!" Lacey was so pleased. "Guess I will have to get the box to her in a secret way, so she keeps it. Might put a letter in there."

"Lacey Brew, you are a fine person," Wild Bill said, pretending to tip a hat at her. They laughed. Lacey was so happy to have someone to confide in about her Time travels. And he seemed relieved to share his extremely unusual story.

As they started back around the ruins, Lacey stumbled on the uneven ground near the fallen tree. She fell onto her knees. When she started to stand up, with him lending her an arm, she put her hand down on a loose flat stone and it came up from where it must have been stuck in the ground for many years. When she tipped it over, they both looked and saw an arrowhead laying there in the red clay.

Wild Bill, or rather, William Hill, Jr., reached down and lifted it up. He held it close to his heart. "It is the one," he cried. "It is the one!" And he held it close and looked up to the skies. "I do not know whose God is there, but today, God, Great Spirit, great spirits of the Indian who shot me, please know I forgive him."

There was a complete hush all of a sudden in the trees. The birds stopped singing. The winds stopped blowing. One hawk flew over. A cast of hawks flew over, dipping low, and the air was full of feathers falling gently to the ground at their feet. And Time stood still.

Will Hill, as Lacey now called him, and Lacey spent many hours together talking. He started to come over to her special office and enjoyed meeting the other *returned souls* who came in almost daily to find new housing. And it seemed, to her, that the more he was there and the more they all talked, and the more he was touched, by her or by Jim Glass or Coy Howe, who knew he was a friend of hers, although they did not know the whole story, the more "solid" and real he became.

They were in her home one afternoon after work when Lacey saw that the painting she had done of her house in 1933 was missing! In its place was a long note, handwritten, as if by a young person.

Dear Lacey Brew,

Mama McCain came right here! She came right into your kitchen and it was in modern time, not in 1933! She saw me! And I was 94. She did not who I was. I went over to her and threw my arms around her, my mama, and as I did, the years fell away and I was 13 all over again, my whole life ahead of me. And she became younger and we laughed and laughed and I had to tell her everything!

We sat in here hoping you would come through the door but you did not. So I asked mama to take me with her to your office as soon as we can, to meet you and to look for a house. I am so happy. Ann and Bobby, she said, had become quite spiritual and went to church a lot, after the moonshining trials, and tried to make a good life for themselves. Little Prilly, also, followed their example. Mama died when Prilly was expecting her first child, in around the time of WWII. And mama said she did not go near any light! She found herself wandering around parks for the longest time. Then she made her way here and came in through your painting of our home! Thank you, Lacey Brew. Thank you!

Your Friend forever,

Jack McCain, 13

Lacey cried when she read Jack's note. She was overcome by the things happening around her, or through her, or because of her. She did not know how to think of it all. Then she heard from Bianca Rose that she was the heir and could keep the house and everything in it! And Mrs. Greer wrote that she had received the box of Hale jewels and they were perfect to help her take care of The Grove until it sold, although she wanted Lacey to have a brooch. Enclosed in the package was a stunning gold brooch with stars in it, stars of diamonds!

That same week, after meeting with the McCains in her office and showing them around town for a new house, Lacey tried her 1864 key at The Grove…and it would not open the door. She tried and tried, with the original old key and its copy. They would not open the house!

She hurried over to Bianca Rose's house, which Bianca was packing up to move to Rose Hall. Without asking, she hurried around to the back door and tried the 1864 McGhee key. It did not open the door. Neither the original nor the copy would work! Nor would the 1925 Mills key!

Taking Will Hill with her, she went to Callaway and tried the 1864 key in the old house she had shown the Prestons. Neither the original nor the copy key would open the house.

"I think the magic is gone," she moaned to Will. "I cannot get into other Times anymore."

"Maybe that is how it is meant to be," Will Hill said gently, taking her in his arms. He hugged her and she let him. And as she did, he became solid as a real person. And he mentioned that he felt different, whole.

When they drove back through the village crossroads of Callaway, and stopped at the weaving studio, Trish Van Weldt spoke to both of them, seeing them both in her doorway. And right then, both Lacey and Will knew something miraculous had happened. He could be seen. He was real. He was here.

They spent much time together. Lacey introduced him to her new friends as Will Hill, or Hillbilly Will, and explained he was a direct descendent of the Robert and Swinfeld Hill family of Fort Hill. They went to the Monacan Village at Natural Bridge and let Duncan Taylor, the Director with Scottish and Cherokee heritage, take their picture standing exactly under the stone bridge where so many years before Edward Beyer had painted Will.

And before long, Alicia Molina, owner of Mysterious Ridge Event Center, in Callaway, booked their wedding for the end of Autumn, when the yellow leaves would be swirling from the forests high above the valley along the Blue Ridge Parkway, and when feathers would fly in the air from hawks circling high over the fields.

Some of the wedding gifts they received included some original art by local artists Lacey and Will had met at galleries and festivals. Philip Sheridan, who traveled the world and painted wherever he went, gave them a Western oil painting he had done of a Cherokee standing on a hill in Oklahoma, looking back east, with a hawk on his wrist.

And author Jerry Ellis presented them with a signed first edition of his book, *"Walking the Trail, One Man's Journey Along the Cherokee Trail of Tears."* Duncan Taylor gave them a Native American collection of totems and prayers. The local DAR Chapter, thinking of William Hill's ancestry, gave them a framed portrait of George Washington, specific to his having checked the frontier forts in the time of Robert Hill. Ellie Sorensen, the jeweler and potter, gave them a set of her trademark pottery with raised green leaves. Young potter Sidra Kaluszka gave them a wedding chalice. Marsha Paulekas gave them a painting of a cabin in the woods. Mary See gave them a painting she had done of The Grove. Suzanne Ross gave them a watercolor of Jubal Early's little law office. Dr. Peters gave them a booklet of the restoration of the colonial Chapel Church. Bianca Rose gave them a lyrical poem of her own framed in a collage of pressed flowers. G & H paid for two nights for them at The Greenbrier for a honeymoon. All was perfect.

At their wedding, which was attended by everyone Lacey had met since moving to Rocky Mount in the Spring, and who knows how many *returned souls*, the minister quoted Psalm 90: 1,

"Lord, thou hast been our dwelling place in all generations."

The End

Epilogue

One might understandably wonder if Will Hill, Jack McCain, and Mrs. McCain lived on, as if they were living their lives in normal time, and not as *returned souls.* Yes. Apparently the key to that transition was in being truly loved. Love bridged the gulf from invisibility and frailty to solid and real and mortal. Brenda Field Marks also was reunited with her *returned soul* military husband Trevor and they moved out of her parents' house—which was in Town, and moved into a house in Callaway, and had a wonderful new life.

Lacey and Will Hill continued on at 33 Cottage Hill Drive and bought the former McGhee home on Autumn Street that Bianca Rose Harriman had rented, and used it for guests. They mostly ate with them at

Bootleggers Café across from The Early Inn At The Grove (once The Grove), a lovely Bed and Breakfast (both places sold by Lacey the realtor) and now owned by a visionary buyer and his partners from out of town.

Once Virginia Tech and their new Medical School and the University of Virginia's Medical School and Philosophy and Religion Department in Charlottesville, learned of *returned souls,* there was quite the competition for grants and studies to learn how many such people were out there. Virginia Tech even created a new Returned Soul Hokie Bird with an ethereal look on its face. The University tried to create a Returned Soul Cavalier but no one was impressed.

Ministers, chaplains, and priests clamored for a piece of the research and many denominations, especially Southern Baptists and Episcopalians, began special *Returned Souls Feast Nights*, to entice these people back into church. Liberty University, surprisingly, began a graduate program in *Returned Souls* before any other university in the world thought of doing that, and also encouraged their law students to get a joint Ph.D./J.D. in the new field, "Not Left Behind." The next to follow their lead was Oxford in England.

Other area colleges and universities such as Hollins, Roanoke, Sweet Briar, Hampden-Sydney, Mary Baldwin, Virginia Western, Longwood, Emory & Henry, Elon, Salem, Virginia Commonwealth, University of Richmond, Washington & Lee, James Madison, George Mason, Mary Washington, Shenandoah, UVa at Wise, and other Virginia and regional schools, are fighting to recruit *returned souls* who never went to or graduated from college. New dormitories are being built.

A few years after Lacey and Will married, and Jess and Bianca Rose married, they were all having dinner at the Hills when Lacey was greeted by a stranger in the kitchen, standing beside a modern art "assemblage" in a shadow box, of a miniature dress form, a small photo negative from the 20th century, fragile bird bones, human hair, and a ribbon, by artist Page Turner. He introduced himself as someone from 3014 trying to find his ancestral home. He had a calico kitten in his arms and handed it to her. They laughed. And so it continued. Lacey secretly wondered what exactly in Page Turner's assemblage had allowed this person from the future to enter their era…And she and Will named the new calico cat, "Celestial."

FINI

Addendum: And Why She Wrote The Book
If you really want to know the details....

Paradoxes. Mind-blowing paradoxes that Ibby Greer kept discovering as she learned more about the history of The Grove, of the Greer family heritage in Franklin County, Virginia, and of her own family's heritage, are the fundamental reasons that she wrote a novel trying to capture Rocky Mount's best, most famous, and most unusual history. Always an outsider, although "mistress" of The Grove for 23 years, the author created a character who was also an outsider, from another place far away, to move to Rocky Mount and "see" it through her fresh eyes. Everyone knows that people who live in a place rarely sightsee or visit the very places nearby that tourists come to see. But a newcomer does.

Fort Hill, the oldest structure in the county, an 18th century blockhouse on the frontier, became a central, even symbolic, location in this story. From Lacey Brew's passion to learn about her new home, come adventures and acquaintances that will change not only her life but also how she views "Time" and history. They come alive.

The author spent decades being a hostess, tour guide, president and regent of various heritage societies in the area, a civic board trainer for regional boards, a supporter of the arts, education, colleges, and activities of the area. She briefly chaired the Board of the Virginia Museum of Natural History in Martinsville, through which she learned, among many other interesting facts, from Curator Elizabeth Moore, about anthropological and archeological digs at sites of the old campgrounds and camp fires of Native Americans in early VA, to see what their diets had consisted of. Her interest in Native American cultures had been piqued.

Ibby ran an independent bookstore, The Blue Lady Bookshop, for 5 years, out of the former law office of Gen. Jubal A. Early, on the grounds of the 19th century plantation house. She sat exactly in the same room looking at the same fireplace and hearth, and through the same two windows, that Jubal Early had. When she and Keister first tried to put books on the old walnut bookcases brought in for the shop, every single book leaped off the shelves, falling on the floor at their feet. It happened again and again. Keister turned to Ibby and said something like, "Jube is not happy with you being in here." But they persisted and eventually the books stayed put. But the door slammed shut and they were locked in. The locksmith (who is in the book) came and got them out, and said he could not figure out what had happened because there was no way that lock could have done what it did, especially on its own. Well, Keister and Ibby knew. Jubal. Ibby's interest in old doors and locks was born that minute.

She owned and wrote for a regional magazine for four years, "Blue Ridge Traditions," which had been started as a black and white publication by Peggy Conklin, trying to highlight the Southern culture. Eventually, the irony that she, from Illinois with a New England heritage, had found herself becoming the quintessential "Southerner" in her ability to quote the history, defend Virginia to visitors, explain the North, and discuss both sides of "The War," while married 18 years to lawyer and author T. Keister Greer, caused her to think about the paradoxes. Had she, like her character Lacey Brew, been "brought" to Rocky Mount by a bigger force than a charming gentleman's courtship and marriage? Had God, Fate, or coincidence brought her there, so she could "see" it and preserve it in fiction? Rocky Mount has been preserved in history books. It was her turn.

A New England and Illinois heritage married to a Virginia heritage, connections to Abraham Lincoln in her own family and to Confederate Jubal A. Early in her Southern plantation home, The Grove, and to Fort Hill, the first structure in Franklin County, through her current romantic partnership, stirred her soul. Ibby Greer's relationship to Rocky Mount has been a kind of love story. A novel was born.

The attention to colonial, frontier, Revolutionary War, Civil War, and other history in this novel is a direct result of the documented heritage of her beloved home for 23 years, The Grove, her own heritage, that of her son Andrew Call, of her late husband T. Keister Greer, and beau William C. Conner.

Keister's ancestor Captain Moses Greer and Bill's ancestor Swinfeld Hill (both are in the novel) served for years on Franklin County's first Court in the 18th century. While they all were doing that, Ibby's ancestors were running New England.

Her late Greer husband's English ancestry included Jamestown families. His earliest English and Scottish ancestors were legislators and judges in Franklin County,

VA, with plantations, and later fought in the Revolutionary War in the South, and as officers and doctors for the Confederacy.

Her Conner beau's Irish Protestant Conner ancestors were settling Loudon County with a Land Grant from the English King, and his Irish Quaker ancestors were building a frontier fort. His various ancestors fought in the Revolutionary War in Virginia with Washington and at The Battle of Guilford Courthouse in North Carolina with Washington. His Conners in Floyd County fought on both sides in the "War Between the States." Many people in Floyd Co. tended to be "Mountain Republicans," non-slave-owning folks who were more sympathetic, perhaps, to Lincoln, than to Lee.

Ibby's English Pilgrim ancestors were settling and becoming governors of Massachusetts, and settling Connecticut, Rhode Island, and New York. One early ancestor, The Rev. John Kewley Prentice Henshaw, was the first Episcopal Bishop of Rhode Island. Her Dutch Stryker ancestors were merchant adventurers and an artist who came over in the 1600's with a Land Grant from the King of the Netherlands. They settled New Jersey and eventually had a mansion in what is now Central Park.

Dr., and General, Peter Stryker, was a governor of New Jersey. General William Scudder Stryker founded the New Jersey Historical Society and wrote *"The Battles of Trenton and Princeton."* In the Civil War he helped organize the 14th New Jersey Volunteers. He also went to the College of New Jersey (later Princeton Univ.), was a lawyer, a banker, and President of the Society of The Cincinnati in New Jersey [Sons of the American Revolution elite]. Both her English and Dutch folks were fighting alongside George Washington in New Jersey.

One of her Illinois ancestors, John Whitfield Bunn, served in the Union Army, as a special spy for IL Gov. Yates. IL ancestor Capt. Benjamin H. Ferguson served under Gen. Grant at Vicksburg. Much of southern IL, ironically, and perhaps understandably, was secretly sympathetic to the South. Many Southern families came up, like the Kelley, Todd, Iles, and Pulliam families, from North Carolina, Kentucky, and Virginia to settle central IL, and still had family back home who fought with the South. Ibby's paternal Jacksonville, IL, cousins had Southern accents and the older ladies were called, in Southern style, "Miss Katie," etc. And her father's hometown was Virginia (IL)....

So, all three—Keister's, Bill's, and Ibby's—ancestors fought alongside George Washington before "North" and "South" parted ways. George Washington, Virginia native, was everywhere! He inspected colonial forts, for instance, in Franklin County.

Her ancestors also include colonial people in history books: the Aldens and Brewsters of the Mayflower; much of the Winthrop Fleet: John Winthrop, Thomas Dudley, and Simon Bradstreet, all governors of MA; the first woman poet, Ann Dudley Bradstreet; Seaborne Cotton; an early theologian, Cotton Mather; Stephen Goodyear, Deputy Gov. of New Haven Colony; Henry Wolcott, co-founder of CT; the first portrait painter in New Amsterdam in the 1660's, Dutch adventurer Jan Stryker from Holland, whose painting is in the Smithsonian. Other early Dutch settlers, the Bunns, in NJ, went on to Il and founded many of its earliest businesses, railroads, and banks. She grew up hearing about colonial history.

Her Illinois heritage includes Hunterdon Co., New Jersey, natives, and residents of Springfield, IL, and Chicago. Paradox: her maternal great-great-grand-father Jacob Bunn and his brother John Whitfield Bunn, who were friends of

Abraham Lincoln before he ever ran for office, were his bankers, and financed his first Presidential campaign. *

[* Call, Andrew T. *Jacob Bunn: Legacy of an Illinois Industrial Pioneer.* Brunswick Publishing Co. 2005.]

Lincoln was her Illinois family's lawyer. Lincoln was a bad word in Franklin County. For that matter, so was New Jersey until recent years.

Mary Todd Lincoln is on record for turning Jacob Bunn's picture to the wall, thinking he, as their banker, had too much to say about their affairs. She later changed her mind. She changed her mind often. But, as a Kentuckian-Illini, married to the President, who was from a North Carolina family and grew up in Kentucky before coming to Old Salem outside Springfield, paradoxes and changing one's mind can be understood!

Another paradox, given Ibby's life in Virginia, is that two of her IL ancestors, Jacob Bunn and Benjamin Ferguson along with Gen. David Hunter, all walked in Lincoln's funeral procession, Jacob as a pallbearer. Hunter had burned VMI and tried to burn The Greenbrier and came close to Franklin County at Hanging Rock on his rush to burn Lynchburg, which Early prevented. Henry DuPont, a Union officer under Hunter, stopped him from doing that and later sent the money necessary to rebuild VMI. Even Keister admired that Yankee DuPont. [Keister attended the University of Virginia in 1939 on a DuPont Scholarship!]

Ibby's Illinois ancestor, Benjamin Ferguson, mustered in at Camp Butler in 1862. He became a Captain, went with his regiment to Memphis, TN, where they were given picket duty. They stayed until the Tallahatchie Campaign, when they were attached to the First Brigade of Gen. Lauman's Division. Eventually he participated with Grant's canal works at Vicksburg, later crossing the Mississippi at Duckfort, Louisiana. He marched with Grant's Army towards Jackson, MS, where they engaged in fighting between Jackson and Vicksburg in the sieges. Upon the surrender of Vicksburg, he helped pursue Confederate General Joe Johnson and his Army across Tennessee.

And Ulysses S. Grant's only daughter, Nellie Grant Sartoris, is buried in Ibby's family's Bunn plot at Oak Ridge Cemetery near Lincoln's Tomb because Nellie's second husband's first wife was a Bunn. Grant, Hunter, Sheridan, and Lincoln were not discussed at The Grove. Ever. (Early is not discussed much in Illinois, either!) And Ibby respected that. Paradoxes.

Andrew Cunningham of Cass Co., IL, Ibby's great-great-grand uncle, had a tannery and contracted to provide leather goods for the Union Army.

Two of Ibby's son Andrew Call's Union Army great-great-great-grand-uncles, Hiram and Edwin Baldwin, both served throughout the War. One of them was active in the battle in which J.E.B. Stuart was killed and the other in the one in which Major Samuel Hale was killed. Hiram Baldwin, from PA, served under Daniel A. Butterfield (credited with composing the bugle-call, "Taps"), in Co. F, 83rd Regiment, PA Volunteer Infantry, Third Brigade, First Division, Fifth Corps of The Army of the Potomac. Hiram fought at Hanover Court House, Williamsburg, Gaines Mill, where he was taken prisoner and sent to Libby and Belle Isle Prisons near Richmond. He was imprisoned 39 days and was exchanged, returned to his regiment, and fought at the 2nd Battle of Bull Run, 1st and 2nd Fredericksburg, Chancellorsville, and Gettysburg. He was discharged in 1863 and re-enlisted for three more years. He was made a Sergeant at the Battle of the Wilderness, fought at Laurel Hill, the Affair at Bethesda Church, Petersburg, Richmond, and Appomattox, and saw Lee surrender.

Edwin Baldwin, his older brother, born in NY, and lived in PA. In 1862 he joined in Capt. John W. Phillips' Company B, 18th Regiment, PA Cavalry, serving as a Corporal. He fought at Fairfax Courthouse, where he was on picket duty and was captured by Confederate Gen. John Singleton Mosby, "The Grey Ghost," in person, but was soon paroled. He fought at Hanover PA, in 1863 and Gettysburg. At Hagerstown, MD, he was captured again, sent to Belle Isle and exchanged again. He also participated in Gen. Judson Kilpatrick's Raid on Richmond, 1864. He next served under Gen. Sheridan at the Battle of Mine Run and Spotsylvania Courthouse. [Could have killed Major Sam Hale...]. He was at Harper's Ferry when Lee surrendered.

Other of Andrew Call's Civil War ancestors include William Call of OH and John E. Burtner of PA, brothers Corporal John A. Criswell of PA, Robert Ross Criswell, William Criswell from Pittsburgh, and others. William oversaw the repair and reconstruction of railroads destroyed by Confederate soldiers. Andrew's great-grandfather from OH, James Custer Call was named in March of 1865 in honor of General George Armstrong Custer, also from Ohio. To balance this, perhaps in some realm of "tit-for-tat" in history, one of Keister's ancestors was named, soon after the assassination in 1865, John Wilkes Booth Greer. He was called "Wilkie" and is buried in the Greer Cemetery, as is Keister, in Sontag.

Andrew discussed his Baldwin ancestors' amazing service for the Union Army once with his step-father. Keister, an accomplished military veteran of what has been called the fiercest battle of WWII, Okinawa, was one to recognize valor. He said that for those two Baldwins to have fought in all of those battles, been captured and imprisoned, wounded, and to have survived to return home, was extraordinary. That was an incredible moment at The Grove: Keister's praise for Union soldiers.

In 1995 a similar thing happened when Keister flew back to Okinawa for the 50th Anniversary of the Battle, and a Japanese Okinawa Veteran missing an arm addressed the Americans, saying, among other things, "I salute you, brave men!" Keister thought that about Andrew's Yankee ancestors: "I salute you, brave men." Losers saluting victors. Although always articulate and bitter about the Union's winning the War of Northern Aggression, to use the name used by many in Rocky Mount,

Keister never really accepted that the South had lost it.

Ibby had grown up with Lincolniana everywhere, but no one she had known in IL talked about "the war." So she re-focused. It lived on at The Grove. Why? Not because Keister supported slavery. Not because he believed in "union." In fact he was a fan of secession. State's rights. Patrick Henry more than Thomas Jefferson. The right for Scotland to be free of England. That kind of thing. The war had been a matter of honor. And loss for his family.

At UVa, a famous history professor, Charles Julian Bishko, once remarked to his star pupil, "Mr. Greer, you are a Monarchist!" Keister was in favor of the American Revolution but, frankly, Ibby wondered if he did not wish there were still Anglican traditions and ideas in Virginia...He often told Ibby that, for Virginians, the real capital was not Washington D.C., the real cultural center was not New York City. They were, for Virginians, London.

And when they were married he chose a pre-Revolutionary 1769 church building which he identified as such in 1950 (a good year) for their tiny wedding. It had been known once as The King's House of Campden Parish in VA [because of the

British monarch when Virginia was a new colony], then the Old Chapel Church. Later it became a Primitive Baptist Church. Then, eventually, it had no congregants. It is owned now and being carefully and meticulously restored to its original 18th century state by Dr. J. Francis Amos, who is the local historian *par excellence*. Dr. Peters in the novel.

Keister, who really personified the South and The Grove, was an Anglophile and his Scots had been wealthy Border Scots in Dumfriesshire (mentioned prominently in Sir Walter Scott's *"The Red Gauntlet"*) and had fought with England on occasion and had not been Presbyterian. But because his prominent Greer (and other names, Webb, Street, and others) family had been decimated, never to recover financially from losing their lands and property in the War Between the States, he never forgot a detail. Not one. Land, remember, was BIG in Virginia.

The Civil War was also very much alive at The Grove because of the house itself, its connection to Jubal Early, and its being raided by Union cavalry after Appomattox. The Yankees (who included Andrew's Baldwins, Ibby and Andrew think) who rode in there looking for Early took all the meats but never found the Hale silver. The silver is in the book, and is safe with the Hale family of Richmond. The buried jewelry is fiction. Ibby thinks. The Grove, to Keister, was a symbol of history, culture, The South, prosperity and civilization. The Grove was a kind of museum, as well as being a great home to live in. There were few discussions, at The Grove, of the Pennsylvania Yankee raider cousins. And none of Lincoln, Grant, etc.

Ibby was the first person, ever, to become an Associate Member of the Jubal A. Early Chapter of the United Daughters of the Confederacy, a category reserved for women with no Southern or Confederate ancestry. That is the UDC Chapter that arranged for the first Confederate Soldier statue at the Courthouse, for which Grove owner Edward Watts Saunders, Sr., gave the dedicatory address in 1906, and for whose fund Booker T. Washington was a donor.

She hosted events for the UDC at The Grove on Lee-Jackson Day. When the replacement statue was dedicated in 2010 (the first having been destroyed by a runaway car), two years after Keister's death, Ibby hosted the reception at The Grove for the public, local dignitaries, and speakers Dr. J. Francis Amos, and Prof. James "Bud" Robertson, of Virginia Tech, national expert on all things Civil War, and other Rocky Mount officials. She did the reception for two reasons: The Grove had been featured in 1906 because of Mr. Saunders, and Keister would have done a reception had he still been living.

There were among the many members of the local UDC those who disapproved of her being in the group because of her familial connection to President Lincoln whose efforts to save the Union caused thousands of troops to march into The Commonwealth. Understood.

Rather than being offended, Ibby understood: the War lived on for the UDC. It did not live on for her, except as mistress of The Grove, but she respected their opinion. Their families had lost much. Her families had hardly been affected. So she resigned from UDC after about two years and stuck with two chapters of DAR, where her ancestors were appreciated. And was twice President of the Henry Corbin Chapter, Colonial Dames XVII Century, a Danville chapter which also had some members not friendly to her Northerness. Sometimes, she thinks, they simply forgot they were at a CDXVII C meeting, and not at UDC. Ibby had a very impressive list of Colonial Officer ancestors already documented and on record, all in New England, and was working on 40 more

Supplemental applications (confirmed already by the New England Historical and Genealogical Society, the best genealogists for New England ancestry), when she resigned, tired of being treated like an outsider. North, South, North, South. Paradoxes. What on earth would George Washington have thought of it all! Right. But...remember, Danville had been a Capital of the Confederacy for a time. And that is the history that mattered to most of the ladies. Understandably.

Ibby's childhood home, the early-20th century Logan-Hay Mansion, modeled in part on Monticello, in Springfield, was wanted by the State of Illinois for the Governor's Mansion in the 1960's. But her father sold it to someone else, who turned it into a school. It was later torn down. Thus, "saving" The Grove after her husband's death became a major priority, and is why The Grove features so prominently in this novel. The Grove and most of its history is preserved in the book and one hopes, in real life, for many years to come.

Her Virginia Gentleman husband, T. Keister Greer, 29 years her senior, had grown up until his third year of high school in the coalfields of McDowell County, WV, where his father, Moses Theodrick Greer and his family had had to move after a fire in 1900 in the Sontag area of Franklin Co., to get work, and as an adult (Moses) worked as a butcher and shopkeeper for the Premier-Pocahontas Collier Co. of WV in Premier, Welch, Coretta, Shaft Hollow, and other coal camps. Keister, raised on the dignified and historic stories of his Scottish and Virginia ancestors (in Scotland and VA), asked that they move back to VA when he was in high school and they did. He finished at Andrew Lewis HS in Salem, but his dad commuted for the rest of his life, dying in 1946. Franklin County was "The South" for Keister. WV was not.

Ibby's families had owned the Stonega Coal and Coke Co. of Big Stone Gap, VA, and the Island Creek Coal Co. of Cleveland, which operated also in far SW VA. She is the first person he ever told, except his first wife, of his childhood in WV. Even his oldest Rocky Mount friends did not know. The only reason Ibby found out was because of a photo tucked deep into a highboy drawer. Unframed little faded snapshot. It was of a worn young woman seated on a train track holding a grubby and chunky little boy of about 3. It looked like Keister, but, surely not!

She asked. It was he. And he, first child of four that would be born in WV, and oldest of the three that survived infancy, was on the lap, of his sweet mother, Goldie Lillian Shaw Greer of Lambsburg, VA. The last sibling was born in VA after the family moved back in the late 1930's. Lots of ancestral silver spoons in that little boy's mouth, actual castles, like Lag Tower and Capenoch in Scotland, and plantations in the past, but he was not born in a castle with a silver spoon in his mouth, as all of his friends had always assumed. Just a few generations before the WV stage of the Greer saga, a little boy ancestor with silver spoons had lived on a plantation with slaves, and a little boy slave's only duty was to fan him with a big hand-held fan.

The reality of Keister's childhood was more interesting for not having a silver spoon involved. His wonderful parents, Mose and Goldie, who lived until she was 90, and died the week before Ibby and Keister met, adored their children and saw that they were educated. They had love. They had books and stories. They had heritage that was kept alive generation after generation. That is something the South may do better than any other region. It preserves what matters.

The little photo and the deep highboy drawers opened a magical box of stories never told. Digging deep into the antique highboy, Ibby found many more discarded, hidden photos of an era kept secret. None of his three children had ever been over to see his childhood homes or their grandparents' many houses tucked along mountainous country roads, by creeks, and by mineshafts. Keister eventually took Ibby, Andrew, and Andrew's dad Matt on trips through McDowell County to see it all, including Courthouse records and cemeteries. Then Keister, his sister Pat, ten years his junior, her husband Ron, and Ibby went on an extensive reconnoitering expedition of where they had lived, hill by hill, hollow by hollow, creek by creek, coal co. grocery by coal co. shop, and Pat took videos of it all.

Ibby got out and stood on the tracks where Goldie had held Keister as a toddler. The contrasts between the shacks up on concrete blocks and Keister's Grove were an epiphany for Ibby. His childhood explained why he was so passionate about his South, his home, his wardrobe (all from London), his English shoes, his collection of fine silver, porcelain, statues, and rare books. The man was a huge success in his legal career, and he had closed the door on McDowell County. Paradoxes. She loved him even more for knowing about his youth. He never would eat a biscuit. Virginians love biscuits. But for him, a biscuit was a reminder of hard times.

Once she convinced him that he should be proud of his heritage, all of it, Ibby got him to tell the stories about growing up there. While she had grown up in a mansion, in a family with three homes (home base in IL, summer in MI, and winter in FL) taking everything for granted, he as a young boy had been walking to school down a steep hill in Welch with a hard biscuit in a metal pail, riding in the back of a pick-up, ordering books from a Sears Catalogue with his precious coins, and delivering news-papers as a child in Shaft Hollow, truly an awful, sad place. Paradoxes. Precious paradoxes. To him, Rocky Mount and Franklin Co., where his ancestors had settled and made huge contributions to the culture, were a heaven.

Out of that highboy came papers. His late wife Dorothy turned out to be Ibby's 12th cousin through Alden sisters, and also had an ancestor, Dr. Burke, in Springfield at the same time as Ibby's great-great-grandfather Jacob Bunn. Ibby and Andrew were related to Keister's children, not once, but twice. Alden and Gill (of NY).

Another set of coincidences that intrigued Ibby, the more she discovered, was the way Southern Keister had brought two very non-Southern wives to The Grove, Dorothy for 46 years and Ibby for 18, and that the two women had quite a bit in common, besides ancestry. The late Dorothy Greer had been raised mostly in Boulder, CO, and Casper, WY, after her mother died in 1924, and Ibby lived in Boulder for 7 years, has family there, and had a sister who lived in Casper and whose children still live in that area. Sharing Springfield, Boulder, Casper, MA, NY and two ancestral families in common with Dorothy, just bound Ibby closer to the intriguing tapestry of coincidences and oddities being woven. For decades people asked Ibby how she could tolerate having a portrait of the late Greer wife in the home. It was a portrait which Ibby had helped arrange, soon after their 1990 marriage, to be painted for Keister because he missed her so. Ibby learned to smile and answer, "Oh, Cousin Dorothy? We would have liked each other. And we both loved Keister."

Ibby's slightly crazy life was a result of education and travel: a Springfield, Illinois, native, she was formally educated first at Miss Duncan's Play School where she was expelled for not eating Fig Newtons. Her rebellious streak went underground. Still hates the cookies.

Towing the line, she completed her pre-school and then attended Blessed Sacrament School in Springfield (Sept. to

Jan., May) and (simultaneously) Gulfstream School (Jan. to April) in south Florida through sixth grade (going back and forth between homes each year and having two sets of friends, two accents, two kinds of education, and little arithmetic…but lots of French, people-watching, and possibly cognitive dissonance from the experience).

Following the tutorial years at Gulfstream School, where each student brought their school books from their Northern school, she was at the very demanding Palm Beach Day for 7th through 9th, followed by three years at the Westover School in Connecticut.

She was then trained in Sociology, Philosophy, and English, a self-designed triple major, with Honors, and Phi Beta Kappa, at Hollins College in Virginia, followed by an M.A. in Comparative Literature (18th century English, French, and German Novel) at the University of Colorado-Boulder. She did post-graduate work in German in Vienna at the Universität Wien in 1976, getting the Second Place Award.

She, her first husband and dear friend, Matthew Baldwin Call (Andrew's dad), several cousins, and Dorothy Greer's mother and aunt all had degrees from CU Boulder. Keister, Ibby's son Andrew, and four of their IL Bunn cousins, and one VA cousin have degrees from the University of Virginia. Distant cousin on Ibby's Irish, Wisconsin, maternal O'Keeffe-Hogan line, Wisconsin native Georgia O'Keeffe, also studied at that University. Both Georgia O'Keeffe and Keister's youngest daughter, Celeste C. Greer, graduated from Virginia's girls' school, Chatham Hall. And about half of all the Confederate generals were Princeton alumni, the university where 99% of all Ibby's Bunn family have gone since it started. They had to have known each other. It is called "The Southern Ivy," because of its students.

Ibby's schools and their vastly different regions, social demography, and traditions gave Ibby a life-long passion for culture and history. Ibby was raised in families who never discussed death or war. She married into a family where her husband discussed both daily. Her passion for story-telling, history, and genealogy was fueled by the hush-hush tragedy of her (Dutch and English heritage) paternal grandmother, of Jacksonville, IL. Charlotte Stryker Taylor (1875-1908), a Victorian lady who had sung Lieder for a hobby, had been educated at a girls' "finishing school" in MA, and had traveled to Europe in 1900 with a chaperone, died in 1908 in childbirth after only three years of marriage.

Charlotte's husband, Robert Cunningham Taylor of Virginia, IL, a tiny town west of Springfield, was a dour, second-generation Scottish-American, a banker and land overseer of Taylor farms. His maternal Edinburgh Cunningham ancestor had fought for the British in the Rev. War and had been captured at Charleston, SC, eventually released and returned to Scotland; his descendants later emigrated to the USA. When she has had to, Ibby has tried to count him as a Southern ancestor. He was in SC longer than anyone at the Roanoke Colony....

That family tragedy, of Ibby's father's Episcopal mother, led to her father being raised a lonely Scottish Presbyterian and becoming an unchurched atheist, who married a devout Roman Catholic. Thus, religion of any kind, God, priests, Popes, death, his mother, and his only brother's death in WWII in Holland, Germany, and any discussion of war, were totally taboo subjects. She saw no WWII movies until she was 15.

On the *U.S.S. United States*, crossing to Europe for her first trip abroad with her father and older sister in 1962, playing in the ship cinema, ironically, given how she had been protected from WWII, was "Judgment at Nuremburg," in which she was suddenly immersed in the aftermath and trial of war crimes for a war she knew nothing about. Then, a month or so later, she stood at a grave in the American Military Cemetery in Margraaten, Holland, and watched her father cry quietly at the graveside of his dear brother, Robert Cunningham Taylor, Jr. (1906-1944). That moment brought Ibby into adulthood, at 12, and may have been a pivotal part of her development as a watcher, listener, and recorder of history and family stories.

In contrast to childhood secrets and silence about family achievements and wars, and to add to the mix of unmentioned tales of loss and war, was her marriage to Keister Greer in 1990. At 40, she married an Anglican-Catholic (Protestant) widower of 69 and a WWII Marine Officer and Pacific Campaign veteran who talked about his personal losses, the Civil War, and his WWII memories daily. He often said that his war experience was what he was most proud of. We won that war. Ibby thinks that being a part of that enormous victory somehow made up for what had happened to his beloved Virginia a century earlier.

Daily, there was a mention or discussion of a battle in WWII or one in the

Civil War. He was the only WWII veteran she knew of who talked about war. Ibby's IL uncle, George Regan Bunn, a Princeton alumnus, who was also a Marine and fought at Iwo and Pelilu, would never talk of it at all. After the war, George created the stainless steel automatic drip coffee machine and company, Bunn-O-Matic, which is still run out of Springfield. When Keister and George met for the first time, Ibby introduced them to each other as fellow Marines. And North-South was forgotten. It was a grand evening. (And Lacey Brew's last name is Ibby's tip of the hat to coffee, to her late uncle's coffee empire, as well as a word chosen for "cooking something up," or finishing and perfecting something, which Lacey did in her life in Rocky Mount).

Paradox. She came from a stoic, quiet Midwest family of all New England Presbyterians with one Irish Wisconsin Catholic line (Regan) who rarely interacted, the one with the other, and avoided the limelight. She married into the world of a prominent "bi-coastal" California and Virginia litigator lawyer and historian in a Virginia estate who wore suits made in London, loved *The Book of Common Prayer* and Evensong in Anglican cathedrals, regularly visited the ruins, towers, castles, and sites of his Scottish ancestry. Ibby found herself doing an about-face, and realized she needed to pay attention and record her new amazing life, a study in opposites.

Ibby's interest in Rocky Mount history comes from her husband's lifelong passion for and two published books about Virginia history. Coupled with her lawyer son's lifelong passion for, and five books about, Virginia and Illinois industrial history, her historical novel of her Virginia home and hometown was to be educational and healing.

"Moonshine Corner" shows the agonies of loss, the confusion of changes, the blending of time periods. It shows hope. It reveals courage, curiosity, and compassion for the Confederacy, and slaves. The novel reveals layers of experience and history that shape a place and shape attitudes. Beauty from ashes. Honor from defeat. Courage. Continuty.

Add to the unusual mix that her beau, since 2010, William Clyde Conner whom she met online on a dating site where he was discussing Franklin Co. genealogy, is a Hill, from the first family to build a structure in Franklin County…and was present as was Ibby back when Keister gave the Dedicatory Speech for the restoration of Fort Hill by the Historical Society, DAR, and other helpers! What, folks, are the *chances* of this synchronicity! A magic realism, time-warp, historical, ghost, love story novel was born. Fort Hill, a central place in the novel, was the one place that Ibby, Keister, and Bill were together, by chance. Or by Fate.

Ibby is the author of a novel, *"Moving Day: A Season of Letters,"* [Brunswick Pub. 2000] set in Boulder and a photographic and poetic memoir, *"Paper Faces: Babyboomer Memoir,"* [Brunswick Pub. 2001] She is an artist with a studio. Her paintings and painted gourds are in area shops and in collections around the country. She makes her home with Bill and their cat Soot in a 1925 Foursquare cottage in Raleigh Court, Roanoke's eclectic neighborhood. Her oil painting of the calico cat is on the cover of the novel.

Acknowledgements

A very special thank you to my partner, William Clyde Conner of Copper Hill, Floyd Co., Virginia, a direct descendant of Swinfeld Hill (a son of Robert Hill in real life), for his patience and help throughout the research and writing of this book, for doing the cooking and bringing food upstairs to my study, countless cups of coffee (in honor of Lacey Brew) and for sharing his Hill genealogy with me.

A very special thank you to all the people who are in the book as characters and as actual named artists and authors. You know who you are! See FaceBook for details.

Thank you to my new neighbor, Matt Musselman, a graphic artist and owner of www.InvokeDesigns.us, for taking the pieces I wanted in the collage for the book cover and designing the cover!

Thank you to Jeanette and Chuck Miller for permission to use the actual bottle, which I bought several years ago, on the book cover, of their "Virginia Lightning" corn whiskey produced at their Belmont Farm Distillery in Culpeper, VA.

Thank you to Robb Hart for allowing me to mention his Paradise Sports Grille in Ferrum and to Bryan Hochstein for mentioning The Early Inn At The Grove (formerly The Grove) and Bootleggers Café in Rocky Mount.

Thank you to my son, Andrew Taylor Call, for providing much of the genealogy and facts about Revolutionary and Civil War service for our families [in the About the Author Addendum]. Thanks to him, as well, for his inspirational books set in Rocky Mount, *Jane Bligh an American Tall Tale; Mariah Miles, Tall Tale of the American Lakes; Grace Gill, Tall Tale of the Franklin County Gold;* and *Trail of the Appalachian Sunset,* [all CreateSpace, Amazon.com. 2013 and 2014] These tales inspired me to do this time-warp historical ghost novel.

Thanks for the encouragement from my Face Book World. You all cheered me on.

Reference Works

Civil War Trust (online). City of Charlottesville: Union Occupation of Charlottesville.

Colonel Washington's Frontier Forts Association. Online.

Crockett, Curtis D. "The Union's Bloody Miscue at Spotsylvania Muleshoe." America's *Civil War Magazine.* History-net.com

Davis, Burke. *Jeb Stuart, The Last Cavalier.* 1957. 2001.

Early, Jubal A. *A Memoir Of The Last Year Of The War For Independence In The Confederate States Of America. Containing An Account Of The Operations Of His Commands In The Years 1864 And 1865.* With an Introduction by Gary W. Gallagher. Toronto: Lovell & Gibson. 1866. University of South Carolina. 2001.

Early, Lieutenant General Jubal Anderson, CSA. *Autobiographical Sketch and Narrative of the War between the States.*

Fisher, Gary. *Rebel Cornbread and Yankee Coffee. Authentic Civil War Cooking and Camaraderie.* Sweetwater Press, Cliff Road Books. 2001.

Franklin County Bicentennial 1786-1986. online.

Greer, T. Keister. *Genesis of a Virginia Frontier. The Origins of Franklin County, Virginia, 1740-1785.* History House Press. 2005. Reprint from 1946 Honors Thesis at the University of Virginia.

Greer, T. Keister. *The Great Moonshine Conspiracy Trial of 1935*. History House Press. 2003.

Greer, T. Keister. Unpublished military and legal memoirs. *Recollections of a Bi-Coastal Lawyer.* 2007.

Salmon, Emily and John. *Franklin County, Virginia, 1786-1986, A Bicentennial History*. Franklin County Bicentennial Commission. Franklin County Board of Supervisors. 1993.

Smith, Captain James Power. "Stonewall's Last Battle." *The Century Magazine*, Vol. XXXII, October 1886. Civil War Trust online.

Stonewall Jackson House Tour. Lexington, 2014.

United States Department of the Interior National Park Service, National Registry of Historic Places, Rocky Mount Historic (District 157-5002) Franklin County. Online.

Trinity Episcopal Church. History. www.trinityrmva.org

The University of Virginia Library. *Socrates Maupin. John B. Minor.*[Professors who kept the Univ. of Virginia from being burned down in 1865. The marker exists because of a petition from Board of Visitors members T. Keister Greer, Esq., and John P. Ackerly, Esq., during their terms of service from 1995-2003]

Virginia Council of Indians. The Powatan Tribes.

Virginia [roadside] Historical Markers. Online.

Virginia Historical Society. Information on Saunders family, churches, plantations.

Washington, Booker Taliaferro. *Up From Slavery: An Autobiography*. 1901.

We Lived in a Little Cabin in the Yard. Edited by Belinda Hurmence. John E. Blair, Publisher. Winston-Salem, NC. 1994. [WPA interviews of former Virginia slaves over 80.]

Wingfield, Marshall. *An Old Virginia Court. Being a Transcript of the Records of the First Court of Franklin County, Virginia 1786-1789.* With Biographies of the Justices and Stories of Famous Cases Transcribed, Annotated, Glossarized, and Indexed. Memphis 4. Tennessee. The West Tennessee Historical Society. 1948.

FINI FINI

About The Author

Born in IL in 1950 exactly halfway through the 20th century, Elizabeth ("Ibby") Taylor Greer, a middle child, is a "watcher," and from that mid-century "peak" has trained her sturdy Baby Boomer Binoculars on the Past, the Midwest, West, East, and South, having lived in each region, and on all of her family's adventures, family stories, late husband, Thomas Keister Greer, Esq's. (1921-2008) ancestry and stories, and those of her current beau. Her education is on-going and she loves her life.

Made in the USA
Lexington, KY
27 October 2015